SOME OF THIS IS TRUE

Michelle McDonagh is an Irish journalist with over twenty-five years' experience, including twelve years as a staff reporter at the *Connacht Tribune*. She now works freelance, writing features and health pieces for numerous Irish papers, including *The Irish Times*.

She is married with three children and lives in Cork.

She is the author of three novels: *There's Something I Have to Tell You*, *Somebody Knows* and *Some of This Is True*.

MICHELLE MCDONAGH

SOME OF THIS IS TRUE

HACHETTE
BOOKS
IRELAND

Copyright © 2025 Michelle McDonagh

The right of Michelle McDonagh to be identified as the author
of the work has been asserted by her in accordance with
the Copyright, Designs and Patents Act 1988.

First published in Ireland in 2025 by HACHETTE BOOKS IRELAND

1

All rights reserved. No part of this publication may be reproduced, stored in a retrieval system, or transmitted, in any form or by any means without the prior written permission of the publisher, nor be otherwise circulated in any form of binding or cover other than that in which it is published and without a similar condition being imposed on the subsequent purchaser.

All characters in this publication are fictitious and any resemblance
to real persons, living or dead, is purely coincidental.

Cataloguing in Publication Data is available from the British Library

Trade paperback ISBN 9781399737876
Ebook ISBN 9781399737883

Typeset in Cambria by Bookends Publishing Services, Dublin
Printed and bound in Great Britain by Clays Ltd, Elcograf S.p.A.

Hachette Books Ireland policy is to use papers that are natural, renewable and recyclable products and made from wood grown in sustainable forests. The logging and manufacturing processes are expected to conform to the environmental regulations of the country of origin.

Hachette Books Ireland
8 Castlecourt Centre
Castleknock
Dublin 15, Ireland

A division of Hachette UK Ltd
Carmelite House, 50 Victoria Embankment, London EC4Y 0DZ

www.hachettebooksireland.ie

For Greg, with love

This book is set in the village of Blarney, County Cork. The village is real as are the iconic Blarney Castle and Blarney Woollen Mills, however the story, characters and the rest of the setting is entirely fictional. So while there's no point in coming to Blarney looking for the Gab pub or Casey's hotel, the village has plenty of real-life hostelries where visitors are very welcome to come for a pint, good food and company. And of course, the gift of the gab.

'Every saint has a past and every sinner has a future.'

Oscar Wilde

PROLOGUE

It all happens so fast.

Her legs pedalling frantically in the air.

That inhuman shriek of terror as she falls backwards into the steep, narrow stairwell.

The heavy thump of soft-tissue-wrapped bone smacking into solid stone.

The sickening crack as she hits the ground at the bottom and then nothing.

I stand in the ringing silence, both hands clamped over my mouth, howling inside.

Then I take a couple of steps, lean forward slightly and I can see her. She's not moving.

I look around in panic, but we're all alone, as I knew we would be.

Shaking so hard, I peer back down.

Still no movement, no sound.

Oh Jesus!

Is she dead?

Should I call for help?

What the hell do I do?

As my mind stutters, my legs take over and I start running.

CHAPTER 1

Friday, 12 January

It wasn't until the following morning that her body was found. The ground had frozen overnight, an Arctic mass having moved south and extended over Ireland, bringing with it a widespread, severe frost. A status yellow ice warning had been issued for the day, with further warnings likely for the coming days. One of the gardeners had been crossing the wooden footbridge straddling the pond on his way to the Water Garden when something at the bottom of the Wishing Steps snagged the corner of his eye. Something pale. Something that didn't belong there and made him pause in his tracks to stare across the pool to the base of the stone steps. But his view was blocked by the mop of climbing creepers that clung to the boulder from which the steps were hewn, spilling over the top like a knotty overgrown fringe. Grumbling under his breath, the gardener continued along the boardwalk, ice crunching beneath his boots. When he reached the willow tunnel, he bent his lanky frame under its interwoven branches.

Keeping the sixty-acre castle grounds looking as impressive as they did was a full-time job for the team of gardeners. In peak season, thousands of tourists came through the gates every day and extra staff were drafted in. Things were much quieter at this time of year, when the vast majority of the visitors were locals making the most of the peace and quiet, who tended for the most part to respect the place and not to leave their rubbish behind. This was his favourite time of the day here, the serenity of the place completely unspoilt. He and the rest of the team had it to themselves for another hour and a half or so before the gates opened.

The gardener made his way around the boardwalk now, passing the miniature willow tunnel for children on his right, before he came to the viewing area at the base of the Wishing Steps. He huffed at the sight of an abandoned, crumpled sleeping bag of what seemed a highly impractical colour, but as he got closer, the condensed plume of his pique still suspended in the air, he realised it was a coat he was looking at: a white, padded, Puffa-style jacket. And then he saw the hand, delicate and white as a snowdrop (*Galanthus nivalis*) and attached to a slender stalk that disappeared into the sleeve of the jacket.

He took a step back.

How very curious.

She, for it was a she – an older girl or very young woman – lay on her back, her feet and lower body resting on the lower steps, arms spread out like a snow angel on the frozen boards. A halo of thick, dark hair puddled her head, ice crystals glinting like sequins in the weak morning sunshine. Her face a washed blue beneath intricate lacework, as if Jack Frost's spider had been up all night weaving her a spangled veil.

The gardener had been fascinated as a child to learn that spiders had silk spinning organs called spinnerets on their abdomens, a collection of spigots that looked a bit like icing nozzles protruding from the ends. The silk was stored in liquid form in internal silk glands, but as it passed through to its spinnerets, it gradually hardened, pulled out by gravity or the arachnid's hind leg to be used as a building material, hunting tool or even a courtship platform.

Even now, after nearly a decade working in this incredible place, the natural world taught him something new every day. He would never run out of things to learn, even if he lived to be a hundred.

Deep in their roots, all flowers keep the light.

Sadly, the same couldn't be said for humans in his experience. He had been a lonely youth, outcast by his oddness, when he had first discovered Roethke's work, and it had been as if the dead poet had reached into his soul and opened up to him an entire new world of possibility.

Around the gardener and the girl, the world shimmered and sparkled and shone, birds squabbled and sang and water rushed recklessly over the ancient rock, splashing ecstatically into the pond. Above them, the flight of damp, mossy steps led to the Rock Close. Shaded by a leafy canopy of primeval yew trees and home to a collection of large rocks that had been in place for over 2,000 years, it was the oldest part of the vast estate, thought to have been the site of an ancient druidic settlement. Acutely sensitive to the frequency of the natural world, he had picked up on a darker energy there, particularly at dusk or early in the morning.

He looked at the girl lying on the ground in her battered grey Converse. There was no blood that he could see. Maybe some discolouring on her face, hard to tell beneath her frosty veil.

Her eyes were closed. She might have been sleeping, although it was clear this was one sleep she wouldn't be waking from.

He took out his phone and called 999. He told the operator he had found a dead girl and gave her the location and the postcode. He told her she wasn't breathing.

Yes, he was quite sure.

She was Dead. As. A. Dodo.

The ensuing silence on the other end indicated that he was after doing it again, being 'inappropriate'. It didn't bother him, though: those things didn't anymore, and at least he had managed to refrain from peppering her with some of the multitudinous facts about dodos that lived in his brain. *Dodo* (Raphus cucullatus), *extinct species of bird, once lived on the island Mauritius. Flightless, slow to reproduce, females only produced one egg a year. Paradox in behaviour and—*

The ambulance people would see for themselves when they got here anyway. The 999 lady told him to stay with the girl, and to send somebody else down to the main gate to open it for the emergency services. He did as he was told.

As he stood there, keeping the young woman company, shivering now in the biting chill despite his fleece-lined waterproof and his sturdy boots, he wondered where she had come from. This frozen angel. And how she had come to fall down here and wind up dead. The castle didn't open to the public until nine and, consulting his watch, he saw it was just gone half eight now. The gates were closed to admission at four o'clock at this time of year, and shut fully at five. He wondered if she had lain here all night, if her death had been instant and merciful or long and terrifying and painful. If it was the fall that had killed her, or the cold. Or something else.

He leaned forward and peered closer. From beneath her death mask, an ethereal beauty lingered.

Not for this snowdrop a new beginning. Not in this world in any case. Her rebirth, if there was to be one, would have to take place on another plane. There could be a poem in that. He could title it 'Dead as a Dodo' and maybe replant the girl's spirit in the kinder, safer place where he imagined the souls of the dodos to have been reborn.

He cocked his head, heard the sirens in the distance. He'd have to work on it later.

CHAPTER 2

Maria
Blarney

From her bedroom window at the back of her house on the hill, Maria had a crow's-nest view of the village laid out below her and the landscape beyond. It was a view she would never tire of: that patchwork of paint-chart greens stitched together with stone and fence and hedgerow, tumbling down to the village.

It was a lovely morning. Clean and clear and crisp. Her favourite kind of weather. There was little she loved more than wrapping up for a bracing walk under a bright sky, returning ruddy-cheeked and revived to the comfort of a crackling fire and a cosy home. From her elevated vantage point, Maria could see right down over the roofs of the Woollen Mills with the bell tower of the Catholic church poking up through the trees and the old graveyard at the front of the Protestant church.

Today though, it wasn't the picture-postcard view she was interested in but the activity going on down there. The village was generally quiet enough at night – not much crime, apart from a recent spate of cars being broken into and some lowish-level drug dealing – but last night with all the sirens wailing and whooping past it had been like downtown New York.

It had been all over the news this morning. An arson attack on the Blarney Lodge Hotel up the old Kerry Road, which had been earmarked to house asylum seekers. The photos online were shocking. Angry red tongues of flame and dense black smoke belched up into the night sky as the hotel was eaten alive. And this morning, a ruined smoking shell all that was left. No good to anybody now. All that destruction carried out on the basis of a rumour spread by far-right rabble-rousers.

And now there was something going on over at the castle as well. An ambulance and a squad car parked on the avenue, according to the *North Cork News* Facebook page. It had been the second item on the eight o'clock news on 96 FM, sandwiched between the arson story and another status yellow warning for ice. *Emergency services attending the scene of an incident at Blarney Castle ... gardaí releasing no further information at this point.*

She hoped nobody they knew was involved. At this time of year, there were very few visitors around, unlike the summer months when the place was thronged with tourists come to kiss the famous Blarney stone that promised to endow them with the 'gift of the gab'. Most of the staff over at the estate were local and in a small village like this, everybody knew each other or knew somebody connected to them.

It was a beautiful place for a walk. Otherworldly in parts. The stunning gardens, botanical woodlands, lake and waterways had been transformed in recent years, and Maria loved to lose herself in the sprawling estate, to escape the outside world for a while.

From her perch, she could see the top of the castle, its familiar grey stone battlement rising proudly towards the sky. A few years back, an American man had to be airlifted from the top after he'd had a heart attack. Maria and the kids had watched the rescue from the window where she was now standing, the helicopter hovering in the sky like a rackety metal dragonfly. The man had come back again afterwards to kiss the stone and to thank the staff and rescue team who had helped save his life. She hoped whatever was going on over there now would have such a happy outcome.

She couldn't see the back gate of the castle from where she stood, or the long avenue inside that wound up towards the Rock Close. That was where all the activity was taking place, according to the comments on *North Cork News*. She swung her gaze away from the castle, back to the neat village square, where a woman was throwing a ball for her dogs, two of those yappy little fluffy yokes.

If they were to get another dog, she'd like another golden retriever or better still, a rescue. She missed the excited skittering of Rupert's claws along the floorboards, his little 'All You Need Is Dog' tag jiggling, his big soft eyes. She missed everything about him really. Tadhg and the kids insisted the best way to get over him would be to get a new puppy, but she wasn't ready yet and as she was the one who would end up looking after him, she held the golden vote. She needed more time to mourn Rupert before she could open her heart again.

The square, where the woman was now trying to wrestle the ball from the mouth of one of her dogs, was bordered on one side by a pretty row of cottages that had originally been built to house mill workers, and on the far side by a row that included the bank, the garda station and the Castle Hotel. The village centre was also home to a chipper, a charity shop, a Centra supermarket, the Muskerry Arms and the Gab pubs, a butcher's, a bookie's, a few restaurants and a handful of gift shops. And around the corner, the Blarney Woollen Mills complex with its hotel, restaurant and huge shop.

There was a knot of people outside the bank, mouths moving urgently, heads nodding in the direction of the castle. A man in a red baseball cap stood outside the bookie's, smoking. She could tell it was Billy Walsh, hanging around waiting for the pub to open at twelve. She often wondered where he got the money for betting and booze when he'd never worked a day in as long as she knew him. Surely his dole couldn't stretch that far.

She looked beyond him to the hotel, where a squat man coming out the main door stopped to talk to another man in a black jacket who was passing. They were joined by a couple who came around the corner, the woman gesturing back in the direction they had come from, no doubt sharing whatever scrap of news they had picked up along their way. Everybody would be wondering what was going on over there, dying to find out more.

'We're off, Mom.' Eva's voice called from the bottom of the stairs.

Crap. She'd totally lost track of time. She glanced at her watch. Eight sixteen.

'Bye, love, see you later.' Tadhg.

A muffled grunt. Ben.

She rushed out to the top of the stairs to say goodbye, but the front door banged behind them. She winced. *Why did they have to nearly pull the bloody thing off its hinges every time?*

She hoped Tadhg was careful driving down the hill. The roads would be lethal this morning and her husband had never lost the invincibility complex of his youth, unlike Maria, who had never really had it in the first place. It was one of the things she'd always loved about him, along with his energy and drive and that innate sense of self-assurance she wished their son had got a bit of.

She went back into her bedroom and sat on the end of the bed that she had made as soon as she got out of it, as she did every morning. She had heard a man on the radio once, a retired navy admiral, talking about how that set you up for success for the day. How beginning your morning with a small success encouraged many more successes throughout the day. There was definitely something in that, she felt.

The house was still around her now, silent. She loved this house, the home where Tadhg had been reared and which they had moved into after his father's death. It was an arrangement that suited everybody, including Tadhg's brother, Gavin, who was settled in New York with his partner Craig, happy in the knowledge that their mother was cosily ensconced in her 'granny flat'. He loved to call it that when he knew Essie was in earshot, she always sure to respond with the threat of a 'clip across the ear'.

She breathed in the calmness before she left to head down the hill to Holy Faith Primary School, where she taught fifth class. It was a tough group this year. She had a couple of very challenging kids who took up a lot of her attention, the ones to whom discipline was a foreign concept. It made her job so much harder and unfortunately meant that the other kids in her class lost out, but it had been the same since she started teaching more than twenty years ago and it would always be thus.

In the hall, she pulled on her quilted navy coat, with a candy pink hat and matching striped scarf. She was rooting in the under-stairs press trying to find a matching pair of gloves when her phone rang.

Noelle.

Unusual for her friend to call at this time of day when she knew Maria would be getting ready to leave for work. She hoped nothing was wrong.

Grabbing two mismatched gloves, she threw her bag over her shoulder and answered the call, closing the door gently behind her.

'Hiya. All o—?'

'It's the American girl, Maria. I'm really worried about her. She never came back last night.'

CHAPTER 3

Noelle

She was probably over-reacting. Wasn't she? The girl, Jessie, was more than likely shacked up with some local lad. She *was* young, free and single, after all. And far away from home.

'Did you check Liam's bed?' Maria had asked. She was only ball hopping, but Noelle didn't find it funny. A bit too close to the bone.

Her son was spoken for now, even if Noelle hadn't initially approved of his choice. In fairness, there weren't too many mothers who'd have chosen one of the Mad Macks from Millview as a partner for their son, even less so as the mother of their first grandchild. Molly McMahon came from a big family of notoriously wild uncles and aunts, most of whom lived on the estate. Fond of their drink and their drugs. Kids with so many different partners it was impossible to keep track of whose were whose. One of the younger lads had been done for dealing drugs and robbing a car last year and it was well known he wasn't the only one of them involved in that sort of thing.

Noelle had hoped Liam would see sense, that the relationship would eventually run its course and that her only son, her baby, would settle down with a nice girl. She nearly died the day he came home to tell her he was going to be a father. She'd been distraught. And furious. With Liam for being stupid enough to get caught, and with Molly Mack for trapping him. She could never have imagined as she sat sobbing into her hands at the kitchen table that day how things were going to turn out. How wrong she had been.

Molly had turned out to be a marvellous mother, a complete natural who doted on her baby, and Noelle had really bonded with the girl over the five months since the birth of her beloved grandson. She had drummed into Liam how important it was that he respected and looked after the mother of his child. Unlike his own sorry excuse for a father.

She stuck her head into her son's room. Just in case.

He wasn't there; he started work at eight and was usually gone by half seven at the latest. She had barely seen him yesterday. He'd popped home for a quick shower and change after work and headed straight back out in the van, no time even for dinner, saying he was going to Dean's house and would get a takeaway. She hadn't heard him come in last night, but he never stayed over in the cramped terrace where Molly lived with her mother and stone-mad younger half-brothers, and where she only had a box room with a single bed and now Leon's cot squashed in. He must have been late. Not good enough on a work night, really, especially when he had responsibilities now. He was a good lad, though, in fairness to him, a great support to her over the past number of tough years.

She pushed the window open as far as it would go, the freezing air rushing in as if it had been hanging around outside waiting, and turned to make his bed.

Oh!

It didn't appear to have been slept in since she had made it yesterday morning.

Noelle checked Liam's laundry basket. The tracksuit bottoms and hoodie he had changed into after work were in there, so he must have been back at some stage. At twenty-four, her son was big and well able enough to do his own laundry and make his own bed, but she didn't mind doing it; he worked hard and she wanted the linen to be fresh for the nights Molly stayed over. The B&B was quiet at the moment anyway, so she didn't have any other beds to do. Apart from Jessie's, of course.

Which reminded her.

She went back around the landing to the room where the American girl was staying. Jessie had booked and paid for a single, but Noelle had given her the biggest of the three empty double guest rooms. She'd be pretty much booked out from St Patrick's weekend in March right through until the end of September, so she appreciated the quiet winter months when she could relax a bit.

Herself and Kevin used to go to the Costa de Sol for a week in October every year, the heat and the cost much more bearable at that time of the year. That had all ended six years ago, along with her marriage, after she found out he was messing around behind her back with one of the girls from the deli in Centra. He had moved in with his deli girl after Noelle kicked him out, had promptly got her pregnant and then left her for an even younger model when the child was still in nappies. Liam and Holly had cut their father off – although her daughter had been in contact with him before she left for Australia – and he had never met his gorgeous grandson. Noelle had gone on a week's holiday to Lanzarote with a newly separated friend a few years back and they'd had a lovely time, but then her friend had met a new man and that was the end of that. All of her closest friends were still married, happily or otherwise, and still in the thick of parenting kids through school and college. Noelle had started her family younger than the rest of them, and had found herself in a very lonely place before Leon came along, bringing a renewed sense of purpose into her life.

Now, what am I supposed to be doing again?

She stood in the middle of the room where her only guest was staying, her brain completely blank, before turning on her heel and wandering back out to the landing. She knew she had gone in there for a reason. It was so bloody frustrating.

Her older sister Grainne, on one of her rare visits back from Dublin, had told her it was time for her to start HRT. The brain fog was only going to get worse, Grainne warned, and her mood was already up and down like a yo-yo, but Noelle wasn't ready to start taking it yet. She was forty-eight but still getting her periods like clockwork every month. Grainne had heard on a podcast that baby girls were born with between one and two million eggs, but more than 10,000 died each month so by the time girls reached puberty, they had between 300,000 and 400,000 eggs. 'Which means that by fifty-one, the average age of menopause, you'll have fewer than a hundred fairly crappy eggs left,' Grainne had informed her sister. Noelle had visualised her remaining eggs shrivelling inside her, her ovaries getting ready to pack up their stalls, good for nothing now her child-bearing years were over. As if her desirability was preparing itself to curl up and wither away along with her fertility. It was all so bloody depressing.

Now, where was she again? Oh yes, Jessie.

She went back into the guest room and surveyed it. The curtains were open in here too. Noelle had listened out for Jessie last night, but she'd fallen asleep around midnight. She wasn't usually this protective of her guests, of course not, but Jessie was different. Only twenty-two and on her own in Ireland, searching for a father she had only just found out about: a Michael Murphy from some place in north Cork with a castle.

Michael Murphy! She might as well try and pull every haystack around the place apart looking for a fine needle. And castles were two a penny in Cork, although Blarney was undoubtedly the most famous.

Young people these days, though. For all the giving out everybody did about them spending too much time online, they were cute out when it came to technology. Much smarter than Noelle's generation in a lot of ways. Jessie had explained that she was *documenting* her search, appealing for people to help her find her father through the videos she posted on YouTube and TikTok. And it seemed to be working too. She might not have found him yet, but her appeal had grown arms and legs. Cathal Cronin in the *North Cork News* had run a full page on her search with a big photo of her: those huge brown eyes and that mop of curls, that gorgeous smile. The story had been picked up by the *Examiner* and 96 FM and was all over social media.

Jessie had been here ten days now and was talking about moving to Blarney for good, to get bar work and maybe go to college at night. 'I know the grass is always greener, but it literally is greener over here,' she had said to Noelle, laughing, before she left the B&B yesterday morning, full of plans for the day. She didn't seem too worried about getting a work visa, was optimistic that she'd track her father down and would then be entitled to an Irish passport. Noelle had advised her not to make any rash decisions, to maybe talk to her family at home first, although there seemed to have been a bit of a fallout there – Jessie had told Liam she wasn't talking to her mother. Well, as Noelle had pointed out to Liam, it was all very new and exciting at the moment and Jessie was enjoying being the centre of attention, a sort of mini-celeb around the place, but the gloss wouldn't be long wearing off once her savings ran out and she had to work for a living and try to find a place to rent in Cork in the middle of the worst housing crisis the country had ever seen.

Noelle had been surprised and a bit put out when Jessie hadn't turned up for dinner yesterday. She didn't usually provide an evening meal for her guests; it was a bed and breakfast she was running after all, not a hotel. But she had taken the girl under her wing and wanted to make sure she was eating right. She'd even gone to the trouble of going down to the butcher's to pick up a nice stuffed pork steak that she had roasted with poppies and veg.

Liam had told her to stop fussing, before he dashed off again himself, saying Jessie was probably out somewhere enjoying herself. 'Ah, would you stop, Mam, she's a young one away from home for the first time,' he had said. 'She probably lost track of time. Just leave it on a plate for her and she can heat it up when she comes in.'

'Well, if she arrives home in the state you brought her home in last night, she'll have no mind for a pork dinner, that's for sure,' Noelle had retorted. 'She's probably not used to drinking like that back home – you can't even drink 'til you're twenty-one over there.'

'At least I brought her home safe. If I'd left her there on her own, you'd be giving out mad about that.'

He was right. She was glad her son had walked their young guest home from the Gab, his own local, even if it was less than a ten-minute walk up the road and it was a safe village. You could never be too careful. He wouldn't want to make a habit of it, though: he shouldn't be out drinking with attractive single women when he was already spoken for. Guests or not.

She looked around at the unmade bed strewn with clothing, the dressing table covered in bottles and sprays and creams, and felt a pang of yearning for her own daughter, who had moved along with her lotions and potions to the other side of the world. She was so conflicted. Glad that Holly was settled in Australia, where she had been nursing for the past two years, but desperately missing her firstborn child. Thank God she had Leon to distract her now.

She picked up a bottle from the dressing table. Victoria's Secret body mist. Coconut Passion. She sprayed it lightly on the back of her wrist, and held it to her nose.

Mmm. She loved the smell of coconut, so evocative of sandy beaches and suncream, of warmer climes. Maybe she would head off somewhere on her own for a week this year, or check out one of those singles holiday packages.

She went into the ensuite, where tubes of foundation and moisturiser lay discarded on the shelf above the sink. In the shower, a disposable razor lay in the tray along with a number of coarse curly hairs that caused Noelle to tut. She turned on the shower, taking down the shower head and chasing them down the plughole.

She went back into the bedroom, and took one last look around, not sure what she was searching for.

It was then she spotted it. The charger plugged into the wall. That girl was never off her iPhone. There was no way she would have stayed out overnight without coming back for it. Then again, maybe Jessie had borrowed a charger from whoever she had stayed with.

She took her own phone out of the pocket of her fleece hoodie and scrolled down until she got to J.

'Hi, it's Jessie. Leave a message and I'll get back to you. Or not.' A girlish giggle. Then the beep tone.

Noelle felt her pulse quicken. Something wasn't right here. She didn't care if she *was* over-reacting. She felt a duty of care to this girl while she was staying under her roof.

She found the number for Blarney garda station in her contacts list and tapped on it.

CHAPTER 4

Dani
Dorchester, Boston

'*Daniela. Svegliati.* Wake up.'

She was down too deep to tell Mamma to go away.

'Daniela.' Her mother grabbed her shoulder and shook her.

'Jeez, Mamma.' What was wrong with the woman? It was the middle of the night. 'Did Laurie have the baby?' she croaked.

Her brother Joe's wife had gone in yesterday to be induced, but that better not be why her mother was waking her at this ungodly hour. Sure, they had struggled to get this far. It was a big deal for Joe and Laurie, she got that, and she was happy for them, but this was, like, the tenth grandchild now – her other brothers' wives were like brood mares, popping kids out all over the place – so the news could have waited until it was daylight at least.

Dani had gone straight to the Bowery for Jenna's fortieth-birthday drinks after her shift finished last night and had only fallen into bed a couple of hours ago. She'd been pretty wasted, still was, but it was a special occasion and she didn't start work again until six this evening.

'It's Jessie, *tesoro. Svegliati. Por favore.*' Her mother's hands were trembling, her voice too. '*Oh che Dio ce la mandi buona!*'

Dani sat bolt upright in the bed, her head spinning.

'Is she here?'

Her mother was prone to be dramatic, regularly calling on God's help for the most minor of crises, but she wouldn't wake Dani at this hour if it wasn't something serious. And why would Jessie be here at this hour of the morning anyhow? She had moved out over a year ago. And she hadn't spoken to Dani for going on three weeks now, hadn't even come home for Christmas. Dani had been giving her daughter time and space, hoping she'd calm down eventually. But had she got herself into some kind of trouble?

'You need to get up and come downstairs, Daniela. The police are here.'

She flung her comforter off and got to her feet. She was wearing only her knickers and bra, had been too wrecked when she got in to throw on one of the oversized t-shirts she usually wore to bed. She glanced at the alarm clock: 5:07 a.m.

'Is Jessie with them?' She'd better not have got herself arrested for some stupid shit.

'No, no. Hurry, please. They say they want to talk to her mamma. I have a very bad feeling, Daniela. Oh, Jessie *cucciola, per favore stai bene.*'

'Okay, Mamma, I'm comin', I'm comin'.'

She rummaged through the pile of clothes on the chair in the corner of her room, grabbing a sweatshirt and track bottoms. Her breath was rank, but she didn't want to waste time brushing her teeth, not even for the cops. Her heart was pounding now. The cops never called to anybody's door at five in the morning with good news.

There were two of them standing in the lounge. Both in uniform, the distinctive navy blue of Boston PD. One taller and wider than the other. Her mother must have buzzed them up from the street. Dani hadn't heard the doorbell: one of those special ones for the hard of hearing that Joe had installed for Mamma, and was loud enough to rouse the dead. She must have been totally out of it.

The sight of the cops standing straight-backed with their caps in their hands sobered her instantly. She felt sweat break out all over her body, escaping from every pore. She wanted to reverse out of the room, get back into bed and fall back to sleep, to stop them from telling her whatever they had come to say.

The shorter of the two stepped forward. He had a forehead that was too large for his face and bumpy acne-scarred cheeks that she tried not to stare at.

'Ms De Marco, I'm Officer Steve Webb and this is my colleague, Officer Jack Ryan. Can you confirm that you are the mother of Jessica De Marco?'

She nodded, blood rushing to her face, the sweat pumping now.

'Could we all sit down?' the cop with the big forehead asked.

Her mother whimpered and blessed herself. *'O che Dio.'*

Dani nodded, mute.

Her mother perched on the edge of the sofa and Dani sat beside her, squeezing her hand. She couldn't remember the last time she had held Mamma's hand. She knew now what was coming, had seen it enacted enough times on TV. She shifted her focus to the crest on the sleeve of the officer's shirt. Blue with yellow writing. Boston PD. AD 1630.

'I'm very sorry to tell you that Jessica has been in an accident in Ireland, ma'am, a fall down a flight of steps, and … I'm afraid she didn't make it.'

The relief. Oh, the sweet, sweet, blessed relief!

'Oh my God! You've got the wrong family, officer. Jessie isn't in Ireland, she's here in Dorchester. She's living just off Blue Hill Ave.'

The cop shook his head, his lips pressed together in a thin line.

'The Garda in Ireland sent us a copy of her passport, and this is the address given on it.'

Her mother covered her face with her hands and began to moan.

'No, this is … Her passport must have been stolen. Jessie's never been to …'

And then it hit her.

Oh God no, surely not!

'Where … where did this accident happen?'

'In a village in Cork called Blarney, in the grounds of a castle.'

Dani sank to her knees on the carpet then, her mouth wide open in a silent, Munchian scream, her mother's wails coming from somewhere far, far away.

CHAPTER 5

Maria
Blarney

'It's desperate altogether. A lovely young girl like that. And I was only reading about her in the paper a couple of days ago.' Essie shook her head, reached for the remote and turned the sound down on the RTÉ news. 'God help her poor mother, having to get that news from the far side of the Atlantic.'

Maria couldn't even begin to imagine the hell of it. The stuff of every parent's nightmare. She glanced over at Eva, who, for once, had lifted her head from her phone to watch the news. Some day, probably not too long away, she could be the one waving her daughter off at the airport as she made her way further out into the world than Maria had ever gone. And much as she'd encourage Eva to spread her wings and experience as much as she could while she was young, the thought of her being so far away from them if anything went wrong was terrifying. A bridge she was in no hurry to cross, that was for sure.

Maria poured herself a cup of tea from the pot on her mother-in-law's coffee table. The room, lit by antique copper lamps and the open fire crackling and spitting away in the hearth, was gloriously cosy. She loved this room, so full of character with its walls painted a shade of deep rich green. Jewel Beetle, Essie said, was the name of it. Inspired by an 1880s John Singer Sargent portrait of the actress Ellen Terry as Lady Macbeth in a spectacular green dress, embroidered in gold and decorated with a thousand iridescent wings from the green jewel beetle. Her mother-in-law had a great eye for interiors; she had done a fabulous job on the apartment.

They had been worried Essie might find her compact two-bedded home a bit small after living in the big house next door for so long, but she was happy out in here. In fact, there were plenty of times Maria would gladly have swapped places with her and moved into this snug little nest where she would only have herself to clean up after. Instead of a husband and two teenagers who left a constant jet stream of crap in their wake whenever they left a room, clothes and shoes and schoolbooks and bags and fake lashes and plates and glasses and empty bottles and cans and crisp packets and ... It was just exhausting. The constant bending down and picking up and putting away. Last night she'd popped into the kitchen on her way to bed, worn out after another long day, only to find the counters, which had been spotless after she'd cleaned up earlier, covered in dirty dishes and cutlery again. The butter and ham and cheese had been left out, a loaf of bread was ripped open down the middle beside a lidless tube of Pringles, and an empty pack of chocolate chip cookies lay abandoned within spitting distance of the bin.

In fairness to Tadhg, his position as principal of the local secondary school was a lot more demanding than her job, the hours far longer. He was also heavily involved in Blarney GAA, coaching the senior team, which often required him to go back out at night to attend meetings and events. Not that he minded: the GAA wasn't work to him, it was part of his DNA, and he wanted to give back to the organisation that had given him so much in his own youth. It meant Maria had to pick up more of the slack on the home front, but apart from Pilates one evening a week and the odd night out with the girls, she was usually at home with the kids anyway.

'Did you see the video she put up on the TicTac yesterday, Maria?' Betty asked. 'Eva was just showing us ...'

'It's TikTok, Betty,' Essie corrected her friend, rolling her eyes at her granddaughter. Betty Byrne had been coming over religiously every Friday night since Maria's father-in-law Jim had died – over five years ago now – to watch the *Late Late*, armed with a bottle of wine and two bars of Cadbury's Fruit & Nut, one each for her and Essie.

'No,' Maria said. 'But I saw the YouTube one she put up last week alright.' She had shown it to Tadhg, who had wished the girl luck finding a man with one of the most common surnames in Ireland, saying, 'She'd have as much luck getting blood out of the Blarney Stone.'

'Here's the last one she posted,' Eva said, holding her phone out towards Maria. 'D'you want to see it?'

On the screen, the American girl was frozen mid-speech, her open mouth showing a row of straight white teeth. Maria both did and didn't want to watch it. Knowing that the girl was now dead, it felt a bit voyeuristic, like a rubbernecker passing the scene of a fatal car crash.

'Here, take it. Nan made some banana bread for me today – I'm going in for another slice.' Her daughter handed her the phone, the video already playing, Jessie speaking directly to the camera.

'Hey, you guys, if you've been following my journey over the past week, you'll know that I did make an attempt to kiss the world-famous Blarney Stone two days ago, but ...' She grinned. 'I failed miserably because, well basically, I'm too chicken shit.'

Jessie was standing in front of a big sign saying *The World's Largest Irish Shop* and Maria could see the familiar green-painted entrance to Blarney Woollen Mills in the background. The girl was wearing a winter white Puffa coat and a red knitted hat, the picture of life and vitality with her luminous skin, huge brown eyes and glossy dark curls.

'So, I don't actually have a fear of heights, but to kiss the stone you gotta climb like over a hundred steps up this narrow twisty staircase to the top of the castle and then lie on your back while some dude helps you dip your head over the side and you hold onto a metal bar. I'm not even kidding, it's crazy, bros. So I wimped out the first time, but I really gotta get me some gift of the gab so I'm determined to do it today. I'll post a photo once I've done it. First, though, I've got to get fuelled up for the climb!'

The video ended on the girl's wide smile.

'It's hard to believe she's dead, isn't it? God love her, the craythurín', Betty said. 'Apparently 'twas the Wishing Steps she fell down. Probably goin' down them backwards with her eyes closed. Aren't they awful eejits too, though, the Yanks? Believin' in all those aul piseógs. Not that I'm callin' that poor young one an eejit now, God rest her and—'

'Ara, that's only aul rumours, Betty,' Essie chided. 'I heard it was the steps over by the waterfall in the tropical woodland.

Nobody knows for sure yet where the poor child fell or how it happened.'

'Well, 'twas Maura O'Donovan told me and she got it from her daughter-in-law Susan who works in the gift shop over there so she'd know,' Betty asserted.

Maria put her daughter's phone down and stared into the fire. It was hard to believe the life of a young woman, so alive and full of plans only yesterday, could be snuffed out just like that. And so tragically too.

The scenario Betty had put forward wasn't as unlikely as it sounded, she thought, given that every year thousands of tourists did walk backwards down those steps with their eyes closed and back up again, in the belief that their wish would come true within a year if they performed the ritual correctly. Legend had it that for hundreds of years the Blarney witch had taken firewood from the estate for her kitchen and in return, she had to grant its visitors' wishes.

The old wives' tale didn't sound half as daft when you were standing in the Rock Close beside the sacrificial altar, under the shade of the majestic trees that stood guard over it. The place had an energy she had never experienced anywhere else – mystical, unearthly, almost tangible.

Poor Noelle was in a right state. She had called earlier to say the girl's mother was flying in from Boston overnight and would be arriving into Shannon early in the morning. She had booked into the B&B, desperate to stay in the room where her daughter had spent her last days. Maria's heart went out to the woman.

'MOM!' Eva jolted her out of her thoughts. 'Are you deaf?' She held her hand out for her phone.

'Did she kiss the stone?' Maria asked, as she handed it over.

'Hmm?' Her daughter had already switched back to scroll mode.

'I was just wondering if she actually got to kiss the stone.'

'Oh, she did indeed,' Betty piped up. 'It was up on the *North Cork News* Facebook page yesterday. Hold on 'til I find it for you.'

She picked up her tablet. Betty had taken to social media like a duck to water. Facebook mainly, but also Instagram. She loved being able to nose into what was going on in other people's lives without even having to leave the house.

'There it is. Ah, would you look at her,' the older woman tutted. 'Proud as punch. She must have asked somebody to take the photo for her.'

There were two photos of the girl. One where you couldn't see her face properly, only her legs, and her shoulders leaning back into the gap between the wall of the castle and the stone itself. The second one was clearly taken afterwards, when she was standing with a triumphant smile on her face beside the keeper of the stone, both giving a thumbs-up. Noelle had been telling her that Jessie had a folding tripod that she took everywhere in her backpack for her 'socials'. Clearly a real pro.

'Did she post anything else after that?' Maria asked.

'She doesn't seem to have,' Betty said. 'I got one of the grandkids to check on the TicTac for me, but that seems to be the last thing she put up. And she so delighted with herself in it.'

'Well, whatever happened to the poor girl, it's just awful – and so sad that she never even got to meet her father after coming all this way,' Essie said. 'And then that fire above in the Lodge last night as well. What's the world coming to at all?'

'Did ye hear there was a child rapist moving into the hotel?'

Eva said. 'One of the immigrants, from Romania I think. Somebody posted a video about it on YouTube and it's all over the internet now.'

Maria took a deep breath.

For the love of ...

'What have we said to you before, Eva? I mean, how many times do we have to have this conversation? There isn't a word of truth in that rumour, just those far-right nutters again targeting gullible kids who believe everything they see online.'

It saddened Maria that her daughter's generation seemed to regard social media as a reliable source of news; that made them a captive audience for all kinds of negative influences. It wasn't all bad, of course – there were plenty of positives to the new digital world – but it was hard not to worry about where it was all going.

'God, I better head inside,' she said, checking the time. 'We have a table booked in Isaac's for eight.'

It was the last thing she felt like now, she thought, as she carried the tea tray into the kitchen, rinsing the cups under the tap before putting them into the dishwasher. She'd much rather get into her pyjamas and stay at home in front of the fire herself, rather than have to get ready and go back out into the cold, but Tadhg had booked it as a treat: it had been their favourite restaurant when they were single and childfree, and they hadn't gone out in town in ages. He'd been looking forward to it and she didn't want to let him down at the last minute.

She took the tea tray into Essie's compact utility room, where she slid it into its slot in one of the built-in units. Everything here had its place, all so neat and ordered, unlike her own dumping ground of a laundry room.

She was heading back out into the kitchen when she noticed the clothes horse standing inside the door.

Isn't that ...?

Her son's black Nike tracksuit was hanging on the airer along with his black North Face t-shirt and boxers – everything he wore these days seemed to be black – and socks. The only thing not his were a bra and couple of pairs of underpants belonging to her mother-in-law.

Why is Essie washing Ben's clothes?

He had stayed over with his nan last night, nothing unusual in that. He stayed a couple of nights a week and was very close to Essie. Both kids were – which was lovely for them, given that Maria's parents had retired to Spain and didn't see much of them – but Ben had a particularly close bond with her. She spoilt him rotten, of course, always having his favourite treats in the press and making him pancakes lathered in syrup and bacon for breakfast.

She didn't usually wash his clothes, though. He kept a pair of the loose bottoms and long-sleeved t-shirts he slept in in Essie's spare room, and he'd been wearing his uniform when he came in the back door of their own kitchen before school this morning.

Odd.

'Essie?' She went back into the sitting room, but her phone rang just as she got there. It was Tadhg, telling her she was running late. 'I'm just coming,' she said.

'You need to get a move on, I've the taxi booked for seven. We said we'd have a drink first in Cask.'

'Oh yeah, totally forgot. On my way.'

CHAPTER 6

Dani
Saturday, 13 January

For as long as she lived, Dani would never forget that interminable flight. When she was a teenager, the body of a young Irish student had been pulled from a quarry out in Quincy and she remembered Mamma praying for the family who had to travel all the way from Ireland to collect their son's remains. It wasn't until she became a mother herself that she realised just how horrific that must have been for them. Bad enough for your child to die close to home, but to die overseas would be an even worse hell. Never, ever had she imagined that she would find herself in that very same situation.

It wasn't the first time she had flown to Ireland. Those previous flights had been happy occasions, full of excitement and nervous anticipation. The first time, as a child, had been her first time ever on a plane. They had flown into Shannon and driven up to her father's homeplace in County Mayo, her and the boys all squashed into the back of their hired saloon. She had folded herself onto Joe's lap, her own shorter legs crushed against the seat in front, as her brothers fought for leg space for their gangly limbs. That had been a great trip: such amazing memories.

Her father's parents had moved to the US back in the 1950s, settling first in New York and then moving further north along the eastern seaboard to Boston. That trip had been her father's first visit to his ancestral home and he had been so excited about meeting all the Irish relatives. They had stayed with his Aunty Annie, bunking down on cots, mattresses and sofas. Dani and her siblings were joined by her father's cousins' kids. They formed a wild posse, spending the days roaming the farmland around them, jumping off haystacks and bouncing around in the back of an ancient jeep driven through the fields by a twelve-year-old. She would never forget the experience of standing in a river so clear she could see the tiny fish the Irish kids called 'pinkeens' nibbling at her feet. Even Mamma had seemed more relaxed away from the restaurant and all its stresses.

It hadn't lasted, of course; it never did. Her father's feet had barely hit the ground at Logan Airport when her mother exploded at him over something he'd said or done, Dani couldn't remember what. Mamma would have been ready to blow after being on her best behaviour for so long; the slightest thing would have set her off.

She shifted uncomfortably in her cramped window seat now. It had been a struggle to fasten her safety belt. She had started to panic when it began to look like it wasn't going to reach across the bloated hump of her belly, even after she extended it as far as it could go. Sweating at the thought of having to ask the air steward for one of those extender thingies, the shame of it, she had wrestled for what seemed an age with it before the stupid thing finally clicked into place. She usually booked an emergency aisle seat for the extra space, but Joe had booked the flights and he couldn't get one at such short notice. She wished again that Joe was with her: her eldest brother, the solid, steady one who had always looked out for her. But he was stuck in the labour ward of Brigham and Women's Hospital right now, mopping Laurie's brow. She had hoped her sister-in-law would tell Joe to go to Ireland with her, that she would insist that Dani needed him more than she did, but she hadn't. Her brother Vincent, with whom she had a fractious relationship at the best of times, had to stay at home to run the business in Joe's absence, and feckless Billy would be about as much use as a toothpick in a tornado. *She'd* end up having to look after *him*. And it would have been far too risky for Mamma to fly, with her heart. So Dani was on her own.

She had the cold air blasting on full, but she was still sweating. She'd taken a couple of Valium before boarding, but they'd worn off and she'd stupidly left the pack in her carry-on bag, which was out of reach in the overhead bin. The man beside her was fast asleep, breathing heavily through his open mouth, caging her in. She thought of Jessie, taking this flight all on her own, the first time she had ever left America, without telling any of them. The moxie of the kid. How fearless and bold she was. Dani had never been to Cork; for a moment her brain glitched and she thought how nice it would be for the two of them to explore the area together. And then, like a resounding smack to the head, the image that she had kept at bay all day broke through the forcefield of her numbness. The horrifying snapshot of her beautiful child's cold body lying in one of those refrigerated drawers that slid in and out like filing cabinets of the dead.

No, no, no!

She grabbed the back of the seat in front of her. *Please, no! It has to be a mistake.*

Somebody else's child ... She didn't care whose, didn't care about their pain, once it wasn't her Jessie. There was probably a simple explanation. That girl, the one who had fallen down the steps, must have stolen Jessie's passport. It suddenly occurred to her that Jessie might not even be in Ireland, that her passport could have been stolen back home and she could still be in Boston. They might all laugh about this someday, unlikely as that seemed right now. About her mad dash across the Atlantic to identify the body of some thieving stranger when Jessie was sulking in a friend's apartment back in Dot.

She released her safety belt and tried to shift in her seat, but she was too tightly wedged in. She reached up and tried to twist the air nozzle above her, but it was open as far as it would go. She needed air. She opened her mouth and tried to take a deep breath in, but her diaphragm felt compressed in the tight space. The man in the seat beside her was no slim Jim himself, his big arm taking over the arm rest between them, which didn't help. Her mouth was dry, her throat parched. She badly needed to swallow, but she couldn't. She was starting to panic now, her breathing too shallow, the sweat gathering under her pendulous breasts and soaking through her t-shirt, her back sticking to the seat. She nudged the man beside her with her elbow, gone beyond worrying about waking him now.

'Excuse me.' He didn't budge. She raised her voice. 'Sir, excuse me. I need to get out.'

She tried shaking his shoulder, but they were so tightly packed in and she was having so much trouble getting air in that it was hard to put much strength into it.

He snorted loudly but didn't wake.

She reached for the call button and pressed it, not caring now about making a scene.

She began to heave.

Jesus Christ, if I don't get out of here, I'm going to pass out. Why is nobody coming to help?

She elbowed the man as hard as she could into his side and he jerked awake.

'What the fu—? What the heck, lady?'

'Please move. Can't breathe.' She pointed to her mouth.

'Oh sure, sorry, Ma'am,' he said, pressing the call bell again and loudly telling the passenger in the aisle seat that he needed to move asap because it was an emergency. People in the seats nearby turned to stare as Dani shakily squeezed herself out of the row.

An attendant in the distinctive green Aer Lingus uniform came down the aisle towards her.

'Are you alright, love?'

'Need air ...' She choked the words out, her eyes pleading. Her head had started to spin now.

'Try and stay calm, you're okay,' the woman soothed in a soft brogue. 'You probably just need a bit of space.' She led Dani down to the back of the plane, past rows of curious eyes. The attendant, an efficient brunette with kind eyes and generous lips painted red, pulled out a jump seat for Dani to sit on in the staff area at the rear of the plane and told her to take a few deep breaths.

'That's it, good woman. You'll be grand again in a couple of minutes.'

How she wished she could take this lovely lady off the plane with her at the other end.

It took a few minutes for her breath to come close to normal again, and a few more for her heart to stop stomping like it was about to bust out of her chest. She took another look at the attendant: according to her badge, her name was Mags.

'Thank you. I got so claustrophobic in there.'

'Ah, you just needed a bit of air. Are you a nervous flier?'

'No. Not usually ... It's ... There was an accident, you see .... my daughter ... I have to go to Cork to ...' She faltered. 'I need to get my pills ... from the overhead bin.'

'Ah, God, was that your daughter? Oh, you poor pet.' Mags hunkered down beside her. 'I'm so sorry. We'd have put you into business if we'd known that. I'll get you your medication and take you up there once you feel steady enough to move. You'll be more comfortable there, at least, and you'll have more ... em, well, comfort.'

Space, she had been about to say. Space for the big fat American, she had probably been thinking. Dani's ankles were so swollen now they were throbbing, the skin stretched tight as sausage casing. She had dyed her hair a colour called Electric Mango last week; she liked to change her colour every few months, to shake things up a little, and it had looked so cool on the model on the box, a funky orangish-red. It didn't look cool on Dani, though; it made her look like a clown. More horror movie than circus. All she was missing was the squeaky red nose and the big shoes. She was a hot freakin' mess.

Once Dani felt okay to move, she let Mags lead her up the narrow aisle, almost tripping over somebody's outstretched foot at one point. The attendant whisked aside the little curtain that separated business class from economy – one world from another. It was only half full and positively spacious compared to her previous quarters. It was a pity Joe hadn't thought of this in the first place, under the circumstances, instead of sticking her in coach. That was the problem with men, even the good ones like Joe: sometimes, they just didn't think.

It was unfortunate that they happened to be one of her two biggest weaknesses in life. Food being the other. Feckless men and fattening food. She had hoped there was a chance that Carl might be the one, or at least that their relationship might have lasted longer than some of the others. But no, barely a month after they had moved in together – to an apartment that she had paid the full deposit and the first and last months' rent on in advance – he had walked out on her without either an explanation or a dime towards the rent. Unwilling or unable to face the thought of trying to find a stranger to share with her, she had ended up moving back in with her mother. At rock bottom. Or so she'd thought. Until two days later, when she was standing in her childhood bedroom amid a pile of unpacked moving boxes, wondering how the fuck she'd ended up here, Jessie had come flying in, screaming and roaring.

Jessie, who had hated Carl. Hated all of her mother's boyfriends and lovers. A 'bunch of users and losers', was how she'd described them, pretty aptly if Dani was honest. She did have shitty taste in men, had never grown out of her teenage attraction to bad boys. Jessie had accused her of being a sex addict, but she was wrong. Sex was just the currency she used to get men, to get love. But no matter how hard she tried, she couldn't seem to hold onto one.

Jessie. Oh God. Jessie.

How much longer until they landed? She checked the time on her phone. Three more hours. Part of her wished it was over, but another part of her wanted to stay in the air, because she didn't know how she was going to get through what awaited her at the end of her journey.

CHAPTER 7

Noelle

Noelle woke at six a.m., dreading the day ahead. Jessie's mother would be landing at Shannon Airport in the next half an hour or so. She was being collected by the gardaí and driven to Cork, due to arrive at around half eight or nine. Noelle had offered to have breakfast ready for her, but the brother who had called yesterday to book her in said she wanted to go straight to the morgue. The poor woman probably wouldn't believe it was true until she saw her child's body for herself.

The whole thing was such a nightmare. Noelle had been so shocked to get the call from Jessie's Uncle Joe yesterday afternoon. The gardaí hadn't even officially confirmed the identity of the dead woman at that stage, although there was no doubt locally that it was Jessie. The guard Noelle had spoken to when she'd called the station in the morning had asked a lot of questions about her missing guest, telling her he'd look into it and get back to her. He had given her a right jolt when he'd turned up at her door a few hours later, until she realised that it had nothing to do with Liam. He was there to break the tragic news about Jessie, asking her to keep it to herself until the girl's family had all been notified.

The call from Joe De Marco had come in on the landline, the guards having given him the name and number of the guest house where his niece had been staying. He wanted to book his sister Dani into the B&B, if possible into the same room as her daughter. His voice had broken as he asked her not to change the sheets on Jessie's bed, saying that before she got on the flight his sister had made him promise to call. Noelle had been aghast to learn that Dani was travelling alone, without a family member or even a friend to accompany her. She couldn't imagine being in a fit state to stand if she were in the same situation, never mind board a plane on her own and cross an ocean to identify her child's dead body. Jessie had talked with affection about her big Italian-Irish family: the grandmother, who had pretty much reared her by the sound of it, the loud, boisterous uncles and their wives, and all her little cousins. She hadn't said very much about her mother, though, apart from the fact that they had fallen out before her trip to Ireland. Noelle hadn't given it too much thought; families were complicated, as she knew only too well herself.

She had assured Joe, of course, that it would be no problem at all, and said that if there was anything else he or the family needed, to just let her know. But she could feel her blood pressure rising at the thought of having his devastated sister under her roof. Dealing with this kind of situation was way outside her comfort zone. Her guests were typically tourists, who were in Ireland to enjoy themselves, and the conversation over breakfast every morning generally rumbled along the same well-worn tracks.

What are your plans for today?

The Blarney Stone? Oh there'll be no shutting you up this evening so when you come back. Ha ha ha!

Make sure to visit the English Market while you're in town.

Hopefully the rain will keep off for ye, but I'd bring an umbrella just in case.

God forgive her the thought, but she hoped the woman didn't stay too long. She'd likely want to get her poor daughter home as soon as possible for the funeral anyway. She wondered how all that worked. It would probably cost a small fortune to have Jessie's body flown home, unless there was some sort of government assistance for this kind of thing. It was unlikely a young one like that would have even thought of taking out travel insurance.

It was just heartbreaking. The girl had come to Ireland with such high hopes of finding a father, maybe even siblings too, a whole new extended family this side of the Atlantic, but instead she'd be going home in a box or an urn, having failed in her search. And to make the whole thing even more tragic, she had been an only child.

She heard the sounds of the baby starting to grizzle from Liam's bedroom. She had suggested to her son that he take his girlfriend out last night and treat her to a meal while she babysat. She had overheard one side of a phone argument between the two of them on Thursday evening before he'd gone out. She had hovered in the landing outside his room, pretending to be looking for something in the hot press as she caught snatches of the conversation.

'Jesus, Molls ... paranoid for fuck's sake ... How many times?'

Noelle had grimaced. How many times had Liam's father convinced her she was being paranoid before the filthy messages on his phone provided her with the incontrovertible truth? If her son ever even thought about messing around on that girl, his life wouldn't be worth living, as he knew only too well. He'd been out drinking two nights in a row this week without Molly when he had work the next day, and he needed to cop himself on. He had a child to provide for now and if that meant he had less freedom than the rest of the lads, tough bloody luck.

She had been all set to tell him a few home truths when he got in from work yesterday evening, but by then the news about Jessie had been confirmed and everything else had paled into insignificance.

Liam had been horrified when he heard. Noelle had tried calling him before somebody else told him, but he had missed her call. He rang her back an hour later, hoping she'd dispel the rumours swirling around the place, and was stunned speechless when she couldn't.

'But I was only out with her on Wednesday night and she was in great form ...'

'I know, love, it's shocking.'

The baby let out another squawk and Noelle got out of bed, pulled her new Christmas Snuddie over her head and put on a pair of fluffy socks. She had offered to keep Leon in with her last night, but Molly still couldn't bear to be separated from him overnight. She was a great little mammy really. Noelle knew she'd probably welcome a lie-in this morning, even though they hadn't been too late last night.

She tapped gently on the bedroom door. No doubt Molly had woken as soon as the baby started to stir. Liam was probably dead to the world beside her.

'I'm just going downstairs,' she said softly. 'Will I take the little man with me and give him his bottle?'

She wouldn't normally get up this early on a Saturday if she didn't have to, but she didn't mind one bit if it meant she got to spend more time with her adorable grandson. She was utterly smitten, she didn't mind admitting. She had heard other people banging on about the love they had for their grandchildren but like everything, it wasn't until you experienced it for yourself that you truly got it.

She heard a rustling inside the room.

'That would be great, Noelle, if you're sure you don't mind. I was just goin' to change him, he's saturated.'

'Leave him, love, I'll do that for you. You hop back in to bed and enjoy a bit of a rest while you can.'

The door opened and Molly handed over her precious bundle, toasty in his soft penguin sleepsuit. A delighted beam spread across the baby's face when he saw Noelle, his dimpled hand reaching for her face.

'Hello, me little puddin'. How's Nana's best boy today? Don't be in any rush to get up now, Molly love, I'm only delighted to have him all to myself for a while. Let Romeo there bring you up your breakfast in bed when you're ready for it.'

Noelle carried the baby down to the kitchen, where the heat had just come on. She shivered. She should have set the timer for a bit earlier this morning; it was Baltic and the house took ages to heat up. With Leon on her hip, she stuck the kettle on and tapped the scoops of formula Molly had already measured out into a sterilised bottle of cool boiled water. Molly felt awful guilt about not being able to breastfeed, but the baby had refused to latch on. The pressure mothers were put under these days was crazy.

Leon began to wriggle and whine in her arms when he spotted his bottle, so she plugged a dummy into his mouth to try and hold him off. He sucked frantically for a few seconds before spitting it back at her with a roar of outrage, his little legs kicking.

'Don't you be givin' out to me, mister. I'm going as fast as I can, it's not Nana's fault you've no patience. Just like your daddy you are – a greedy little guzzler.'

She smiled to herself as she stuck the dummy back in his mouth, thinking of Liam at that age. He had always been a great feeder, unlike Holly, who was as picky then as she was now. Maybe Australia would force her to expand her palate a bit.

The kettle came to a boil and she dropped the bottle into a jug of hot water as she bounced the baby on her hip. She would have to buy one of those electric bottle warmers, but for now, the old-school way would have to do.

The dummy hit the floor with a thunk and the baby took a sharp breath in, the red warning for an almighty roar on the way. She shifted him to her other hip and jigged him up and down faster.

'Alright, alright, baba, it's nearly ready now.'

Liam had been a right placid little lump, with his Buddha belly and chipmunk cheeks. Leon must get his temper from the other side of the family. Hopefully he'd take after his mammy and not those cracked aunts and uncles of his.

She grabbed the baby's changing bag and did a swift change on the sofa at the end of the kitchen, dropping his heavy nappy to the floor, where it landed with a soggy thump, the acrid stench of ammonia stinging her nostrils. She patted him dry with powder, inhaling his delicious baby scent and blowing raspberries into his soft belly while he gurgled and kicked in delight. It was too cold to leave his legs free this morning, so she buttoned him back up quickly before he had time to start giving out.

She took the bottle from the jug and, saying a silent prayer, squirted it inside her wrist, relieved to find it was warm enough. His gums clamped around the bottle and he started to gulp, gripping it with both hands.

'Ah, ah, slow down now, there's nobody going to take it away from you,' she said, smiling down at him. 'You'll get a pain in your tummy.' She loved watching the baby as he fed, his eyes closed in bliss, his cute little groans of contentment. She remembered watching Liam like this. How could that have been twenty-four years ago? Where had all that time gone? He had been a beautiful baby too. Her precious boy.

She glanced at the clock on the wall: just gone half seven. Dani De Marco was probably on the road now, battling jet lag on top of her shock and facing into an inconceivable task ahead. She had probably gazed down adoringly on her baby daughter once like this too, never imagining what lay ahead for them both.

CHAPTER 8

Maria

Maria woke with a splitting headache and a horribly dry mouth. She couldn't remember the last time she had drunk so much and boy, was she paying for it now. Mixing wine and cocktails, too, a recipe for disaster.

But she had felt the need for a blow-out. It had worked too: she'd been in flying form. The two glasses of wine before dinner had her nicely merry and she had polished off another couple over the meal, before dragging Tadhg back into Cask afterwards for cocktails. Happily ensconced on a stool at the bar with the alcohol buzzing nicely through her veins, she'd been able to enjoy the trendy vibe, to admire the stylish young people around her instead of feeling awkward and out of place as she would if she were sober. She had felt good in her AllSaints cargo jeans and the Marco Moreo wedges that added inches to her height. She was loving the shorter, blunt bob her hairdresser had convinced her to have before Christmas, her highlighted blonde hair styled in a gentle boho wave that took years off her, and Eva had worked some kind of sorcery with her Charlotte Tilbury contour wand that made Maria's cheekbones look higher and more defined. It used to be that daughters raided their mother's makeup bags, but these days it was the other way round.

She couldn't afford to let herself go, not when she was married to a man like Tadhg. It wasn't that she worried about him cheating on her, despite what had happened to Noelle. He wouldn't have the time, even if he had the inclination, and as much of a charmer as her husband was, he'd never shown the slightest interest in another woman. He invested so much of his passion in the GAA, there wasn't much left over, even for her sometimes. She'd have to be blind not to see the way other women looked at him, though: at forty-eight, he was still a fine-looking man and kept himself in great shape, with no sign of the paunch or receding hairline that so many men his age sported. There weren't many women she knew who could say that after twenty-two years of marriage, they were as physically attracted to their husband as they had ever been.

She had practically ripped the boxers off him last night when they fell into bed. She hoped to God they hadn't made too much noise, cringing at the thought of their daughter hearing her parents having sex on the other side of her bedroom wall. It was hard when you had teenage kids living under your roof, but she hoped they hadn't let go too much last night, their inhibitions unlaced by alcohol. She hoped she'd at least held onto the headboard to stop it banging off the wall.

She had fallen into a deep, drunken sleep, only to be woken at four a.m. by the Fear. Always top of her playlist of worries, of course, was Ben. Those new friends of his were a genuine cause for concern, in fairness, but she couldn't say a word to him or he'd take the head off her, telling her she should be happy he *had* friends to hang around with. And she had been: herself and Tadhg had both been thrilled, until they found out who they were. There was no telling him, though; Ben would have to learn for himself. She just hoped that happened before those lads got him into any serious trouble. Covid had been particularly tough on her youngest child. While some kids had sailed through the pandemic, delighted with the breaks from the school routine, others like Ben had really struggled. He had missed out on a good chunk of his first year of secondary school, and had found it hard to settle in when school reopened, pulling away from the small band of pals he had hung around with since Junior Infants.

It had broken Maria's heart to see the other lads heading down to the GAA pitch with their hurleys or cycling around the village while her son refused to leave the house, growing paler and quieter as the months passed. She had asked him a few times if something had happened, some kind of falling out, but he just shook his head. She had even asked the mother of his closest friend, Jamie – former closest friend now – if she knew what was going on, but she hadn't heard anything, telling Maria not to lose sleep over it and saying they'd all be back friends again before they knew it. It hadn't happened, though.

People assumed that being a teacher bestowed some kind of advantage upon you when it came to parenting, that she should somehow have all the answers, but the truth was that she was in the same rocky boat as everybody else. As anxious as any other mother would be when her child existed largely in the virtual world he accessed through his PlayStation. One of the worst decisions they had ever made was to get him a TV for his bedroom. He had begged and begged for it until they finally gave in, but while they had at least been able to see him when his console was in the playroom, now he rarely emerged from behind the closed door of his bedroom unless driven out by hunger.

They had been so relieved when at the start of last term he started hanging out with Harry and began to come out of himself again. He had enjoyed the more relaxed structure of transition year after the Junior Cert, and then this year, through Harry, a new addition to the school, he had gained a whole new group of friends. But they had turned out to be a pack of brazen pups who had no respect for authority of any kind, spending more time in detention than any other kids in their year; their parents were the type that either didn't care or went on the attack against the school, claiming their sons were being picked on for no reason. The speed at which those boys had influenced her own son's behaviour had shocked Maria. She understood it wasn't easy being the principal's son, especially as a teenage boy, but his attitude towards Tadhg had deteriorated to the point that he was barely civil to him, and things seemed to be getting worse.

She had lain awake in the early hours wrestling with images of her son being drawn down dark paths which saw him dropping out of school, ending up on drugs and even in prison. Or worse, dead in the wreck of a stolen car. She didn't know what time she had finally fallen asleep, but some of the stress of the night's anxiety was still trapped in her body.

'Morning, sunshine. Thought you could do with some caffeine.' Tadhg, looking fresh and well rested, came in the door with a tray, the newspaper under his arm. He never got hangovers; it was so bloody annoying. 'Sit yourself up there. You're getting breakfast in bed today, a special treat.'

Jesus Christ. I can't remember the last time I got breakfast in bed and he waits until I'm dying sick from drink to make it.

As she pulled herself up in the bed, a wave of nausea hit her. 'Oh God, love. I'm not sure if ...'

He propped the tray over her lap. A mug of coffee. A plate of bacon, eggs and a lumpy browning mush of avocado on a soggy bed of sourdough toast.

The muscles at the back of her throat contracted. 'It looks fab, thanks,' she said weakly, reaching for the glass of water on her bedside table. There was definitely no way she could get this food down; she'd have to wait for her husband to leave and hide the evidence. If only Rupert was here: he'd have gladly taken care of it for her.

Instead of leaving, though, Tadhg got back onto his side of the bed with a mug of coffee and the paper, propping the pillows up behind him.

He never went back to bed.

'Is training not on this morning?'

'Nope. Cancelled 'cos of the weather. The pitches are all frozen.'

Shite.

Now she was going to have to at least pretend to eat something.

The nausea rose again. She cut through the glistening belly of a poached egg, its yolk erupting onto her plate like gloopy orange pus, then cut the bacon into small pieces, surreptitiously shoving both the bacon and the egg under a slice of toast.

Tadhg began to rummage through the paper, putting the weekend sections to one side for her. 'There's a big report on that fire up at the Lodge. Two security guards were assaulted, one hospitalised, and a squad car had its tyres slashed. Isn't that disgraceful?'

'Desperate.' She tried to tune him out as she pushed her tray to one side and gingerly moved to the edge of the bed. Her husband had a habit of reading out bits from various articles that he thought she might find interesting. She usually didn't mind, but she wasn't usually dying from drink.

'Shocking stuff altogether. I hope they catch whoever's responsible and make a bloody example of them.' He shook his head. 'Wouldn't the ignorance sicken you? You can be damn sure they all had family who emigrated for work over the years, but they're very quick to forget that now. I must try and get somebody in to talk to the kids about it, like we did with Andrew Tate last year.'

Her head hurt too much to give a shit about arson or the far-right agitators or Andrew bloody Tate right now. If only she could fast forward to the end of the day until she felt normal again.

'Oh, there's an article on that girl who died at the castle. They've named her, used her photo and all. God help that family, it's very sad. When did Noelle say the mother is due to arrive?'

'This morning some time. Poor Noelle is up to ninety over it. Did I tell you she's booked into the B&B? She wants to stay in the room where her daughter was staying.'

'You're not serious?' Her husband grimaced. 'That's a bit ghoulish, isn't it? Typical OTT Yank.'

'I don't think it's ghoulish at all. I'd probably do the same thing in her situation. The poor woman ... Oh God, I really don't feel well. I think I'm going to be sick.'

She got out of bed and headed for the ensuite. At least her husband wouldn't follow her in there.

CHAPTER 9

Dani

If anybody asked her afterwards, she wouldn't be able to tell them much about the drive from the airport to the hospital in Cork where the mortuary was located: her thoughts were muffled behind a barrier of diazepam, shock and jet lag. The cop who was waiting for her when she landed at Shannon Airport looked like she'd come straight from central casting for the role of Irish *cailín*. Auburn hair pulled back off her face, with freckles to match. Green eyes. She said her name was Amy, but Dani thought she looked more like an Erin or a Caitlyn. She pulled Dani's hastily packed case to a cruiser parked outside the arrivals department, where the male cop sitting in the driver's seat got out and shook her hand robustly, before stowing her baggage in the trunk. Dani sat slumped in the rear seat, staring dully out the window at a blur of green fields and grey sky, punctuated every now and then by a house or a row of low-rise buildings on either side as they passed through a village or town.

The cops had offered to take her to the B&B in Blarney first so she could freshen up after the flight, but as much as the thought of a hot shower and a fresh set of clothes appealed,

Dani had insisted on going straight to the morgue. She couldn't bear to stretch the agony out a single second longer than necessary.

The balding male cop, whose name Dani hadn't caught, started to make small talk as they hit the outskirts of the city and were slowed down by traffic lights. His cousin played for the Cork Boston Gaelic football club; he'd been out to visit him a few years ago. They had gone on a whale-watching tour one day, he told her, and he'd been so seasick they had to cancel their plans to go to James Hook afterwards for lobster. Dani said what a pity that was, because James Hook lobster rolls were the absolute best, but the flat, deadened sound that came out of her mouth was unfamiliar to her own ears. Talking about lobster and Gaelic football with cops en route to a morgue – the whole thing was surreal.

Her phone pinged from her purse. Joe.

Hope you arrived safely. Call me when you can. Thinking of you xx

Another ping.

Just wanted to let you know, the baby arrived at 10.35 p.m. our time while you were in the air. A little girl, eight pounds, one ounce. Mom and baby both doing good.

Her brother's message yanked her back in time to the night twenty-two years ago when her own little girl had been born in the same hospital. She had come out purple and hollering: a mop of spiked black hair, huge, shocked eyes, tiny fists waving, ready to take on the world. As if Jessie De Marco had somehow known that life was going to be no bed of roses.

Dani had been so terrified at the thought of having to tell her mother she was pregnant. At seventeen years of age. She had pictured Mamma's face curling in disgust, a look that would be mirrored in the faces of Dani's aunts. Never mind telling her the truth about who the father was. Getting rid of it had seemed like the best way out: that way, as her baby's daddy had pointed out, nobody else would ever need to know, especially her family. She hadn't been able to go through with it, though; not even the fear of Vittoria Antonelli Doyle's reaction was enough to make her. She had been the youngest one in the waiting room that day, the only one on her own. Everybody else had somebody: a mother, a boyfriend, a friend. She'd had no-one because she had told no-one; *he* had made her swear not to. Maybe if Pops had still been around, she'd have told him.

As the youngest of the Doyle kids and the only girl, Dani had always been her father's pet. A born entertainer, Mick Doyle had a politician's knack for remembering faces and names, for making every person who came in the door of Vittoria's feel special. Handsome and charming in his tailored tuxedo, he could have been a member of the Rat Pack he loved so much. Nat King Cole, Sammy Davis Junior, Dean Martin, Frank Sinatra. A natural on the piano with a voice like caramelised sugar, Pops knew how to hold an audience. 'You should be playing Carnegie Hall, Mick,' he'd been told on more than one occasion by a customer, and while he might have laughed those compliments off at the time, even as a child Dani had sensed the sadness in her father: a sense of disappointment, perhaps, that his stage was the corner of an Italian restaurant where all around him his audience slurped spaghetti and devoured his wife's famous gnocchi gorgonzola, and not a more illustrious venue. To their customers, Mick and Vittoria were the glamorous couple who ran one of the most popular Italian restaurants in all of Boston, the perfect team. She looked after front of house, greeting customers and managing the business that had been in her family for generations, and he kept them all entertained with his songs and his wit and his storytelling. Their party piece was Sinatra's 'The Way You Look Tonight' and when Dani watched them sing the words to each other, her mother leaning over the piano and gazing into her father's eyes, she used to imagine it was real. That it wasn't a charade put on for their customers and that her mother really did adore Pops, as much as Dani did.

Like a bird flying low and seeking refuge when it senses a storm on the way, Dani had learnt at a young age how to gauge her mother's anticyclones and depressions, to flee or hide before she blew. Somehow Pops had never learnt to read his wife's moods though, to scent danger on the wind, or maybe he had and he chose to take the brunt of them to protect her, because it was rarely the boys Mamma unleashed upon. Her mother was like an unlit pyre doused in gasoline – the slightest slight or wrong word or look all it took to ignite her – and Dani lived in a constant state of red alert.

One of Dani's most vivid childhood memories was of running to her mother in tears after she had fallen yet again and skinned her knee – she had been an awkward, clumsy child, always tripping over nothing and walking into things. She would only have been about four years old. Mamma had been sitting at the round table in the kitchen with Zia Giulia and her own namesake Zia Daniela. The two women were permanent fixtures in their home, drinking strong black coffee, puffing on Camels and chattering volubly in Italian, often derogatively about Dani's father, even as he sat in the next room watching TV. *Coglione. Pezzo de merda. Stupido cretino. Imbecille.* Pops hadn't needed to speak Italian to know they weren't paying him any compliments. No wonder he had turned to the booze for comfort.

He hadn't been there that day when she fell, which was why she had run to her mother, in pain and whimpering at the sight of the blood on her knee. She had pulled at Mamma's arm to try and get her attention, but her mother, annoyed at being interrupted in the middle of whatever story she was telling, had flung her away irritably and Dani had landed hard on her bum on the kitchen tiles, the shock making her cry even harder. Mamma had got to her feet, caught her by the arm and dragged her out of the kitchen and down the hall to her bedroom, fingers digging into her skin, yelling that she was *la idiozia*, just like her father, while Zia Giulia shouted after them, 'What the hell is wrong with that child?' Mamma had shoved her into her room and slammed the door on her.

Her father had found her hours later, lying on the floor inside the door, having cried herself to sleep. The tears had started again when she saw him and he had taken her in his arms and lifted her to the bed. He had gone to get something to clean the grit and after he'd wiped the congealed blood from her knee had offered her the pack of Disney princess Band-Aids to choose from. Then he had held her, rocking her gently, as she tried to tell him what had happened, between sobs and long shuddery breaths, showing him the red marks on her arm where Mamma had hurt her. Her mother never usually got physical. She had felt a warm raindrop plop on to her forehead and when she looked up, Pops was crying too and that made her feel even worse.

After a few minutes, he had lifted her chin and looked into her eyes. 'You are the most special little girl that was ever born, Daniela Doyle, and don't you ever forget that. I'm so sorry for what happened to you today. It was wrong and I'm going to tell Mamma that. You're beautiful and smart and funny and someday, you're going to go out into that world and do great things. I just know it.'

She didn't know if Pops had ever said anything to Mamma; it made no difference if he had. Part of her was glad he hadn't lived long enough to see how wrong he had been about her. Dani had fucked her life up. She hadn't been a good mother to Jessie – had been pretty shit, if she forced herself to be honest, which she didn't like to do too often as it was so painful. The truth was she'd left Jessie to be raised by her mother, dropping in and out of her daughter's life over the years of her childhood – conscious that as much as she loved Jessie, she had no clue how to be a mother to her.

Please, God, let it not be too late for me to make up for that now.

I swear, God, I'll get my shit together.

I promise I'll bring her home and start afresh and look after her properly this time.

I'll quit the booze and the men, I'll start cooking healthy for her, I'll find a nice home for us both.

Just please, God, I beg you, don't let it be her.

She'd know if Jessie was gone, wouldn't she? Didn't they say mothers knew, that they sensed when their child's soul left this world? She had no feeling, not even a tickle in her gut that her daughter's beautiful, brave spirit was gone. That had to mean something, didn't it?

And then it was time.

And they were there.

She got out of the car and her knees started to tremble real hard. The red-headed cop asked her if she was sure she was up to this and she said she didn't know, but she had to do it anyway. There was a corridor, strip lighting, a row of doors. Her head felt floaty, her feet heavy. The nice officer linked her arm.

They were brought into a small room with white walls.

A bitter, chemical smell.

A trolley, a white sheet, the shape of a body underneath.

She gripped her fingers tightly. Swallowed.

There was a whirr and a hiss and the room filled with a fresh, citrusy aroma that failed to mask the bass note of death.

Somebody asked her if she was ready and she must have nodded because a man in scrubs gently pulled the sheet back, and still none of it felt real.

For one brief, euphoric moment, she thought *It's not her* and the relief nearly floored her. This girl was too young, her hair too dull, her skin too waxen, her—

And then she saw the beauty spot on her right earlobe ...

And the tiny scar beside her eyebrow where she had been pushed off the top of a slide when she was five by the youngest of Cindy Miller's brats ...

And, vaguely, the bluish bruises on her temple and cheekbone.

A chair was pushed under her and she collapsed onto it.
God, no, no, no.
Her baby.
So pale, white as the walls.
So cold, she hated the cold.
So still, she never sat still.
So dead.

CHAPTER 10

Noelle
Blarney
Sunday, 14 January

She was woken by a howl. The baby. She scrabbled around on the bedside locker for her phone to check the time. Just coming up to six again. He was like clockwork, that lad.

Hang on, though.

Molly and Leon hadn't stayed here last night.

'NOOOO!! No, no, no. Oh God, please, no!' The anguished cries shattered the early-morning quiet; a mother waking to a fresh hell.

Jesus Christ. That poor woman.

Noelle jumped out of bed and pulled her dressing gown on, tying the belt around her waist.

What should I do? Should I knock on her door and see if she needs anything? Oh Christ, what do I even say?

The woman was a complete stranger. Noelle knew nothing about her except that her only child had just died at the age of twenty-two, that there had been some falling out between the two of them before Jessie came to Ireland, and that she was here all by herself. She had no idea whether Dani would want to be comforted by a stranger or left alone.

If it was Holly ...
She shuddered.

She knew it was horrible of her, but she wished Jessie had booked into some other B&B and that her mother was waking up under somebody else's roof this morning. If Maria was here, she would know just the right thing to say to the woman, the right thing to do for her. Maria was a natural empath: people were always telling her she should have been a counsellor. It was too early in the morning to call her friend for advice, though.

Noelle's phone hadn't stopped buzzing yesterday. There was such a sense of loss and disbelief around the village in the wake of Jessie's death. Even people who hadn't met her felt they had come to know the girl through her stories online and her interviews in the local media. A group of locals had even organised a candlelit vigil for Jessie this evening, over in the village square.

She opened her bedroom door quietly and stepped out onto the landing. Her room was at the front right of the sprawling dormer bungalow; the room she had given Jessie, and now her mother, was at the front on the other end. The house was badly in need of a makeover. She had done what she could with paint and wallpaper and soft furnishings, but she'd love to have the money to do a proper job. It wouldn't be happening any time soon, though, despite the fact that things had got a bit easier since Liam had started working and contributing to his keep. He was a good lad, really; there were plenty his age still living at home with their mams and not handing a penny over. She hadn't had to ask for it either: he had offered, batting away her feeble protests. She put a bit aside each week out of what he gave her; it would go towards a deposit for his own place some day. Only for him, she probably would have lost the B&B, but that was all in the past now and her ex-husband couldn't hurt them anymore. Please God, anyway.

She moved soundlessly across the carpet, past the staircase and over to her guest's room. Silence now. Maybe she had fallen back to sleep. Hopefully. Noelle began to back away. She wouldn't disturb ... Oh Jesus Christ. A wretched sound like a honking seal stopped her. She pressed her hand against the wall beside the door.

Christ!

Taking a deep breath, she tapped gently.

'Dani?'

No answer.

Should I walk away? Does she want to be left alone? Should I knock again?

'Em, sorry ... I was just wondering if you needed anything, Dani,' she said. 'Tea or coffee? Some toast or a bit of breakfast maybe?'

A throat cleared inside the room. 'Come in.'

She pushed down the handle, and stuck her head around the door. It smelled as if Jessie had literally just walked out. Pistachio, salted caramel and vanilla: Jessie had told her what the lovely scent was. She took in Dani sitting at the dressing table amid the clutter of her daughter's cosmetics and realised that she must have just sprayed the body mist.

Dani turned to her. She looked dreadful, her face swollen and blotchy under that garish orange hair. Her dark roots were coming through; she had the same natural colour as her daughter and Noelle wondered why on earth she would destroy it like that.

'Did you manage to get any sleep at all?' she asked.

'Yeah, I crashed out as soon as I hit the pillow. What time did I actually go to bed? I kinda lost track of time yesterday.'

'It was around four in the afternoon. I knocked around six to see if you needed anything, but there was no answer and I didn't want to wake you. Then I knocked again around nine to see if you were hungry, because you hadn't eaten all day, but you said no, you just wanted to sleep. You were exhausted, God love you.'

'I woke around ten and took a couple of ... um ... pills to help me sleep. I knew I'd be up all night otherwise and I just couldn't bear ... I just needed to knock myself out.'

'I know. I can't even begin to imagine how you must be feeling.' *Very fucking helpful, Noelle, good girl yourself.* 'If there's anything at all I can do for you, just let me know. You must be starving. Will you have something to eat? I can bring a tray up, or you might prefer to come down?'

'Yeah, I could eat,' she said groggily. 'I'll just shower first and get dressed. I need to figure out ... I need to call home.'

She sounded so like her daughter, it was uncanny. Noelle loved the accent, the way Bostonians ignored their r's. She had cousins in Boston who had come over to Cork when they were kids and the older Irish cousins used to keep asking them to say 'I park my car in Harvard Yard', cracking up when they said, 'I pawk my caw in Hawvad Yawd.'

'You get yourself ready and then, once you have a coffee and some food inside you, I'll sit down with you and help you make a list of what you need to do.'

'Thank you, Noelle, that would be great. I need to go through her stuff and choose something for her to be ... Oh God, I don't think I can do this.' She slumped over the dressing table, her shoulders shaking.

Noelle crossed the room, laid her hand awkwardly on the other woman's back. 'Don't worry about that right now, Dani. I'll help you later. I'll go down there and put the kettle on. You take as long as you need.'

Dani gripped her hand as if it were a life buoy. 'I feel so awful,' she gulped. 'The last time we spoke, she was so angry with me.'

'Oh, Dani, I'm so sorry.'

Christ. Could this get any worse?

'But I'm sure she'd forgotten all about that. You can't beat yourself—'

'No.' Dani shook her head. She turned to face Noelle again. 'You don't understand. She'd just found out I'd been lying to her for years. She grew up thinking my ex-husband was her dad. We split up when she was very young and he moved out of state; she had no relationship with him. But one night, a couple of weeks before Christmas, this cousin of his goes into the bar where Jessie works downtown and gets talking to her. When Jessie found out they had the same surname, she asked the woman if she knew her dad, Ricky De Marco from Dorchester. The woman put two and two together right away and figured out who Jessie was. She told her I was a lying skank, that Riccardo wasn't her father and had no idea who was.

'Jessie was so upset she had to leave work. She came straight over to the apartment to ask me if it was true. I had to tell her it was. She demanded to know her real father's name and where he was and I had to tell her that I didn't know exactly. I was so young, only eighteen when I had her and, well, myself and her dad hadn't exactly spent a whole heap of time talking. He was in the US working on a J1 visa and all I knew about him was his name and that he was from some place in north County Cork with a castle. The way she looked at me that night ... And oh God ...' She squeezed Noelle's hand harder. 'That was the last conversation I ever had with her. I'd no idea she'd even left Boston. She wouldn't answer my calls, ignored all my messages. I knew she was okay 'cos she visited with my mom over Christmas – when she knew I'd be out – to exchange gifts, and she'd been calling and messaging her, but none of us knew she was actually in Ireland. I just thought I needed to give her some time and she'd come round, but ...'

'Oh, Dani, I'm so sorry.'

Bad enough to lose a child under such tragic circumstances, but this was just horrific. If Dani hadn't lied to Jessie about her father, then the girl wouldn't have come to Cork when she did, and she wouldn't have fallen down those steps. The guilt of that would kill you.

Why, Noelle wondered, had Dani not just told her daughter the truth about her father in the first place?

CHAPTER 11

Maria

'Why did they have a vigil for her, though? I mean, it's terrible sad an' all that, but it's not like the young one was murdered. Not like that poor girl up the country.'

'God Almighty, Betty, will you keep your voice down? The whole place can hear you,' Essie said, elbowing her friend.

It was a bit late for that. You'd hear Betty Byrne a mile away, even if there was an All-Ireland hurling final with Cork playing Kilkenny turned up to full volume on the TV in the hotel bar. The woman was half deaf and had zero filter. She could no more read a room than she could the Latin translation of *Ulysses*.

Eva, who much to Maria's surprise had accompanied them over to the vigil, sniggered. She got great mileage out of Betty, who she regularly said was 'so unwoke, she's comatose'. Five foot nothing, the older woman was all out today in a head-to-toe-purple glittery skirt and top under a faux fur jacket, a feathery boa coiled around her neck.

The bar was packed. Casey's hotel, just off the square, was always busy, between christenings and funerals and the many different life events in between, but there had been a huge turnout for the vigil. Most of those who had left their warm homes to stand in the village green on a bitter January evening were there to show their solidarity with the family of the American girl, and to mourn the loss of a life so young and filled with promise. There were always the few, of course, who were only there for the nose, and the free finger food that Dermot Casey had been persuaded into 'offering' by Alice Cummins and her formidable band of helpers on the Blarney Community Forum.

The girl's mother had turned up, to the surprise of everyone. Maria didn't know how the woman was even standing, never mind at a vigil for her own daughter. Maybe she had thought she'd find some comfort here, in the midst of strangers who wanted to offer her their heartfelt sympathies. It had been such an emotional and moving event: dozens of night lights flickering and glowing in the dark square like battery-operated fireflies. Fr Gerry had said a few words that Maria couldn't hear from her spot at the edge of the crowd, and then Alice had led the hymn-singing.

The sweet, mournful wail of the uillean pipes rang out across the square, where droplets of warm breath floated in the air like dozens of tiny ghosts and even the trees seemed to bow their heads in sorrow. Maria had brushed the tears away from her eyes and hugged Eva closer to her side.

She spotted Tadhg threading his way through the wedged bar now, balancing three drinks in his hands. She stood to take them from him, and he dived back into the crowd to collect the rest. She handed Essie, who was driving, a sparkling water with lime, Betty a vodka and Coke, and Eva a Lucozade.

'Have you been on to Noelle, Maria?' Betty asked. 'How's the mother doin', did she say? She must be in bits altogether, God love her.'

'She hasn't said much, to be honest,' Maria said. In confidence, Noelle had told her that Dani had been informed of the cause of her daughter's death – a traumatic brain injury due to the fall – but she had no intention of telling Betty that.

'Did you see her at the vigil?' Betty asked, butting into her thoughts. 'Dani, she's called. A fine-sized girl, I'd say she likes her grub, but she has a gorgeous face, the same colouring as the daughter.'

'Jesus, Betty, you can't say things like that,' Essie scolded, looking around her to see if anybody was listening. You wouldn't know what the woman could come out with next. Even Eva had the good grace to look appalled.

'What? Didn't I say she had a lovely face? Feck's sake, you'd be afraid to open your mouth these days.'

'Well, it wouldn't do you a bit of harm if you kept yours *shut* the odd time.'

Maria let the conversation drift around her as she craned her neck to see where her husband had got to. Where on earth was he with her drink? She was gasping.

She spotted him standing at the bar with Paul O'Donovan, throwing his head back in laughter at whatever his friend had just said. He was wearing the blue-striped Boss shirt she'd bought him for Christmas, knowing when she'd seen it in the shop that it would bring out the colour of his eyes. There weren't many men around who looked as good as he did at his age, although she'd bloody well strangle him if he didn't hurry up with her mineral. She couldn't face the thought of alcohol after her day of hangover hell yesterday. Wedged in beside

Essie and Betty on the inside of the table, she was about to pick her phone up to ring him when she spotted Noelle threading her way through the packed bar from the far end, her face flushed and tense looking.

Maria waved to get her attention. Her friend must have changed her plans. She'd said she had to bring Dani back to the B&B after the vigil and she didn't want to leave her on her own there.

Noelle widened her eyes at her as she got closer.

What was wrong with ... Oh!

The woman following in Noelle's wake, as the crowd parted before them like the Red Sea, had to be Dani De Marco. She had the same huge brown eyes and full red lips as her daughter, although the resemblance ended there. Her hair was a weird Fanta orangish colour and she was wearing some sort of a clashing animal print chiffon thing that did nothing for her. Maria couldn't believe she had come into the bar; she'd have thought it was the last thing the girl's mother would have wanted to do. And by the look on Noelle's face, it was the last thing *she* had wanted to do too.

'Noelle, over here,' Betty trilled. 'Squish over, Essie and make some room,' she said, before sliding along the faux leather bench and nudging the man at the table beside them. 'Sorry love, would you mind movin' down there a bit to make space for the mother of that poor girleen who died at the castle? If ye put your coats under your seats, ye'll free up some room. Good lad yerself.' The man and his female companion shuffled along obediently as much as they could.

'Squeeze in here, Noelle love. And Dani, isn't it? I'm Betty. Come on, girl. There's plenty of room.'

The woman really was incorrigible. Eva bent her head.

'Sit yourself in here.' Betty patted the seat beside her, taking Dani's hand hostage between her own as she told her how sorry she was for her 'trouble'.

The American woman looked dazed. She probably thought the over-familiar older lady, dressed as if she were going to a wedding and now bellowing out introductions to the rest of the table as if they were all deaf, was on day release from some kind of mental unit.

Landing heavily on the seat beside Maria, Noelle muttered, 'Just when I thought things couldn't get any worse, Betty bloody Byrne throws herself into the mix.'

'You look like you need a drink, girl.'

'You can sing that. I'll go to the bar in a minute. Jesus, it's mental in here.'

'Stay where you are, Tadhg is at the bar. I'm waiting ages for him to bring my own drink, he's too busy bloody yapping. I'll try ringing him there. Are you on the G&Ts?'

'Yes, thanks.'

'And how about …?' She nodded towards Dani, who was sitting the other side of Noelle, her hand still held captive by Betty.

'An Irish coffee. I said I'd make her one at home, but she insisted on coming in here.'

The Yanks were mad for their Irish coffees. They came off the tour buses clutching their complimentary vouchers like winning Lotto tickets, keen to imbibe as much of the local culture as they could and not seeming to notice that none of the locals were knocking back whiskey-infused hot drinks at brunch.

Maria rang Tadhg's phone, hoping it was on vibrate; he'd never hear it over all the noise.

'Shit, sorry love. I got chatting to Paul and—'

'I saw that. I wouldn't want to be dying of feckin' thirst. Noelle is here now as well. Can you order a gin and tonic and an Irish coffee as well, please? And make it a bit faster this time.'

'We better try and rescue the poor woman,' Noelle said, turning to Dani and touching her arm. 'Dani, this is my good friend Maria. Her husband is getting us some drinks at the bar.'

'Nice to meet you, Maria,' the American woman said. 'That's so kind of him.'

'Lovely to meet you too, Dani, though I'm sorry to have to meet you under such sad circumstances. If there's anything we can do for you, anything at all, please make sure to let Noelle know.'

'Thank you, I appreciate your offer. It's all just so …' She splayed the fingers of her free hand against her breastbone like a fan. 'The American embassy have given me a contact person who I'll be talking to in the morning about arrangements and stuff. It's not straightforward. There'll have to be a cremation and—'

'Oh Lord, I don't know about those cremations at all, doll,' Betty interjected. 'I mean there's no goin' back you know if you change yer mind …'

'BETTY!' Essie and Noelle cried in unison. Eva looked mortified.

Dani dropped her head into her hands, her back shaking.

Oh, for Christ's sake. Betty bloody Byrne.

'I'm so sorry, Dani,' Noelle said. 'Betty didn't mean to upset you. She just doesn't think sometimes before she opens her big gob.'

'All I said was—'

'Betty!' Essie warned, index finger to her lips like a junior infants teacher.

Dani held up a hand. 'No, it's fine ... This is all just so ...' She lifted her head, and Maria realised the tears on her face were of laughter.

Noelle looked at Maria from concerned eyes that mirrored her own. She was probably wondering the same thing. Was the woman having some kind of emotional meltdown?

Where the hell was her husband with their drinks? It looked like Dani could do with that whiskey.

'Oh, here's Tadhg now,' Noelle said.

'Thank Christ.'

'Sorry about the wait, guys. It's bedlam up there,' Tadhg said, holding the gin and tonic and Maria's Club Orange in one hand, and the handle of the Irish coffee glass in the other. He placed the drinks on the table and wiped his brow. 'Christ, the heat in here'd knock ya. I'll head back to the lads and my pint, leave ye ladies to it.'

'Thanks for saving us the trip, Tadhg, you're as good,' Noelle said, pushing her guest's drink over to her. 'Here you go, Dani. Be careful now, that glass is roasting.'

Dani ignored Noelle and the drink in front of her. She was staring up at Tadhg as if in shock, her rosy cheeks turning even redder.

'Dani,' Noelle repeated. 'Your drink.' She pointed to the steaming glass in front of her, but the other woman still didn't acknowledge it. She didn't take her eyes off Maria's husband. Just sat there staring weirdly at him while the others, apart from Tadhg, who hadn't seemed to notice and was turning to go, all made eyes at each other.

Just when Maria was about to break the awkward silence, the American woman opened her mouth and said, 'It's you! Oh my fucking God, it's actually you!'

CHAPTER 12

Dani

She had doubted her own eyes at first. Thought he might have been a figment of her imagination, barfed up by her traumatised brain. It had been over twenty years since she had last laid eyes on the man, after all, and she'd never expected to see him again. When she had shared with Jessie the embarrassingly scant information she possessed about Jessie's real father – *A village in north Cork with a castle? I mean, come on!* – she had never imagined that her daughter would succeed in finding him. Not with such a common name and so little to go on. This was Ireland: every town and village probably had a castle of some sort. She had told Jessie her dad had been over in the US on a temporary work visa, and that was true. She just hadn't mentioned that he happened to be a teacher: *her* teacher. Her daughter's opinion of her had been low enough already.

When she'd lifted her head to thank Noelle's friend for the drink, her instant reaction had been to freeze. The hubbub of the bar around her faded away, as if somebody had covered her ears with noise-cancelling headphones. She hadn't been able to take her eyes off him, only vaguely aware of Noelle saying something to her, of the steam rising from the glass in front of her, the sweet smell of whiskey.

His hair was longer now, thick and wavy, with peppery streaks. He had worn it tight back then; she had loved how the bristles felt under her fingers. A real man, not like the geeks she went to school with. And so goddamn fucking hot. Tall and ripped. Those devastating eyes that made her tummy all jittery when they singled her out. Topaz – the colour of her birthstone, as if he had been created especially for her – framed by long, dark lashes.

This whole situation was already so wacky: that weird Betty lady beside her, her words running into each other and coming at Dani so thick and fast that she kept having to ask her to repeat herself. There had been a strange moment when the teenage girl across the table from her, whose name she hadn't caught during Betty's breathless introductions, had looked up from her phone to say hello and smiled at her. There had been something so familiar about her, as if Dani knew her from somewhere when, of course, she couldn't possibly. It was only later that she realised what it was. She had her father's eyes: that same mesmerising shade of blue. The girl had quickly turned her attention back to her phone and Dani had been distracted by the gabby Golden Girl again.

Noelle had interrupted Betty mid-flow at one point to ask Dani if she was alright, suggesting that if it was all too much for her, they could have a quiet drink back at the B&B instead, but Dani had assured her hostess that she was fine. She had been so moved by how many people had turned out for her daughter, all those strangers who had stood in the cold, visibly affected by the death of a young woman most of them had never met. She had taken comfort from the simple ceremony, from the warmth of the people who had come up to her afterwards to shake her hand and offer their condolences. She had needed it after the call from her mother.

And then that man had approached the table with their drinks and she had looked up and for the second time in ten minutes, she was looking into those eyes. This time, set in a face she did recognise, albeit slightly jowlier now and a bit more crinkled around the eyes and mouth.

It was *him*!

The shock of it had sparked an intense visceral reaction in her body. Every muscle, from her jaw to her toes, stiffened and it was as if her mind had disconnected from its network and all she could focus on was him.

She had no idea how long she sat there.

Staring.

Until she came back online and she was finally able to open her mouth and make some words come out of it.

He stood gaping back at her, a look not of recognition but of confusion. As if he had never set eyes on her before. Below him, the girl on the stool with the matching eyes was looking at her too.

'I'm sorry, wha—' he began as Betty jumped in with, 'What's wrong love, are you alright? That's Tadhg, Maria's husband. Ah, you're probably all over the place, God help—'

'It's him,' Dani said, 'but I don't und—' And then it hit her. 'Oh my God! She found you.'

'I don't ...' He put his pint on the table and shrugged his shoulders at his wife.

'What's she on about, Tadhg? Who found you?' Betty asked.

'Will you stop, Betty?' Noelle said. 'Look, clearly this is all too much for you, Dani, why don't you and I—'

'NO!'

Noelle looked shocked at her raised voice. They all did, except for the girl, who just looked embarrassed. Dani didn't care. She couldn't believe he was standing here right in front of her.

She made an attempt to get to her feet but was boxed in on all sides. She could feel the sweat on her back, above her lip, glueing her thighs together. It was far too hot in here, too crowded.

'I never thought she'd actually find you. But ... why didn't she post anything about it?' She had known nothing about her daughter's public search until the guards told her. As well as blocking her from all her accounts, Jessie had apparently set up new ones. Dani hadn't been able to make herself watch her daughter's final videos yet, but from what she'd been told, Jessie hadn't posted anything about finding her father.

Michael just stood there, looking flummoxed.

His wife got to her feet then, grabbed their coats and began to try and push her way past the drink-laden table. 'I think it's time we left. I'll give you a buzz later, Noelle ...'

'I'm talking about your daughter, Michael. Our daughter.' Her voice rang out loud and shrill across the bar, causing heads to turn in their direction, conversations to pause mid-stream. 'Jessie De Marco. She came to Blarney to find you. I just didn't think she had.'

You could have heard a beer mat drop.

'I'm sorry, you must be mistaken. I've never met you in my life ...' Michael looked at Noelle, his hands raised, as if hoping she could intervene.

'That's not true though is it, Michael? Or should I call you *Mr* Murphy?'

CHAPTER 13

Noelle

The chatter of the crowd around them stalled as if somebody had pressed a mute button, the spotlight shining on Dani as her spellbound audience held their breath. Casey's wasn't really the kind of place for drunken rows or embarrassing shows like this one, not unless you wanted your private business spread round the village like a dose of the clap.

Tadhg looked at Noelle helplessly, as if she was the woman's keeper and not just someone unfortunate enough to find herself front and centre in a drama she had no wish to be part of. Had she imagined that flash of something in his eyes when he saw who the hot whiskey was for? Surprise, maybe, that the grieving mother was in any fit state to be sitting in the pub drinking hot toddies with them.

'Dani.' She reached across Betty and tapped Dani's arm. Her eyes were still glued to Tadhg, wide, unblinking. 'I really think it's time we left.'

'You're right, Noelle,' Betty said. 'It's all been too much for her, the poor girl,' and for once, Noelle could have hugged the older woman. 'A good rest will do her the world of—'

'NO! I'M GOING NOWHERE!'

More heads turned, from further down the bar, to see what the commotion was all about. Betty's mouth fell open and the Murphys looked like a family of rabbits caught in the headlights of an articulated truck.

For fuck's sake.

She had to get Dani out of here before she lost it completely. She reached under the seat for the coats she had shoved there.

'Come on, Dani,' she said, gently.

'NO!' Dani pushed her hand out in front of Noelle, as if she were trying to stop traffic. 'Sorry to be rude, Noelle, but I need to find out what the hell is going on here. This is frickin' … Did she make contact with you?' she asked Tadhg. 'Did you meet her?'

'Okay, I'm sorry, but that's enough. We're going to leave now. I know you're upset,' he said to Dani, 'and we're very sorry for what you're going through, really we are, but I have no idea what you're talking about.'

Eva was already pushing her way through the bar, abandoning her jacket on the stool behind her. Maria, with a squeeze of Noelle's arm and a quick goodbye, grabbed her daughter's jacket as she left with Essie. Tadhg followed behind them, picking up the rear.

Most people turned their heads away as they passed, pretending to resume their conversations; others kept a side eye on Dani, wondering if the show was over. Noelle threw daggers at Sinead Keogh, who had turned right around on her stool to watch the entertainment, the nosy cow.

'GO ON. RUN AWAY. You're good at that, MR MURPHY,' Dani roared in Tadhg's wake. All heads now whipped round in her direction, every un-injected eyebrow in the place raised. 'You won't get away so easily this time. I'm going to find out exactly what the fuck is going on here.'

Mr Murphy? Sweet Mother Divine.

Why the hell had she agreed to bring her in here in the first place? It was clearly all too much for her. Noelle was pumping sweat now, her shirt stuck to her. The place was hotter than hell; her blood pressure must be sky high. She had to get out of here. Handing Dani her jacket, she squeezed awkwardly out between the tables, just catching a glass before it overbalanced.

There was no sign of Dani moving. Instead she reached for the drink that Tadhg had bought her and knocked half of it back in one go.

Right, that's it.

'I need to get some fresh air before I pass out, Dani. I'll wait outside for you, okay?'

The other woman nodded, before lifting her glass to her lips again.

Noelle made her way out through the bar, making eye contact with nobody, as Betty's booming voice trailed after her.

'Lookit, I know you're in a bad way, girl, but you can't be goin' round sayin' things like that. Tadhg is the principal of the secondary school over the road there, his mam's a great friend of mine, and I'm tellin' you now, you couldn't meet nicer people.'

She had almost made it through the small foyer to the front door when she felt somebody grab her sleeve. She turned: her friends Fiona and Lorraine were right behind her.

'Jesus, Noelle, what the hell was that all about?' asked Fiona.

'I honestly don't know. I think the poor woman's crackin' up,' she said.

'She must be going through hell, sure. I don't know how she's even putting one foot in front of the other,' Fiona said.

'I know. I should have brought her straight home after the vigil, but she was adamant she wanted to come in here.'

'She probably doesn't know what she wants. Is she here on her own?'

'Yeah.'

'That's awful,' Lorraine said. 'You'd think there'd have been somebody that could have come over with her.'

'I know. I wish she had somebody with her, then I wouldn't feel so responsible for her.'

She took her leave of the girls and went outside, where a small knot of smokers had gathered, the freezing air a welcome balm. She moved away from the entrance and leaned back against the icy wall of the hotel, noticing that Essie's car, which had been parked opposite the garda station when she arrived with Dani, was gone. She pulled her phone out to call Maria, but there was no answer. She didn't leave a message; her friend would phone back when she saw the missed call.

She was starting to shiver now in her light cotton shirt, although her chest was still burning. She hoped this wasn't the start of the hot flushes Grainne had warned her about. She shrugged her coat on, wishing Dani would hurry the hell up. Over in the square, the night lights twinkled along the path that cut through the middle, and above her in the clear black sky, stars glistered and winked, like sequins stitched into the Milky Way. She remembered Holly, when she had been going through her astronomy phase, telling her that there were about two hundred billion stars in our solar system alone; they were there during the day too, but the sun made the sky so bright, we couldn't see them.

That had been a happy time: Kevin still at home, her family yet unbroken. She could clearly picture her daughter, aged eleven or twelve, turning to her from the telescope Santa had brought that Christmas, bright-eyed and enthused, firing facts at her.

'If the centre of our galaxy was a city, Mom, we'd be living in the suburbs, about 26,000 light years from the centre. There's this supermassive spinning black hole in the very centre called Sagittarius A. It's a monster that's more than four million times the mass of the sun and sucks up passing light beams and gas and dust, basically anything that gets too close.'

Holly had assured her that the black hole wasn't a threat to Earth, 'not for about four billion years, at least, when the Milky Way will collide with the Andromeda galaxy, scattering stars and planets across the cosmos like glitter'. Even so, it still came into Noelle's head whenever she looked up at the night sky. The idea of that insatiable dark hole lurking out there somewhere.

The telescope was in the attic now, gathering dust, along with Liam's guitar and Holly's rollerblades and the rest of the abandoned detritus of their childhood. Kevin was long gone and Holly had settled into her new life on the far side of the world, a place that right now felt as far away from Noelle as the stars above her. No matter how much she tried to be happy for Holly, to be glad she had escaped this small village on this little island on the edge of Europe for a bigger, more exciting life, inside, not so deep down at all, she ached for her daughter. She selfishly hoped Holly didn't fall in love with an Aussie: if that happened, she'd never come back.

'There she is. NOELLE!' Betty yelled as if she was on the far side of the square and not standing mere feet away. Dani was with her, thank God. Hopefully the American woman would go straight to bed when they got back and knock herself out with some more sleeping pills. Her body clock was probably still all over the place; sleep deprivation would drive anybody mad. She'd be horrified in the morning when she remembered the scene she'd caused in front of everyone.

'See?' Betty was saying to Dani. 'Didn't I tell you t'wouldn't be open at this hour?' She pointed at the door of the garda station, a few doors up from the hotel. 'That's it there.'

'What the actual—? So what the heck happens when somebody commits a crime round here?'

'Well, there wouldn't be a lot of crime around here now, love, although havin' said that, my friend Nuala's son Brendan, he works for the ESB or whatever the hell 'tis called now, anyways wasn't his car taken from outside his front door in the middle of the—'

'Well, how do I contact the cops then? Noelle, is there a number I can call or something? I need to talk to that officer Amy, who brought me to the mortuary yesterday. She gave me a card with her number, but I don't know what I did with it.'

'Well, the station will probably be open again in the morning,' Noelle said. 'They close early in the—'

'But I gotta talk to somebody now!'

Oh Christ. This is all I need.

'I'll help you look for that card when we get back to the

house, and if we can't find it, I can bring you down here in the morning. I'm sure it can wait until then.'

'I gotta talk to her right away,' Dani said, her speech rapid, chest heaving. 'I gotta let her know that Michael Murphy is here in the village. There's no way that's a coincidence.'

Jesus, it was more worked up the woman was getting, not less.

'Tadhg has lived here his whole life, Dani,' Noelle said in as sympathetic a tone as she could muster. 'You must have mistaken him for somebody else. We've known him for years, haven't we, Betty?'

'We have, girl.' Betty nodded sagely.

'Well, if you've known him for years, then you'll know that he spent time teaching in Boston back in the early two thousands. Maybe he goes by the name Tadhg now, but back then, he went by Michael.'

'No, Dani, he's always been Tadhg. I'm telling you, you've got the wrong guy here.'

Hang on, though, it was coming back to her now. It had been a long time ago, but Tadhg *had* spent a couple of years in the States before he and Maria got together. And now that she thought about it, she was pretty sure it had been Boston. He had never gone by the name Michael, though.

'Well, Michael – or Mr Murphy as he was to us then – was my English teacher,' Dani said. 'As well as my lover. He did a runner when he found out I was pregnant and that was the last I saw or heard of the guy until today.'

Noelle just stood there. Gobsmacked. Even Betty was lost for words.

No way. Not a chance.

Dani continued, her voice getting louder, more agitated: 'I guess he just forgot all about me and got on with his life, so he must have been real shocked when Jessie turned up here out of the blue all these years later searching for him. It was all over the local papers and online; he couldn't not have known about it. Then ten days after she arrives, her bruised body is found dead at the bottom of a staircase in the castle grounds with no witnesses and no CCTV. You can't seriously tell me that don't stink to high heaven. I gotta talk to the cops who investigated Jessie's death and tell them about this.'

This couldn't be right. She had to have the wrong person.

Her phone started vibrating in her pocket and she fished it out. It was Maria calling her back.

CHAPTER 14

Maria
Monday, 15 January

'Quiet please, Dylan O'Leary, I'm watching you. Stop annoying Aoife; she's trying to do her work and you should be following her example.'

'I didn't do nothin', miss, I was—'

'*Dylan.*'

'But miss, I was oney askin' could I borrow her rubber 'cos someone's after robbin' mine again.'

'That's such a lie, miss. He's writing in pen – what does he need a rubber for?' Aoife said hotly.

Maria took a deep breath. 'Alright, Aoife. Just get on with your own work, please.'

It was futile to even try to argue with Dylan. She knew that if there was any thieving going on in her classroom, he was the most likely culprit, and he knew that she knew. Barely a day went by when he wasn't forced to return some item of property to one of his classmates. The school provided him with his own supplies at the beginning of each term, all of which disappeared within the first week. It wasn't the child's fault his mother had no interest in his schooling and gave him crisp sandwiches for school every day; it had been Nutella until that was banned due to nut allergies. Nor was it his fault that his mother chose to spend whatever benefits the family got on vodka and vapes and chipper takeaways rather than proper food for Dylan and his siblings; nor that he was allowed to stay up until the early hours gaming and arrived into school late and half asleep on the days he did turn up. It wasn't really his mother's fault either: it was all she knew.

On the days when Dylan really pushed Maria's patience, she reminded herself that the child was already on the back foot in life compared to the kids who had pencil cases filled with fancy pens and rubbers and lunch boxes full of healthy snacks. He hadn't chosen to be born into that family; nor had his mother, a bould strap if ever there was one, chosen to be born into the chaos of her own upbringing. And the constant fidgeting and squirming, difficulty paying attention, impulsive behaviour and excessive talking that made Dylan so exhausting at times were not his fault either. Today, though, her patience with him was running thin. She was dog-tired, his SNA had called in sick and a leaky tap was driving her insane drip-drip-dripping into the sink. She made a note to call the caretaker to sort it out. She shivered. The classroom was chilly this morning, the central heating sluggish after the weekend. She should have worn a heavier jumper.

She looked down over the row of bent heads and sighed. She felt jaded at the thought of the day stretching out ahead of her. Maths followed by Gaeilge. Small break at 10.30, then *Mental Maths* and tables, followed by English, religion and big lunch at 12.30. SPHE in the afternoon and then SESE. Her life corralled into square boxes on a timetable. She usually didn't mind this, thrived on the routine of it, in fact, but since they had returned after Christmas break, she'd found it hard to get back into it. She just hadn't been herself, and felt a real lack of energy and motivation.

There had been an article in one of the weekend supplements about women changing careers in mid-life, some of them leaving stable, pensionable jobs for something more financially precarious but rewarding, like life coaching or psychotherapy or candle making. She didn't know any teachers who had changed career, though. Like every job, it had its pros and cons. People were always going on about what an easy number teachers had, with their short working days and long holidays, but when her kids were younger there had been plenty of days over the long summer months when she would have loved to be one of those mothers going out to work and dropping her kids off to childcare. Keeping kids entertained all day was one of the hardest jobs you could do, especially when the weather was bad, as it so often was in this country, and she had always looked forward to the return to work in September. This was the first time she could remember that she hadn't been glad to get back at the start of a new term. The article had made her think about what she would do if she was ever to change career. She hadn't been able to think of a single thing. When she was much younger, she'd had vague aspirations of being a fashion designer – she'd always been creative and good at art – but she was too old for that now. She was forty-five years of age and for the first time in her life, she felt stuck in a rut.

She'd love to just walk out the door and back up the hill, climb into bed and call in sick for the rest of the week. Of course she never would. She'd have to be dying before she took a sick day. This wasn't like her at all, but she hadn't slept well last night after that scene in the hotel. It had been so disturbing, the way that woman had looked at Tadhg, as if he was a ghost. And the things she had said.

Tadhg hadn't even been at the vigil – he'd had some GAA business to attend to – and had only come to meet them for a drink in the hotel afterwards. She was sorry now she had coaxed him to come over.

Ben had been in the kitchen taking a frozen pizza out of the oven when they arrived home, and Eva had proceeded to fill him in on all the drama. 'And then she starts saying that Dad was that girl Jessie's father. It was so cringe, like the whole place was watching and she was roaring at him. I mean, what a weirdo.'

Ben had stared at his sister in disbelief. 'Actually?'

'Yeah and then Dad said he'd never met her before and she started shouting even louder and calling him *Mr* Murphy. She totally lost it, like, it was so bad we had to leave. I mean I feel sorry for the woman and all, but she's psychotic.'

'Crazy, bruh,' Ben said, pouring himself a glass of water and heading back up the stairs.

Maria called after him. 'Ah, Ben, are you forgetting something?'

'Huh?'

'Your pizza, idiot,' Eva shouted.

'Oh yeah, actually I don't really feel like it now. You can have it if you want.'

'Cheers.' Eva picked up the pizza her brother had left on the counter and disappeared with it before he had time to change his mind.

Hoping Ben wasn't coming down with some kind of bug, Maria had followed Tadhg into the sitting room, where he was hunting for the remote control, and closed the door behind her.

'That bloody thing, why is it never where it's supposed to be? Who had it last?'

'Just leave it a minute, will you?'

He had continued lifting cushions, reaching down the back of the sofa.

'Tadhg,' she said.

'What?'

What?!

How was he so unfazed by the upsetting incident in the hotel?

Her husband was a hard man to rattle. It was a temperament that served him well in his chosen career. She often wished Ben had inherited some of his father's personality; the two of them couldn't be more different: Ben was a born worrier and, to Tadhg's utter disappointment, hadn't a sporting bone in his body. Eva was more like her father, for the most part: even-keeled and coolheaded – although she had a tendency to fall apart when she was tired, like Maria – and good at every sport she put her hand to.

Why had Dani looked at Tadhg like that, though? Why had she seemed so convinced she knew him? And the way she had said 'Mr Murphy'. How did she even know his surname? Was it just a coincidence that Tadhg happened to have worked in Boston all those years ago? Or that Michael was his middle name?

Her husband had often talked about the wild partying he had done over in the States with his fellow Irishmen. He had been a young teacher, fresh out of college and living away from home for the first time.

'Is there any way you could have met that woman Dani and forgotten?' she'd asked him. 'When you were living in Boston?'

'What? Jesus, Maria, Boston's not like Blarney, you know. The population of Greater Boston is nearly as big as the entire population of Ireland. And even if I had met her back then, well ... let's just say she's not exactly the type of girl I'd have gone for.'

'She might have looked very different back then, though. It's so long ago.'

'Nobody could change that much, Maria. Look, I'm not saying I was an angel while I was over there. I wasn't. None of the lads were. And there was a lot of very heavy boozing that went on. Some of those girls literally threw themselves at us; they used to say the accent turned them on. Remember the one I told you about who shagged her way through nearly all the lads in our house?'

Maria had remembered that story. She had been disgusted at the time, not at the lads, for taking advantage of the girl, but at the girl herself. Last night, though, looking back from the perspective of the mother of a teenage girl in a very different world, she had felt very differently.

Tadhg had kept rummaging under the cushions. 'Ah, there it is.' Settling onto his side of the sofa, he'd pointed the remote at the TV. The conversation was clearly over as far as he was concerned.

As the ancient radiator at the back of her classroom clanked and gurgled, Maria wondered now if it had been a genuine case of mistaken identity, or if the American woman was on the verge of some kind of breakdown. Maybe her daughter had come over here to get away from her. Maybe she had serious mental health issues. It was very strange that she had known nothing about her daughter's trip to Ireland in the first place. God only knew what was going on in that family.

    Noelle hadn't called her back last night; she'd try her again after school.

CHAPTER 15

Dani

She shifted uncomfortably on a hard, varnished bench that would have looked more at home in a church than in the lobby of the police precinct where she was waiting to speak to a member of the Garda Síochána. She had followed the instructions hand-written on a sign to 'PLEASE RING BELL AND WAIT' and a uniformed cop had come out from a door behind the screened-in counter. He'd told her he would let the sergeant know she was there and had then disappeared back to where he'd come from. She could hear hoots of laughter from inside, voices rising and falling. Surely, these people should be out investigating crimes right now, not sitting on their butts sharing funny stories. It wasn't right. They should be more respectful of her, a bereaved mother waiting outside, who was only sitting here in the first place because they weren't doing their jobs properly. They'd been far too quick to rule her daughter's death an accident.

She had a missed call from her mother. It had come in at 4:11 a.m., Mamma not taking the time difference into consideration. She couldn't face the thought of calling her back. Her mother's words, her heart-rending cries, had been ringing in her ears since yesterday's call.

'This is your fault, Daniela, all your fault. My Jessie is dead because of you. You did this!'

Joe had taken the phone off her, telling Dani he'd call her later, to take no notice, that Mamma was in so much pain she didn't know what she was saying.

Dani's mother knew exactly what she was saying, though, and awful as it was to hear, there was a lot of truth in her words. It was her fault that her daughter had made this mad, impulsive dash to Ireland, and she needed to find out if the man Jessie had come here in search of had anything to do with her death.

Another loud burst of laughter came from behind the door, the woman's voice rising in hilarity. If somebody didn't come out soon, she was going to ring that damn bell again. She had asked Noelle to give her a ride – the woman had told her only yesterday to let her know if there was anything she could do for her – and had been disappointed when Noelle didn't offer to accompany her inside, saying she needed to pick up something in a nearby supermarket and would wait outside the precinct. Dani thought she had detected a slight cooling in the temperature of her host's hospitality this morning. She understood it was awkward for her: Blarney was a small village and she was good friends with Michael Murphy – who Dani was now trying to get her head around calling Tadhg, pronounced like tiger without the r at the end – and his wife. But Jessie had spent her last nights alive sleeping under Noelle's roof, so surely the least this woman could do was support the girl's mother in finding out whether the fall that had killed her had really been an accident?

The consular officer she had been assigned at the American

embassy, Larry Duggan, had answered her call yesterday evening after two rings, despite it being a Sunday. His slow, soothing drawl on the other end of the line had helped to quell the horrible, twitchy agitation that had taken hold of her body and that two Valium had barely taken the edge off.

She had called the mortuary first thing this morning and insisted on talking to the manager, informing him that she would not be consenting to the release of her daughter's body to the undertaker until she was satisfied that her death had been properly investigated. The original plan had been for Jessie's body to be collected this morning by a local funeral director and brought to the cremation due to take place Wednesday. Dani had been shocked to find out that the cost of transporting a body back to the US could run up to $20,000 and that the Irish government didn't help out with the cost of repatriation. Whereas, as Larry had explained to her on Saturday, a cremation here in Ireland would cost hundreds, and most people in such a situation opted for this.

Her mind kept torturing her with screenshots of her beautiful baby girl lying on a shelf in a cold steel fridge. Each time the image flashed into her head, she shook it away. That way lay insanity. There would be plenty of time to grieve later. For now, she had to try to stay strong. To focus on finding out how Jessie had ended up at the bottom of those steps.

She had called the undertaker earlier as well, to tell him about her change of plan, and he said he'd let the crematorium know. Then she had finally managed to root out the card that nice officer Amy had given her and called her. There was no answer and she hadn't wanted to leave a message – it was too complicated to explain – so she tried again ten minutes later and kept trying until the cop answered. Dani had expected the guard to be blown away at her bombshell revelation and to say she'd be sending somebody straight round to Tadhg Murphy's house to question him. Instead, she had seemed quite nonchalant, reiterating slowly and carefully, as if Dani was some kind of dimwit, that the gardaí who had attended the scene of her daughter's death had determined that there was no foul play involved and that the coroner had decided it wasn't a state case. So the state pathologist hadn't been called to do a post-mortem, as would happen in the case of a suspicious death. The autopsy had instead been carried out by a regular pathologist at the hospital morgue, who had determined that Jessie had died from a traumatic brain injury due to a fall. This did nothing whatsoever to allay Dani's concerns. Toxicology samples had been taken and sent for analysis to see if Jessie had alcohol or drugs in her system that might have caused her to be unsteady on her feet; Dani had been shocked to find out that it would take about three months for these results to come back.

As Amy had explained this morning, it was very difficult to give an exact time of death, particularly given the freezing weather conditions that night, but having taken several factors into account – the CCTV footage at the castle, statements from the few witnesses who saw her that day and Jessie's own social media posts – the pathologist had ascertained that the death had taken place between three p.m. on Thursday afternoon, when Jessie was last seen on CCTV, and 3.34 a.m. on Friday morning.

She had told Amy that she wanted to talk to the cops who'd been at the scene at Blarney Castle on Friday morning and ask them to explain how it was that they were able to determine so quickly that her daughter's death was an accident and that foul play wasn't involved. Surely it couldn't be that cut and dried? Even without the revelation that the man her daughter had come to Ireland on a mission to find, Michael Murphy, was living in the village.

Amy had gone off to make a call and had come back to her within the hour saying that it would be the following day, Tuesday, before the guards from Gurranabraher station on the north side of the city, who had been working the scene on Friday, would be back on duty again. Dani had kinda lost it a bit then. There was no way she was waiting until then to talk to somebody about this. Anybody who had ever watched a true crime documentary – and Dani was completely addicted – knew how vital the first few days following a suspicious death were when it came to finding the perpetrator. She told Amy that she'd be at the precinct at ten a.m. and wouldn't be moving her ass from there until she talked to somebody in charge. The guard had gone off to make another call. She had been back again within ten minutes to tell Dani that the sergeant who'd attended the scene at Blarney Castle on Friday would meet her at the station at eleven o'clock this morning.

It was 11:09 now and there was no sign of him.

Fuck this shit.

She got to her feet and was about to reach again for the bell when a heavy door on her side of the counter opened and a bulky man in plain clothes came over to her.

'Dani Doyle?'

'That's me.'

'Detective Sergeant Colin Ryan.' He stuck a hand out, and shook hers vigorously. 'I'm very sorry for your loss, Dani,' he said. 'Come on through with me.'

CHAPTER 16

Noelle

'Jesus, Maria, you'd want to have seen her. She came out of Gurranabraher like somethin' possessed. She asked me to give her a lift and then asked if I'd mind waiting for her. I felt like saying it's a B&B I'm running, girl, not a taxi company, but sure I had no choice but to do it. I thought she'd be in and out in half an hour but nearly an hour I was waiting in the car for her twiddling my thumbs, and then out she comes like a bat out of hell. I was full sure the guards would put her mind at ease and that would be the end of it, but God Almighty ...'

Noelle hadn't wanted to alarm her friend unnecessarily. She had hoped that after a decent night's sleep, Dani would have realised she'd been mistaken about Tadhg. She hadn't been able to put off calling her any longer, though.

'But why was she so annoyed? Did she not get to speak to anyone?' Maria asked.

'No, she did. She wouldn't have left the place without speaking to somebody, the mood she was in. She met the sergeant who was at the castle last week when Jessie was found, and a detective as well, from what I could make out between all her giving out. She thinks they're not taking her seriously enough, so she's going to go over their heads. She said she's going to *demand* another autopsy. If the cops won't do it, she'll get one done privately, she's saying, but either way her daughter's body won't be leaving that morgue until it's done. I doubt very much you can just go off and get your own autopsy done, but there's no talking to her. She seems to have it in her head that there's some conspiracy going on.'

'God, she really seems convinced her daughter's fall wasn't an accident so.'

'She really does. And …'

'What?'

'Well, she's still ráiméising about Tadhg being Jessie's father. She's saying he used to be her teacher, Maria …'

There was a sharp intake of breath on the other end of the phone. Noelle hated having to be the one to tell Maria what the American woman was saying about her husband, but she had to warn her at the same time.

'Oh my God.'

'I know, it's mad. I get the impression that the guards said as much to her too, but it was like a red rag. She has that poor man at the American embassy hounded. Liam heard her on the phone to him when he came home for his lunch: she was going on about getting proof that Tadhg had taught her at some high school in Dorchester and that they—'

'What did you say?'

'Sorry, Maria, I know how upsetting this must be for you. I don't know why she's saying all this stuff; she seems to be fixated on him for some reason. I don't know. Maybe she had mental health issues already and Jessie's death just tipped her over—'

'No, the school. Where did you say the school was?'

'In Dorchester – that's what she said, anyway.'

'But that's ... How would she know that?'

'Sure nothing the woman's saying makes any sense.'

'Noelle, that's where Tadhg taught when he was in Boston. In a high school in Dorchester. How the hell would she know that?'

What?

'Em ... I don't ... She's from Dorchester herself, maybe she googled him and saw his name on the school website or something.'

This had to be a massive coincidence. Didn't it? Jessie hadn't said anything about her father being a teacher or working in Dorchester. Why would her mother not have told her that if it was true? It would certainly have narrowed her search. Definitely a coincidence. Noelle might not have been quite as bedazzled by the great Tadhg Murphy as everyone else, but she knew there was no way he'd ever have gone near one of his own students.

'Yeah, you're probably right,' Maria said. 'I feel awful for the woman, she must be going through absolute hell, but you can't just go around saying stuff like this. Things might be different in the States, but we have laws here to protect people from this kind of thing.'

'Look, hopefully she'll run out of steam soon and go back to Boston to bury her poor child. I just hope to God she's gone from under my roof by the end of the week.'

Noelle hadn't said anything to Dani about Liam drinking with Jessie in the Gab on Wednesday night. The last thing they needed was the guards sniffing around their door.

CHAPTER 17

Maria

Maria had been waiting to get a quiet word with her husband since he'd come in from work, but Eva had chosen that evening to have a mini meltdown over her upcoming pre-Leaving Cert exams when she got home from study at half six.

'It's just all too much. I can't take it.' Her daughter had flung herself onto her bed, face sunken into her pillow. Maria made a mental note to change the fake-tan-stained sheets that stank of stale biscuits.

There was far too much pressure on kids to achieve high points in the Leaving Cert, but she suspected her generally chilled-out daughter's stress was fuelled in no small part by tiredness.

'What time did you put your phone down last night?' she asked. She had popped her head in to say goodnight at around half ten, when she was heading to bed herself, and told Eva not to stay up too late, reminding her she had a long day of school and study the next day. 'You were obviously awake too late and—'

'Mooomm, you're really not helping. And I wasn't even awake that late,' which meant she was. 'I'm just really stressed, okay?

I know I'm going to fail Irish, I'm not able for higher level, it's just too hard and Dad won't let me change to lower. I'm trying to study, but nothing's going in.'

'I know, love, sure I went through it myself. Things haven't changed much since then.'

That wasn't really true, though. So much had changed since Maria was in secondary school. On top of the pressure of the points race to get a university place, kids nowadays had the world of social media to contend with, a massive additional source of stress that Maria and her peers could never have contemplated. It would have seemed positively dystopian, if that had even been a word back then, that one day, instead of ringing each other in the evening from the one family phone (on which call time was strictly monitored) or meeting each other face-to-face, their children would instead communicate primarily via their own personal mobile devices.

There had been talk of reforming the Leaving Cert and college points system for decades: it was far too narrow and inflexible, the emphasis lying on academic success only. A very unfair system that meant a person's future was pretty much dictated by the results of one major exam taken when they were seventeen or eighteen years of age. Tadhg, as a secondary principal and a teacher himself for over two decades, would be one of the first to agree that the current system failed far too many kids.

Not for the first time, Maria felt grateful that both of her kids were smart and had always done pretty well in school. But if the Evas of the world – with brains to burn, parents to turn to for support and money to pay for grinds if needed – found it a struggle, what hope was there for the poor kids with additional needs and no support at home, like Dylan O'Leary? How would he survive in secondary school? She really feared for some of her pupils, wished the world they were being decanted into after the relatively cosseted years of primary school could be a kinder, safer place for them.

'Mom, are you even listening to me?' Eva had turned around and was hugging a pillow to her tummy.

God, when does parenting start to get easier? When will they ever start needing less of me?

'Sorry, love, I'm wrecked myself this evening. Look, why don't you get into your jammies? I'll bring you up a hot chocolate and a couple of biscuits. Did you get all your homework done in study?'

'I still have some Business to do and I only got one hour of study done. I just can't focus properly … I'm so—'

'Does the Business have to be in tomorrow?' Maria needed to nip her daughter's stress in the bud now.

'No, not until Wednesday, but if I don't do it, I'll have even more to do tomorrow.'

'There's no point in trying to do homework or study when you're this tired. You're better off taking it easy for the rest of the evening and getting an early night. Everything will seem a lot easier after a good night's sleep. Okay, love?'

Tadhg would have told Eva to take a bit of a break, then finish her homework and get the extra hour of study done, but she was hard enough on herself without her parents piling even more pressure on her. And Tadhg could be far too hard on the kids at times. There was simply no point in Eva trying to study when her brain wasn't in a fit state to take any information in. Unlike her younger brother, Eva had always been a diligent, hardworking student. Ambitious and competitive like her father, keen to have the highest marks in her exams. She had done very well in her Junior Cert and was hell bent on getting her first choice of Pharmacy at UCC, the points for which had been over 600 last year. Hopefully she would achieve it, but it would take a lot of work. Ben, on the other hand, had to put far less effort in for his results, which drove his sister insane. He was a natural at maths: his teacher had told Maria at his last parent–teacher meeting that he had it in him to get a distinction at honours level in the Leaving Cert. It was just as well learning came so naturally to Ben, because he was lazy by nature and tended to give up anything that didn't come easy to him – like sport, much to Tadhg's frustration.

She delivered Eva's hot chocolate to her with a few of her favourite Jammie Dodgers on a plate. Then she popped her head into Ben's room to check if he had finished, or even started, his homework – he was in fifth year, facing into the Leaving Cert next year – and got a thumbs-up, which could have meant anything. She headed back downstairs to talk to her husband. But he wasn't in the sitting room, where she had expected to find him, one eye on the TV, the other on his phone screen. She checked the kitchen and the office, but there was no sign of him.

She stood at the foot of the stairs and called his name in case he was upstairs somewhere. She could hear Eva laughing and chatting on her phone, clearly recovered from her meltdown; there was silence from Ben's room, apart from the odd mumbled expletive. Too much time gaming did him no good, but at least they knew where he was, and that he wasn't roaming the village with that gang of messers. He hadn't been out with them all weekend, in fact, had barely left his room. Maybe he'd seen their true colours. She went back into the sitting room and lifted the blind to look outside. Her husband's car was still there, so he hadn't popped back down to the school as he sometimes did.

He must be in with his mother, which suited Maria because she didn't want the kids to overhear them. She went out her back door and through the door at the rear of her mother-in-law's kitchen a couple of hundred yards away. Their back doors were always left unlocked, except when they went to bed at night, although after a spate of break-ins in the local area the previous year they had started locking the side gates and had smart doorbells installed. The heat of Essie's sitting room enveloped her like a warm hug when she walked in.

Essie paused the TV, where two people sitting on a sofa were frozen in time on the screen. They were watching *Gogglebox*, one of their favourite shows. A box of After Eights sat in front of her husband on the coffee table, paper-thin black wrappers scattered around. His favourites; Essie always kept a stash in the press.

'So this is what you're up to. Snaking in here to be spoilt by your mother,' Maria said, smiling at the pair of them. Tadhg had always been close to his mother and their bond had become even tighter since he'd moved his family into his childhood home. Her mother-in-law was a great support to them, she doted on her grandkids, and they were always there for her too if she needed anything.

'Ah sure, I'd be a long time waiting to get a bit of TLC inside.' He nodded towards their own house. 'Isn't that right, Mam?'

'Oh yeah. You're fierce badly off alright, my heart bleeds for you,' Essie said, throwing her eyes up to heaven. 'How are you, Maria? Will you have some tea? I'm making a fresh pot.'

'I won't, Essie, thanks. I'd only be awake all night. I wanted to talk to you both away from the kids; Eva's already up to high doh about the exams ... Anyway, I was on to Noelle earlier. She was telling me that Dani De Marco seems to have convinced herself that her daughter's death wasn't an accident.'

'Ah, sure the poor woman must be half mad with the grief,' Essie said.

'I know it's terrible what she's going through, and I don't know if she's trying to distract herself from the reality of her daughter's death, or what's going on with her, but it's getting a bit worrying now.'

She filled her husband and mother-in-law in on her conversation with Noelle, about the American woman's visit to the garda station and her talk about getting a second autopsy.

'The cremation was supposed to be tomorrow, but she's cancelled it,' she said. 'Noelle is in the horrors over the whole thing, as you can imagine.'

'I wouldn't worry about it too much, love,' Tadhg said. 'She can't stay here forever; I mean surely she has a life and a job to go back to in Boston. As Mam said, it sounds like she's gone a bit mad with grief. Not surprising really, I suppose.'

'I am worrying, Tadhg, because she's after telling the guards and Noelle and God knows who else that you were her teacher and you had a sexual relationship with her ...'

'You're not serious?' Essie said, appalled. 'Why would she say something like that?'

'Ah, that's mad stuff altogether. That woman's clearly not in her right mind,' Tadhg said, dismissively. 'Even so, she'd want to be careful. You can't just go round making those kinds of accusations, especially about somebody in my position.'

'I don't understand though how she knew you were a teacher, because Noelle didn't tell her. *And* she knows the school where you taught was in Dorchester.'

Her husband looked perplexed. 'I've no idea. Maybe she did a search online. You can find anything out these days. I bet the reason she came up with the name Michael Murphy was because there's so bloody many of them out there. Didn't her daughter say she'd only just found out who her father was? So her mother must have kept it from her deliberately: maybe she wasn't sure who he was and didn't want to admit it, so she made up this whole story about the village with a castle, never actually expecting the girl to come to Ireland.'

'Well, I typed Tadhg Murphy teacher Boston into Google and did a search but found nothing about you, so then I checked schools in Dorchester and Holy Cross came up and I remembered that was the name of the school where you taught.'

'Yeah, but—'

'So then I decided to search Holy Cross High School, not for one minute thinking I'd find her there, and I came across this site called Classmates.com. Look, I screenshotted some of the photos of the yearbook for 2001, when you were working there, and I found this one. I'm not sure – I want you to check – but see this girl here? ... Daniela Doyle ... I mean it was over twenty years ago and she was obviously a lot younger and ... well, different, but she's the image of Jessie, isn't she? I wonder if De Marco could be her married name?'

The blood drained from her husband's face. And that was before he had even looked at the photo.

CHAPTER 18

Dani
Tuesday, 16 January

She was dragged to the surface in the early hours of the morning by a piercing yowl. It took her a few moments to get her bearings. To realise she wasn't in her own bed. She wasn't even in her own country. She was lying on the sheets that her daughter had slept on, that still smelled, ever so faintly now, of her.

Jessie. Oh God!

She lay frozen in horror, groggy from the pills she had taken to get to sleep. It was probably cats that had woken her: they made such godawful noises when they were mating, like babies screeching in distress. There it was again, another high-pitched squawk. She remembered then that Noelle had told her that her grandson was staying over the night before. It didn't just sound like a baby; it was one.

And her own baby was dead.

How can she be gone?

How can this be real?

Grief kneed her deep in the gut, the memory of the last time she had seen her daughter haunting her. Jessie's lovely face twisted in anger, her vicious words slashing at Dani like shards of glass. Going straight for the jugular.

... never a mother to me ...
... nothing but a drain on the family ...
... living at home at your age ...
... from one fucked-up relationship to the next ...
You're a mess, Daniela, a hopeless frickin' mess!

She couldn't remember when her daughter had stopped called her Mom: some time in her teens when she had started to lose all respect for her. Dani had pretended it didn't bother her – the removal of a title that she had probably never deserved – but it had hurt. She'd tried her best, she really had, but the men she went for had all turned out to be duds, every last one of them; a string of dysfunctional relationships trailing behind her like noxious contrails.

After they lost Pops, Dani had slipped right off the rails she had already just about been clinging onto. She'd started skipping school, scored herself a fake ID at sixteen to buy liquor, went to the wildest house parties, where she drank 'til she hurled and then started all over again. She was brought home by a friend's father black-out drunk on one occasion, and ended up in the Emergency Department on another, with Joe called to collect her. The boys had moved out by then, and Dani was living for the day that she'd be old enough to go too.

She had known, though, that she'd never be the same again in her eldest brother's eyes if he heard she'd got herself knocked up at the age of seventeen without as much as a steady boyfriend to show for herself. And she couldn't bear the thought of the revulsion in the eyes of her mother and the aunts, as they sat around the table harping on about her cousins' academic and career successes, all the while judging her and her ripening body. Her baby's daddy had made it clear that he had no interest in standing by her, and everything that came after that – getting engaged to Ricky De Marco the day of her eighteenth birthday, getting married a few months later – was *his* fault.

Joe hadn't been at all happy when he heard the news about her engagement. He had sat her down and warned her against marrying Ricky De Marco, said he was a boozer like Pops and she was far too young. She had loved her father, though, and unlike Mamma, she had no intention of pushing her husband into the arms of hard liquor. She often wondered what would have happened if she had told Joe the truth, the reason, then about the size of a lime, that she was rushing into marriage with a man she barely knew.

She'd had to learn the hard way that Joe was right about Ricky De Marco. Dysfunctional would have been a kind description of their marriage. Ricky could be charming and funny and generous when he was sober, or at least not hungover. The problem was he spent less and less time in either of those states after Dani moved in with him. The third time he hit her, she packed up her stuff and moved back in with her mother, who proceeded to pour into her granddaughter the love she had somehow never been able to give her daughter. Dani's divorce came through the day after her twenty-first birthday and since then, she had lurched from one toxic relationship to another, each one ending the same way. In her tears.

Her daughter's words, although harsh, contained plenty of truth. Dani was a fucked-up mess. She had failed at relationships, failed at motherhood, failed at life. She was a failure.

She turned on the lamp on her nightstand, pushed the comforter off and got out of bed, pulling back the curtains and opening the window. She stood there, breathing in the chilly air. It was so quiet now that the yowling had stopped, not a thing stirring. No sirens or taxis or loud drunks falling out of bars. She had never realised before how noisy their apartment at home was, even after the restaurant below closed and their customers and staff went home to their beds. This place was so peaceful in comparison. How could her daughter have come to harm here? In this mecca for Irish Americans who came to search for their roots, kiss the stone and buy knitted sweaters and shamrock souvenirs to bring back home?

It was too much of a coincidence. That Jessie had come to this village, carried out a very public search for her father and that somehow he hadn't heard about her and put two and two together. Maybe Jessie hadn't found out who he was, but he had to have been aware of her quest. Surely he kept up with the local news, read the papers? One look at Jessie's photo would have been like walking back into that classroom in Holy Cross and setting his eyes on Dani. She had been a stunner back then, just like her daughter, not that she had known it at the time. The way he had acted on Sunday evening, though. As if he'd never set eyes on her before.

From what she had learnt so far about him, *Tadhg* was a real 'pillar of the community', deeply involved in the local GAA club. Some things hadn't changed. He had been Mr Popular in Boston too, all those GAA lads hanging off his every word. And girls, of course. She and a couple of her girlfriends had gone out to watch him play at the Irish Cultural Centre in Canton a few times. They had nicknamed him Neo for his resemblance to Keanu Reeves in *The Matrix*, albeit a blue-eyed, and slightly less perfect, version. He had stood out on the pitch. His imperfections – teeth that could have done with being straightened by a brace and whitened, and a slightly bent nose – had only added to his attraction for Dani back then. All the girls had crushed on him so bad, but she was the one he had chosen.

At least Larry at the embassy was taking her concerns seriously, telling her he could get her a recommendation for a good attorney in Cork if she felt she needed some legal advice. She was flat broke, as usual, but it was beginning to look like she wouldn't have much choice if the cops continued to dismiss her concerns. She'd have to ask Joe to cover the cost of the lawyer as well as the cremation, which she didn't like doing when he and Laurie were stressed over the baby. He could well afford it, though. They owned two rental apartments as well as their own home, so they had plenty of cash coming in on top of both their salaries. She had spoken to him briefly yesterday to let him know what was happening, but he had been distracted, rushing back to the hospital. She knew Joe would have her back, though; he always did.

She picked up her phone to see if her mother had left any more messages. She knew she shouldn't listen, but she forced herself, as if Mamma's ranting and wailing was some form of penance. Sometimes her mother was angry and accusatory, at others anguished, her babbling punctuated by heaving sobs. Dani forced herself to listen to every single one. She didn't call back. Her mother didn't even seem to want her to; she just wanted to let Dani know how much *she* was suffering.

Not once did she wonder how Dani was doing over in Cork on her own, but then Dani would have been more shocked if she had.

She dialled 171 and put the phone to her ear, her mother's cries crashing over her despite the big wide ocean that separated them.

Why? Why? Perché Dio? Why did you have to take her? Why could you not have taken—

She ended the message, afraid of what she might hear and decided to go downstairs to make herself a mug of cocoa. Noelle had made her some last night and even though she didn't particularly like the taste, the hot milky drink might help her get back to sleep, especially if she washed down a couple of Valium with it.

The kitchen door was closed, but she was surprised to see light spilling out around the frame at this hour. They must have gone to bed and left it on. She was inside before she realised there was somebody else already there. She yelped in surprise and the man standing in front of the sink turned round. It was Noelle's son Liam, the baby propped against his shoulder.

Liam, who had been so sweet to her since she had arrived at the B&B and who was clearly upset about Jessie. She could imagine her girl's eyes widening when they took in her landlady's cute son; he rocked a kinda young Mark Wahlberg vibe. Jessie was a sucker for sexy eyes, just like her mother.

'Oh, I'm sorry. I wasn't expecting anybody to be up.'

'Dani. Sorry, I hope this guy didn't wake you,' Liam said,

rubbing the baby's back in gentle circles. 'He gets a bit colicky at night sometimes; we have to walk him round to try to get his wind up.'

'The kid's got a mean set of lungs, for sure,' she said, smiling. 'I just came down to make some cocoa.'

'Sit down there and I'll make it for you, since it was this lad who woke you up.'

Holding the baby in the crook of one arm, he moved easily around the kitchen while she watched, heating the milk in the microwave and stirring the brown powder into it. He carried the cup over to the table.

'Would you like a slice of toast or anything?'

'No. I'm all set, thanks.'

The baby had fallen asleep in his father's arms, his delicate head cradled in Liam's big hand, content now his pain had eased. He was a cute kid. Dani had met Liam's girlfriend Molly when they arrived yesterday. A tiny thing, she couldn't have been more than a size six and she had given birth less than six months ago. Dani had never gone back to her pre-baby weight after Jessie, didn't know how women like Molly seemed to just snap back into shape.

'I better put this guy back down before he wakes up again,' Liam said.

'Before you go, I was wondering if Jessie said anything to you while she was here, about what happened between us, her and me, before she left Boston?'

'Am, well …' He shifted the baby from one arm to the other, looking awkward. 'She mentioned it alright.'

'The last time I saw her, well, things weren't good between us.' She sighed deeply. 'If I could turn back time and stop her finding out the way she did ... It was Ricky's cousin who told her he wasn't her father.'

'Yeah, Jessie did tell me about that. She was very upset, as you know yourself, and she did mention there'd been a bit of a falling out between the two of you, but I really got the impression that she was feeling bad about it, you know, that it was just the shock of finding out and the way she found out ...'

'Do you think she was planning to contact me?'

'I'm sure she would have eventually if ... Jesus, I'm so sorry, Dani. What happened to her, it's just so ...' He shook his head. She saw him glance at the clock on the microwave: 3:28 a.m. He was probably calculating the amount of time left before his alarm went off for work. 'I really need to get this guy back to bed.'

'Just one last thing before you go ... Do you have any idea if she'd made any progress in tracking her father down?'

'No, not by Wednesday night anyway. That was the last time I spoke to her and she'd definitely have told us if she had.'

CHAPTER 19

Maria

She had called in sick this morning. It was practically unheard of for her, but there was no way she could possibly focus on teaching her class today: on dealing with Dylan O'Leary's antics and Ella Hogan's constant tattling and trying to act normal in front of her colleagues in the staffroom at break. Not after the hellish night she had just put down. She'd sent a text message first thing to Evelyn, the principal, saying she'd been up half the night with a vomiting bug and wouldn't be in today. And it was true, apart from the vomiting bit.

Her mind had spun round and round all night, a whirling big wheel of catastrophic thinking.

Tadhg couldn't deny now that he had taught Dani De Marco, or Daniela Doyle as she had been back in the early 2000s. Hearing Daniela Doyle's name and seeing her yearbook photo last night had drained the colour from his face, shocking him into silence. Maria, watching his reaction, had felt an icy shiver zip along her spinal cord and up the back of her neck, and she had known, in that moment, that this was bad. Really bad.

The big wheel started spinning faster again.

What's going to happen now?

How are we going to stop this from coming out?
If it comes out, what then? Could Tadhg lose his job?
Will he be suspended pending investigation?
How would we cope on one income?
And the kids, oh God, the kids, how could they face going into school if this became public?

She didn't understand. How could he, *her Tadhg*, have done something like this? And how the hell could he have just got on with his life, thinking there would be no repercussions?

She had lain beside him pretending to be asleep for hours, wondering if he was pretending too, and thinking back to the early days of their relationship. He had only been back from the States about six weeks when they had started going out. He had pursued her determinedly, although admittedly she hadn't made it too hard for him. She'd been so thrilled that *he* had singled *her* out for his attention. He had been two years ahead of her back in school. His younger brother, Gavin, who had been in Maria's year, was the better looking of the two boys, although he didn't have Tadhg's sporting prowess and wasn't quite as popular. All the girls in her year had fancied the arse off Gavin and were stunned when they heard he'd come out after he moved to New York.

Maria and Tadhg had only been going out together a year when he proposed. She was twenty-four and he was twenty-seven. They didn't get married for another couple of years after that, but she was the only one of the girls settling down at the time. Three of her closest friends had gone off travelling for a year and if she had been single, she'd have gone with them. Whenever she had felt a bout of FOMO coming on, she'd reminded herself how lucky she was to have Tadhg.

It was through Tadhg that she got to know Noelle, who had been in his year in school; Noelle's then husband, Kevin, had hung around in the same gang as Tadhg, The two women had got talking to each other on a night out in town and instantly clicked, their friendship solidifying over the coming months and years. Noelle had started her family earlier than Maria; Tadhg hadn't been in any rush to have kids, wanting them to enjoy their time together first before being tied down. Last night, her husband had stared at the photo on her phone, blinking rapidly, as if he was hoping to somehow unsee what was in front of him. Daniela Doyle, who with her dark eyes and hair and that flawless skin, could have been Jessie De Marco's sister.

'What is it Tadhg, love? Did you know her?' Essie had asked.

'I don't ... This is crazy ... She looks completely different now, but yes, I did know her. But I'd never have ... Jesus Christ ...'

'What do you mean you knew her?' Maria had asked, hoping there was another explanation, one that wasn't about to make their lives implode. 'You didn't actually teach her, did you?'

Please say no.

'I did. Just for one year, though. Her last year ... I think she'd transferred from another school. Oh God!' He dropped her phone onto the sofa, covered his face with his hands.

The viper coiled in Maria's stomach had raised its head, hissing loudly. She had looked at her mother-in-law, seen her own worry and confusion reflected back at her.

Tadhg had started shaking his head, one hand clamped over his mouth.

'Tadhg? What's wrong?'

Surely not, there was no way ... But why was he so upset?

'I never had a baby with her.' He had sounded panicky. 'That part isn't true.'

That part? Oh God.

He had leaned forward then, his hands on his knees, head hanging. Essie had moved closer to him, put a hand on his arm, giving it a quick squeeze.

'What happened with that girl, Tadhg? Please tell us you didn't ...'

He had looked up then, directly at Maria, his horrified eyes filling her with dread. 'It's not like it sounds. You have to understand. Nothing ever happened between us while she was still at school; it was after she graduated. It was the Christmas holidays; I was out drinking every night with the lads. It should never have happened, but please, you have to believe me ...'

'No,' Maria said. 'No, this can't ...' She looked at the photo on her phone, the girl, so young in her candy-pink Juicy Couture tracksuit, her long hair pulled into a side ponytail.

Most likely to: Win an Oscar someday!

Funniest moment: When she faked a note for gym class saying she had meningitis so would have to sit it out.

Wins award for: Drama queen

The words blurred in front of her.

Her brain struggling to compute what her husband had just said. There was just no way, not Tadhg, not with one of his own students, a child. No. This couldn't be happening.

'How old?' She had choked the words out.

He had his head in his hands again.

'How old was she, Tadhg?'

'Eighteen. At least. She'd finished school that summer.'

'And you'd have been ...' She tried to do the maths in her

head … He was forty-eight now; he'd have been around twenty-five back in 2001. 'Twenty-five, so seven years older than her.'

Essie took a sharp breath in.

'A year older than Eva is now,' Maria had said, causing her husband to moan into his hands. 'Jesus Christ. You were her teacher; she was your student only a few months earlier – that's wrong on so many levels. Look at me, Tadhg.'

He had lifted his head, forced his shame-filled eyes to meet hers.

Please let there be some explanation, don't let this be what it sounds like.

'I know – it should never have happened,' Tadhg said, 'I was paralytic drunk and stupid, so fucking stupid. I should have said no, but it was a moment of weakness … but you have to believe me, that child was not mine.'

'How on earth can you say that if you were *paralytic drunk?*' Her voice was shrill with panic.

'I used protection; I was always careful that way. There's no way I got her pregnant, just no way. And … this is going to sound awful, but the way she was with me, well, she clearly knew what she was doing. That baby could have been anyone's.'

It didn't matter what his excuse was, though. The bottom line was that he had been a teacher, a person of authority who had slept with a teenaged former student. They read about scandals like this in the papers all the time, about teachers abusing their positions. But those people were monsters, despicable human beings, the complete opposite of her upstanding, decent, law-abiding husband, a man who didn't even have a single penalty point on his licence.

Weren't they?

CHAPTER 20

Dani

She had almost deleted the message when she first saw it, assuming the missed call from a weird number she didn't recognise was a scam. Thank God she hadn't. It had come in just after midnight, but her phone had been on silent. After she'd listened to the WhatsApp voice note the first time, she had sat there in shock. Even though the niggle in her gut had been telling her there was more to her daughter's death than met the eye, her gut feelings didn't exactly have a great track record. They'd led her astray too many times, especially when it came to men.

She had begun to wonder if maybe it *was* just a huge coincidence that she had bumped into Michael, that maybe Jessie hadn't met him. Coincidences happened all the time. Look at that case in Colorado back in the eighties, when two women were killed in one night. The husband of one of the women was the prime suspect for years because his business card was found on the body of the second woman. Turns out he'd given her a ride while she was hitchhiking once months earlier and passed on a card for his new appliance repair business. In an even crazier twist, it turned out that the real killer, who had finally been convicted in 2022 after a cold case review, had been rescued from the mountain the night of the murders when he was caught in a snowstorm.

However, the message from Ari, her daughter's best girlfriend, confirmed that something hinky *had* been going on here. Ari was volunteering on an environmental conservation project in the Mindo cloud forest, on a remote site outside of Quito in Ecuador. Jessie had toyed with the idea of going with her to the rainforest to help rescue and rehabilitate wild animals that had been abused and trafficked, but she'd decided to stay in Boston and save some money to go travelling the world instead. If only she had gone with Ari, she wouldn't have met Ricky's cousin that night in the bar, and she wouldn't be dead now.

Ari had been out of coverage until yesterday, when she'd gone on a trip into the nearest big town, nine hours away from the project site, to stock up on provisions. She'd been in an internet cafe, catching up with the folks back home, when the messages about Jessie from their mutual distraught friends had flooded into her phone. Ari had known about her friend's trip to Blarney – they told each other everything – but Jessie had warned her not to tell her family where she was if they tried to contact her. The girls had been keeping in touch on a messaging app called Discord – sporadically on Ari's side, as she had no access to wi-fi in camp.

In a long voice note, punctuated by sobs, Ari told Dani that she had sat in that stifling cafe, tears pouring down her cheeks as she read the most recent emails and messages that she'd received from Jessie. Then she had picked up her phone and called the restaurant in Boston to get Dani's number.

I just can't believe it. She can't be gone. She was saving so hard, she was going to come down here, we were going to travel South America together. She was so excited about finding her dad. It looked like she was really close too, according to the last message I got from her. I know things weren't great between you when she left Boston, but they would have gotten sorted out. I know they would. I'm so sorry, Dani.

Dani checked the time: 7:22 a.m. She had no idea what time it would be in Ecuador, but she had to try and talk to Ari. She went into her recent calls and dialled the number starting with +593. It rang and rang, eventually going to a generic voicemail system. *Crap.* It was probably the middle of the night there. It could be hours before Ari called back. What if she had already gone back into the rainforest, taking Jessie's last messages with her? Dani went into WhatsApp and recorded her own message, asking Ari to please forward her a screenshot of that last message from Jessie as soon as she could.

Less than a minute later, her phone notified her that she had a new WhatsApp. It was a text message from Ari who apologised for not being able to take Dani's call as she was sharing a dorm in a hostel overnight and didn't want to wake her room mates. However, she said she'd send the screenshot right away. While she was reading the first message, the second one had come through.

Even though her daughter's final words to her best friend only confirmed her own suspicions, she sat in stunned silence after taking them in.

Think I may have found someone who knows my dad, meeting later today. Getting closer now. Have feeling will have found him by time I talk to you again.

The message had been sent at 1:27 p.m. last Thursday, the day her daughter had last been seen.

CHAPTER 21

Noelle

They were sitting in Maria's sunroom, the baby on his blanket on the rug between them, kicking his pudgy little legs, delighted to be free of the constraints of his Baby-gro. Maria's house was always so cosy; they'd had it retrofitted with insulation and triple-glazed windows. Not like the B&B, with its creaky back boiler and condensation running down the windows. It cost Noelle a small fortune to heat the place.

'Doesn't it feel like another lifetime since ours were that small?' Maria said, looking wistfully at Leon.

Noelle had been astounded when her friend rang to say she'd called in sick to work and really needed to talk to her. The only time Noelle could remember Maria missing work before was when she'd tested positive for Covid. She'd bundled the baby into the car – she was minding him while Molly was at work today – and driven straight over to her friend's house.

Maria was pale and tired-looking, dressed in black leggings and an oversized hoodie, her blonde bob in need of a wash or at the very least, a good brush.

'It sure does,' she replied. 'Imagine, I was only a year younger than my Holly is now when I had her; that one is only just about able to mind herself, never mind a baby.'

'It's mad when you think of it, isn't it? You were far more mature than her at twenty-four, though, far more mature than I was at that age too. Remember how broody I was after you had Holly? I was mad to have a baby but Tadhg wasn't ready ...' She tailed off, her eyes welling up.

'Oh, Maria.' Her friend wasn't a big crier; she was usually too busy mopping up everybody else's tears. She had such a big, soft heart. And was so genuine. A couple of years below Noelle – and Kevin and Tadhg – Maria hadn't grown into her gawky looks until after she left school. She'd never been one of the *in crowd* – unlike Tadhg, one of the most talented hurlers the village had ever produced, captaining Cork to three Munster Senior Hurling Championship successes and two All-Ireland titles.

Noelle remembered the first time Tadhg introduced the young teacher to the group as his new girlfriend, on a night out in town. She had barely recognised Maria: her sleek, layered Rachel bob framing her pretty face and a new wardrobe that flattered her enviable figure, with those gorgeous long legs. It wasn't only her looks Maria had grown into during her time away in Limerick at teacher training college: she had grown into herself, and the three-year age difference, which had seemed so big when they were in school, seemed like nothing at all in the bar that night. They had gravitated towards each other, and their friendship had strengthened over the years through marriage and babies and the ups and downs of life – Noelle didn't know how she'd have got over the breakdown of her marriage without Maria – to the point where they confided in each other about everything. Almost.

'It's Tadhg,' Maria said, biting her lip, the skin cracked and sore-looking. 'God, Noelle ...'

'What is it?' She hoped Maria wasn't about to say he'd cheated on her. Tadhg had always had a bit of a twinkle in his eye, but Noelle had never heard any talk of him messing around and Cork was a small place. Even so, nothing would shock her after her own experience; and while, even after nearly two decades of marriage, Maria still inexplicably seemed to think the sun shone out of her husband's arse, Noelle wouldn't trust any man as far as she could throw him.

'That woman. Dani. What she said—'

'Ah, Maria, don't mind that one. The carry-on of her, in front of everyone ...'

'Some of it is true, though.' Her friend's voice was so faint a draft could have carried it away.

'What do you mean?'

No, surely not.

'It's true. Not about Jessie, but about her. Dani.'

No way!!

Leon, who was due a feed soon, started to grizzle, kicking his legs harder now. Noelle picked him up and jiggled him on her lap.

'That he was her teacher?'

Maria nodded miserably, chewing her lip.

'But not that he ... that anything happened between them?'

Maria nodded again.

'Oh no, Maria.' Noelle had never been one of the many worshippers at the altar of the mighty Tadhg Murphy, but she'd never in a million years have thought he'd go near one of his own students.

'He went by Michael over there, it's his middle name. He knew the Yanks would butcher *Tadhg*. In fairness, it's a name anyone who's not Irish would struggle with. He says it didn't happen until after she'd left school, the following Christmas, and it was just one night, but it's still really bad.'

If their roles had been reversed and it was Noelle who had just found out this earth-shattering news about her husband, Maria would have known exactly what to say to make her feel, if not better, at least a bit less shit. She was such a positive person, able to spot flecks of silver lining in the darkest of situations, a glass half full to Noelle's 'never even got a glass in the first place'. And not only had Noelle no clue what to say to her friend, Leon was now arching his back, his little fists clenched, ready to start roaring for his feed. 'I have to heat this lad's bottle for him. Come in with me and I'll make us both a cup of tea.'

Maria followed her obediently into the kitchen, slumping onto a stool at the breakfast bar, while Noelle put the kettle on and got the baby's bottle and formula out of his nappy bag. She lay Leon in his pram, ignoring his howls of protest, while she made up his feed, willing the kettle to boil faster.

Poor Maria. No wonder she hadn't been able to face work today.

'So, they were only together the one night? After she finished school?'

'Yes. She graduated in June and it was the Christmas after.'

'Jesus, what the hell was he thinking?'

'I don't know, Noelle, I really don't know. She was only eighteen, he was twenty-five – and her teacher, for Christ's sake.'

'But he wasn't Jessie's dad?'

'No.'

'Well, thank God for that at least,' Noelle said, wondering how he could be so sure: according to what Dani was saying, the timing of Jessie's conception would have coincided with his time in Boston.

Jesus, so she's been telling the truth after all. Partly, anyway.

'I know but it's still awful, Noelle. If this gets out, he could lose his job. I mean, what if he's not allowed to work with kids anymore? It's just so ... I can't believe he could have ... I was awake all night going over it in my head.'

'He won't lose his job, Maria,' she said, although she had no idea whether or not this was true. 'And hopefully, it won't get out ...'

How the hell could she tell Maria that Dani was in with one of Cork's top criminal law solicitors as they spoke, demanding a second post-mortem and an investigation into her daughter's death? Dani had asked Noelle for a *ride* into town earlier for her appointment and hadn't looked a bit impressed when she gave her the number for Blarney Cabs. Much as Noelle felt sorry for the woman's loss, Dani needed to realise that Noelle wasn't her personal driver.

'Why did Tadhg let on he didn't know who she was in the bar on Sunday?'

'He didn't. He knew her by her maiden name, Doyle – he genuinely didn't recognise her. And she's changed an awful lot. I saw a photo of her from back then: she was the image of Jessie.'

'Jesus.'

'Here. I'll make the tea, you take care of the baby.' Maria nodded towards the pram, where Leon was frantically gnawing on his fist, seconds from a full-blown hissy fit.

She brought a spotty tea pot over to the granite kitchen island and left it there to brew, returning with two coordinating cups and saucers and then the milk jug and sugar bowl to match. Noelle loved Maria's kitchen, loved her whole house. Her friend had put her own stamp on the place when they moved in but had kept Essie's country-kitchen look – washed in creamy neutrals, with its Belfast sink and cream range.

Noelle scooped the baby from his pram and stuck the teat of the bottle between his little lips. He began to suck greedily, swallowing in panicky gulps as if he'd never been fed before.

'Slow down or you'll get another sore belly, silly billy,' Noelle said, and as if he understood her, the baby relaxed his death grip on the bottle. She turned her attention back to her friend. 'How on earth did they end up getting together?'

'The lads were on a mad bender: they were all off on Christmas break. Tadhg and another guy were the only teachers in the house, the rest of them were all in construction. All illegal, of course, cash in hand, so they had plenty of money to throw away on drink. And these lads were serious drinkers. Tadhg was always well able to drink, but he said this was a whole different level altogether. Starting at lunchtime and going on into the next morning. He said Dani, or Daniela as he knew her, was hanging out of him in the bar and they were all doing shots. He couldn't remember how he got home that night, but when he woke up the next morning, still pissed, she was straddling him and instead of pushing her off, the stupid, stupid man ...' Maria interlaced her fingers, squeezing so tight the blood began to pool under her nails.

Shit, this is awful.

'Oh, Maria, you poor thing. No wonder you're so upset.' Noelle took the bottle away from the baby, sat him up straight and began to wind him.

Maria opened the lid of the tea pot to give it a stir, then dropped the spoon and started to cry. 'God, I'm so thick.'

'Ah, Maria, this isn't your fault.'

She shook her head. 'No, the pot. I never put the stupid bloody tea bags in.'

'Ah, shur your head must be all over the place', Noelle said, getting to her feet with the baby on her hip and going to the cupboard where the tea caddy was kept. She put two bags into the pot and gave it a stir. 'I'll pour some more hot water in on top – it'll be grand.'

As they waited for the tea to brew, Maria explained that according to Tadhg, Dani had turned into a bit of a stalker in the weeks following that night they were together, bombarding him with calls and texts. He said he'd stopped going out in case he bumped into her – acutely aware of how much he'd fucked up – just going to work and training and straight home again. She'd turned up outside the school a couple of times, which had really freaked him out, but the final straw was when he came home from the gym late one Friday evening and found her waiting in his bed without a stitch of clothing on.

'He told her that what had happened between them should never have happened, and he was sorry, he really regretted it. She lost the plot altogether then. Started screaming and throwing things at him and telling him she'd make sure he did regret it. Grabbed her clothes and left the house in floods of tears. He was terrified the school would find out and his teaching career would be over. But they never did and even more surprisingly, he never heard from Dani again. He did end up coming home early because of it, though; he was back in Blarney the following month.'

'What a nightmare. It's no wonder she got such a shock when she saw him on Sunday. And he must have got even more of a shock when he copped on to who she was. Christ, Maria, I can see why you couldn't face going into school today. Where's Tadhg? Did he go in?'

'Yeah, he had a meeting this morning so he had to. Essie knows – she's all upset too – but we haven't said anything to the kids. I'm sick with worry over it, though. What if it comes out and we have to tell them? She was the same age as Eva is now.' Maria looked across the island at her, agonised.

Noelle got off her stool and went over to give her friend a one-armed hug, the baby sated and drowsy in her other arm. 'Look, there's no point in borrowing trouble from tomorrow. That probably won't happen and at least she wasn't still his student – that would have been an awful lot worse.'

And it would have, but Tadhg had still crossed a very serious line, no two ways about it.

CHAPTER 22

Dani

'Well, I can certainly see why you'd have concerns, Dani, under the circumstances you've just outlined to me.'

'I'm glad to hear you say that, Brian, because the cops don't seem to be taking me seriously at all.'

She was sitting in the attorney's city centre office and had just filled him in on everything that had happened since her arrival in Cork on Saturday while he jotted notes down in a legal pad.

Jessie's message to Ari had swept away any doubts she'd begun to harbour about her own instincts. She had called the police precinct straightaway and asked for the sergeant she'd spoken to yesterday but was told his shift didn't start until nine. She had called back again at 9.15 and left another message, but an hour later she still hadn't heard from him, so she'd got back on to Larry in the embassy. He had managed to get her an urgent appointment with Brian Fitzpatrick, an attorney who had been involved in a number of high-profile murder cases, at noon.

She had taken to Brian right away. He had come out of his office to greet her, shaking her hand. A slim, well-groomed man, in a beautifully cut dark blue suit, a dazzlingly white shirt and a blue tie with deep pink pinstripes that tied in with the colour scheme of his modern office. One wall was lined with navy floor-to-ceiling cupboards, and behind his sleek white desk was an expensive-looking hot pink swivel chair.

'Do you think it's possible that Mr Murphy didn't recognise you when he saw you in the hotel bar?'

'No, I don't. I mean, sure, I don't look the same as I did when I was in high school,' she said, 'but I haven't changed completely and I recognised *him* straightaway.'

'Just so I have this straight,' he had said, 'you're telling me that this man taught you for your final year of high school and that after you graduated, you had a sexual relationship with him?'

'Yes.'

'What age were you when it started?'

'Um, well, I was seventeen when we slept together.'

'And was that the first time he'd had any sexual contact with you?'

'Well, it was the first time he touched me, if that's what you mean, but he'd started singlin' me out from pretty early on after I transferred into his class. It was just the way he looked at me at the start, ya know? Real subtle, so I wasn't sure if I was just imaginin' it. I liked English in school, only subject I was ever any good at. He encouraged me to take an elective in creative writing that he was teachin', said I had a real talent. It was a small group, so I had a lot more one-on-one contact with him. He used to stand beside my chair with his thigh touchin' mine, not so as anybody else would notice and man, it sounds so cheesy now, but it felt like there was sparks flyin' between us. Or sometimes he'd put his hand on my shoulder and squeeze real gentle and the hairs on the back of my neck would stand up.'

'Did he ever touch you sexually while you were still in school?'

'No, but it was pretty obvious that he was attracted to me. The chemistry between us was off the charts. He started askin' me to hang back after class to discuss my work and then the questions became more personal, about my family, whether I had a boyfriend. He'd say stuff like surely all the guys must have been linin' up to be with me. That a girl like me deserved somebody who'd treat me like a queen.'

She used to lie awake at night visualising the two of them together, wanting him so badly it hurt, not that she was going to tell the attorney that. The night of senior prom, she had been hyperalert to his presence, his eyes tracking her round the hotel ballroom, burning through the satin fabric of her gown. She had followed him to the restrooms, casually walking past as he came out, feigning surprise. With a tilt of his head, he had beckoned her around the corner to a dimly lit corridor leading to the bedrooms and she had followed, heart pounding, legs like rubber. When he'd lifted her hair away from her ear, his fingers sparking little fires all over her body as they brushed lightly off her skin, and he'd leaned forward, she'd been so sure he was going to kiss her. What happened next had been nearly as good, even though his lips made no contact with her flesh. 'You,' he had whispered into her ear, 'are the most beautiful girl in that room tonight.' Then the sound of voices approaching caused him to take a step back from her, to press pause and walk away, turning at the corner to look back and gift her one of his special smiles.

The attorney tapped his pen on his pad. 'What contact did you have with Mr Murphy after you graduated from high school?'

'None whatsoever, until the weekend we got together.'

He raised an eyebrow.

'It was nearly six months since I'd seen him. Coming up to Christmas 2001. I was in a bar with my cousin and her friends; they were older than me, in their twenties, and I had a fake ID. Michael ... um, I mean Tadhg ... was with a big group of guys, all pretty wasted. He came straight over when he saw me, offered to buy me a drink, even though he knew I was underage. I was trying to act all cool around him. I'd cried myself to sleep for months over this guy because I'd been so sure he'd reach out to me after I graduated school. I'd even sent him a thank you email with my cell number on it, but he said he never got it.'

He'd pulled her into a corner and told her she was even more beautiful that night than she had been at the prom. He bought her a double vodka and Red Bull, saying that's what all the girls back home in Ireland drank, and then he bought her another one and she kinda lost track after that. They had sex for the first time in his car outside the bar, and again in his bed after she went home with him that night. The following morning, she had woken first and lain on the pillow beside him, gazing at him. Drinking in every feature of that handsome face, his long black lashes, his perfect jawline ... and then his eyes had popped open and there was no mistaking that initial flash of horror when he saw her.

'He went home the following week for Christmas and even though he said he'd call me, he didn't, so I called him and sent messages but he didn't reply. That was such a miserable Christmas, me watching my phone constantly. He just ghosted me. If it was now, I'd never have contacted him again – that would have been the end of it – but I was seventeen and madly in love so after the holidays, when I knew he'd be back, I went round his place one evening. The door was open, so I just went into his room and waited for him.'

The look on his face when he'd come in and seen her lying on his bed – butt naked, expecting him to be turned on, all on for another night of wild sex – shock, curdling into revulsion and then rage. The things he had called her. *Psycho*, *stalker*, *freak*. Each word a dagger to her heart. He had gathered her clothes up, thrown them at her, told her to get dressed and get out.

'He was furious. He basically threw me out, like a piece of trash. I was devastated. I never wanted to see him again after that, but a couple of weeks later, I found out I was pregnant and I had no choice but to tell him. I think a part of me still hoped there was some chance ... that it might change things ... but he just wanted me to get rid of it.'

'I hope you don't mind me asking this, Dani, but are you absolutely certain he was the father?'

'One million per cent. I wasn't sleeping with anybody else at the time. I was only seventeen, remember, just a stupid kid really. So stupid that I still thought there was hope for us after that, that maybe he just needed time to process the idea of being a daddy, of us being a little family. I left it a couple more weeks: I knew he'd be mad that I hadn't gone through with the abortion, he'd made me swear on my mom's life I wouldn't tell anybody, but I still thought ... Anyway, that's when I found out he was gone. One of his roommates said he'd just upped and left his job mid-semester, said he'd moved to Canada and he didn't have a forwarding address for him or an address back home. I never saw Michael Murphy again until two days ago in Blarney and far as he was concerned, I'd gotten rid of his baby.'

Devastated at the realisation that Michael had done a runner, Dani had called Nicole. Her closest friend had known about her infatuation with their teacher, but she'd had no idea that anything had happened between them. It had nearly killed Dani to keep the secret from her friend – she had done it for Michael – but she no longer cared. She needed to talk to someone. Nicole wasn't home, though; she was over at her boyfriend Shawn's house. His parents were out of town for the weekend and Nicole had told Dani to call round. The party was in full swing when she got there and her friend was already half tanked. When Nicole handed her some kind of alcoholic punch in a plastic glass, Dani drank it and it nearly blew her head off. And when somebody else passed her a bong, she took a deep drag. Uncaring of the baby growing inside her belly, she proceeded to get drunk and stoned, her feelings for Michael souring over the course of the night.

At some point, she'd staggered down to the basement, where a group of guys she knew were playing pool and knocking back beers. Ricky De Marco came over and handed her a bottle. A couple of years older than her, he had filled out a bit since she'd seen him last, and was looking a lot cuter. He had recently broken up with Ashley Wilson, after finding out she was cheating on him with one of his team-mates. They'd cried on each other's shoulders for a couple of hours and then ended up in Shawn's little sister's bedroom, screwing frantically, too wasted to even think about using protection.

He may not have seemed quite as cute to Dani the next morning, but Ricky De Marco had adored the ground she walked on. Back then, at least. And she'd needed to be adored, after the way Michael had treated her. Although shocked when she told him a few weeks later that she'd missed her period, not once had Ricky suggested that they end the pregnancy. Instead, he'd gone to a jewellery store and bought her a cheap ring and by the time her family found out she was pregnant, she was eighteen and they'd been engaged for two months.

Ricky's devotion to her hadn't been long wearing off once the baby weight started to pile on, though. After Jessie was born, he'd pretty much reverted to living the life of a single man, leaving her alone in their shitty one-bed apartment, comforting herself with carbs while he went out boozing. He'd proved about as good a father as he was a husband. Her parting shot as she walked out of their grotty apartment that last time was that it didn't matter that he was such a crappy dad as he wasn't even Jessie's real father. The look on his deadbeat face had been hilarious and at the time, she felt it served him right for the way he'd treated her, but how she wished to God she'd kept her big mouth shut now. Ricky had moved out of state soon after that and she'd never heard from him again. She'd kept his name, though, and the story that he was Jessie's father, which was on her daughter's birth cert.

Back living with her mother, who was only too willing to watch Jessie while she went out, Dani had started to get her social life back and soon got into a relationship with Doug Winters, which had lasted on and off for the next four years until he was killed in a car wreck on his way home from a weekend bender. She had missed Doug, but she hadn't missed the chaos of their life together. Heavy drinking and drugging and screaming rows, the odd punch thrown on both sides.

Since then, it had been one fucked-up, chaotic relationship after another, with her moving in and out of her mother's place, eventually leaving Jessie there permanently. Her mother had pointed out that she was able to give the child the stability that Dani couldn't. Three healthy meals a day, a safe, warm home and help with her schoolwork. The basic stuff that any half-decent mother would do for her kid, but that Dani couldn't seem to manage.

And Dani, believing that Mamma was right, hadn't thought to question why it was that she had so much love to give her grandchild and yet so little for her only daughter. Dani had tried so hard to be good, to make Mamma love her, or at least like her, but nothing ever seemed to work. And when Pops went, she had given up trying.

Her father's death had come as a complete shock to them all. An aneurysm in his brain exploded as he lifted his five iron to take a shot at the seventh hole and he had crashed to the ground, his head landing on the grass with a thud. A drooping eyelid was the only sign of this ticking time bomb Pops had been carrying around in his brain, not enough of an annoyance to necessitate a trip to the doctor. Unknown to him, a weak spot in the wall of a blood vessel in his brain had stretched and thinned and bulged, growing to the size of a large blueberry. As he lifted his club that fateful day, the pressure finally became too much and the blood-filled berry had burst, taking away the person who loved her most in the world.

She realised the attorney was staring at her expectantly.

'Jeez, sorry, Brian, where was I again?'

'I was just asking why you didn't try to track Michael Murphy down over the years, or tell your daughter about him.'

She let out a long breath. 'It wasn't that simple, ya know? Firstly, I had no idea where he was from – the only reason I even knew it was some place in Cork with a castle was 'cos he'd mentioned it in class one day. And when things went south with Ricky, I couldn't just turn round and admit I'd lied to everyone, so I just kept schtum. By the time Jessie was old enough to start asking questions about her dad, I'd been telling that story so long, I nearly believed it myself.'

CHAPTER 23

Maria

The shock of hearing from Noelle that not only was Dani De Marco not going to be out of their lives any time soon, but that she was refusing to move her daughter's remains from the morgue and had engaged one of the top criminal attorneys in Munster had sent Maria into a tailspin.

Tadhg had sounded as horrified as she felt when she rang him at work to tell him.

'We have to do something, Tadhg. She's not only going round alleging you're Jessie's father – she's saying you may have had something to do with her death. That's slander.'

'I think we need to get some legal advice ourselves now, before this thing gets totally out of hand. Maisie O'Connor's daughter Justine specialises in defamation law. She went to St Vincent's and she comes back every year to do careers day for us. I'll give her a call right away.'

'Tell her it's urgent, won't you? The sooner we find out where we stand, the better,' Maria said.

Justine O'Connor had got back to Tadhg within ten minutes of getting his message, asking him to quickly outline the situation. She was going to be coming through the village on her way back from visiting her mother that night around eight, she'd said, offering to drop into them then if it suited. Tadhg had arranged to meet her at his mother's house, away from listening ears.

It had taken all of Maria's strength to act normally in front of Ben and Eva when they got in from school. Ben seemed even more subdued than usual today, his spirits not even lifting at the smell of the roast chicken dinner that had greeted him when he came in the front door, dropping his schoolbag in the hall where it landed like a sack of wet cement. He always arrived home ravenous, and she liked to have his dinner on the table for him when he got in.

She had pottered around the kitchen, washing up the pots and pans and wiping down the countertops, while he pushed petit pois and chunks of roast potato around his plate, staring at his phone. He usually inhaled his dinner. She hoped to God the rumours about Dani's outburst in the hotel hadn't reached the kids in school.

'How was your day, love?'

'Fine.'

'Did you get much homework?'

'Yeah.'

'Would you like some more gravy?'

He shook his head, his attention fixed on his screen. If things had been normal, she'd have picked him up on his manners, but she had more on her mind today. She had learnt to pick her battles: it was hard enough to get the kids to eat at the table and not in their rooms or in front of the TV without trying to enforce the 'no devices at the table rule' as well. It was like school lunches: after years of the same rows, you eventually just gave up.

By the time Eva had come in from study two hours later, Maria was fizzing with nervous tension, one minute hoping the solicitor would reassure them that they had nothing to be worried about, the next anxious that things might go the other way. Thankfully, Eva was in a much better mood this evening.

Maria had had to force herself to act interested in her daughter's inane chatter.

'I mean, he cheated on her so many times, Mom. She said she hated him like and she even started seeing Jayden Cunningham to get back at him. Jamie and Jayden are like arch enemies, they both got suspended for fighting in the boys' toilets last year, and after all that, Katie gets back with him. What the actual? I just don't get it. I mean has the girl no respect for herself? And then ...'

Maria nodded and tutted in what she hoped were the right places. She really didn't have the head space for her daughter's 'spilling of the tea' today; it felt like there was just about enough room for her own brain. She wished Eva would stop talking, eat her dinner and disappear up to her room. Eight o'clock couldn't come quickly enough.

The solicitor was one of those women who managed to rock the effortlessly cool look that Maria had always envied. She was dressed in a pair of wide-legged black pants and a fitted black waistcoat with chunky platform runners. Her short, platinum-blonde hair was cut tight at the sides, longer on top, and was clearly the work of a really good hairdresser.

She was chatting to Essie when Tadhg and Maria arrived at

ten to eight, Maria not having been able to wait in her own house for another second.

'You could probably have done without this tonight,' Tadhg said. 'But we really appreciate you calling to us so late.'

Justine waved a hand. 'Not at all, Tadhg. As I said earlier, I'm in court tomorrow and Thursday and I was passing on my way home. I might just get you to fill me in again from the beginning, and I'll take some notes if that's okay.' She pulled a yellow lined A4 pad from a black Zadig & Voltaire crinkled leather tote bag that under normal circumstances Maria would have been drooling over.

As Tadhg told her the whole story, starting with the scene in the hotel on Sunday and then going back to when he first met Daniela Doyle in 2001, Maria studied the solicitor's face intently. Her expression remained deadpan as he spoke and she interjected with questions. She didn't so much as bat an eyelid at Tadhg's revelation that he'd had sex with one of his students when she had barely graduated, even though Maria felt every muscle in her body cringe in shame. Justine had probably heard a lot worse.

She stared at her notes for a few moments after Tadhg had finished speaking.

'Okay,' she said, 'so my initial thoughts here are that firstly, we only have Ms De Marco's word at the moment that Brian Fitzpatrick has taken her case on. I know Brian well, so I can put a call into him in the morning to find out what the story is. Secondly, it's rare enough but not unheard of for family members to request a second post-mortem if there's any level of suspicion about a death. In a situation where a coroner agrees to facilitate this, the family would have to bring in their own pathologist and I can tell you those guys don't come cheap. It would have to be done within a tight enough timeframe too – I think it's about five working days. There's a shortage of space in the city morgue, believe it or not, so a body can't just be left there indefinitely. If a family or next-of-kin doesn't claim the remains, the coroner can arrange for burial and it's paid for by the local authority.'

How sad, Maria thought, to be so unloved in life that your body could be unclaimed, like a pair of glasses or a piece of left luggage. Buried by strangers, mourned by nobody.

'In terms of the garda investigation,' Justine continued, 'while you did have a sexual relationship with this woman and she's saying you could be the father of her child—'

'She's saying he *is* the father,' Maria said, 'no could about it.'

'Right. Which has to beg the question, why has she not tried to track you down before this? Even if only for the maintenance payments. It would have been easy enough to do it through the school, surely, if she had explained the situation. And why not tell her daughter who her real father was if she believed it was you? Why allow her to believe her dad was this De Marco guy who just abandoned them both?'

'Exactly, Justine,' Tadhg said, raising the palms of both hands like a priest on the altar. 'It makes no sense. I mean, the woman was turning up at the school where I still worked, in my bed, even; there isn't a hope in hell she wouldn't have let me know if she'd been pregnant.'

'Well, even if you were this girl's father, the crime scene guys know their stuff and they'd have called the coroner if they had any suspicions at all that the girl's death was anything other than an accident. They're clearly satisfied there was no sign of foul play involved and by the sound of it, the PM didn't show up anything that would suggest otherwise.'

Comforted by the solicitor's pragmatic, unruffled demeanour, Maria felt the viper in her stomach uncoil. She must come across situations like this all the time.

'What about the stuff she's saying about Tadhg, though?' Essie asked. 'Telling people he's the father, hinting that he might have had a hand to play in her death. Surely she can't just go around saying things like that?'

'Well, the law on defamation is much stricter in Ireland than it is in the US,' Justine said. 'It's actually among the harshest in Europe. That makes my job defending claims for the paper a lot harder, but it's positive for you. There's very strong protection afforded to freedom of expression by the US Constitution: it's not subject to a constitutional balance with the right to the protection of individual privacy or the right to reputation and good name, in the same manner as it is under the Irish Constitution. The bottom line is Irish and English law is much more favourable for somebody looking to protect their reputation.'

'So how do we get her to stop slandering me around the village, then?' Tadhg asked.

'Firstly, it's not called slander anymore. Since the Defamation Act of 2009, the term defamation has replaced both slander and libel. Just to explain, a defamatory statement is a statement that reasonable members of society would think damages your reputation. It's not defamatory if it's true or substantially true. To make a case for defamation, you have to show that the statement you're complaining about was published to at least one other person. And published includes any type of communication, including a conversation with another person, comments made on social media, newspaper articles, blog posts and speeches.

'One defence to a defamation claim could be that the statement is true; under Irish law, the onus on proving that statement rests on the person defending the action. The biggest issue we have here is that some of what Ms De Marco is saying *is* true. You *were* her teacher, Tadhg and you *did* have a sexual relationship with her. Even if the two facts were not concurrent and you didn't have sexual relations with her while you were still her teacher, they are both fact. What is not fact is that you are the father of her child, so the onus would be on her to prove this, not on you to disprove it.'

'Could she make him take a paternity test to prove it?' Maria asked. Despite her husband's adamance that he couldn't be Jessie's father, how could he know for sure? He swore he'd used condoms that night, but condoms didn't always work. What if, out-of-his-face drunk as he had been that night, he hadn't used one each time or hadn't put it on properly?

'That would be highly unusual in a situation like this,' Justine said, 'and not something I've ever come across. In cases where the paternity of a child is disputed, the district court can order the alleged father to do a DNA test, but that generally only happens in cases where maintenance or custody is an issue. That's obviously not the case here. It's not a family law case and the child in question was an adult and is deceased. The main issue here would appear to be the defamation, which clearly damages Tadhg's reputation, particularly given his position. If she's also saying or even intimating that you may have had a part to play in her daughter's death, that's pretty serious. You could send a very strong shot across her bow in the form of a legal letter reminding her that she's not in the US now; she's in Ireland and is governed by Irish law.'

Justine pursed her lips and paused for a few moments before speaking again. 'You also have the option of applying for an injunction to compel her to refrain from making any further such claims, in the hope that this would be enough to make her stop what she's doing. However, the last thing I'd advise you to do at this point is to institute defamation proceedings, because from the type of person you've described to me, I think it would be like a red rag to a bull. My advice is to hang tight for now, not add any fuel to the flames and hope this will all calm down.'

Tadhg nodded. 'That sounds like a sensible approach to me.'

'But what if she doesn't stop?' Maria asked.

'I'd still advise you to bide your time. Everybody who knows Tadhg knows he's a person of good character, and you really don't want this to hit the media. It's entirely up to you, but if I was in your shoes, I'd speak to the board of management at the school and let them know what's going on. Sometimes it's better to be open about these things, before they hear it from somebody else, if they haven't already. Blarney is a small village, as you're only too well aware.'

CHAPTER 24

Maria
Wednesday, 17 January

'Miss, miss! Dylan has a Nutella sandwich in his schoolbag. He just showed me.'

'I don't, miss, I swear on Scrapper's life. She's such a f—' For once, Dylan managed to control himself enough to mutter whatever choice adjectives he was about to describe his classmate with under his breath.

Not quite low enough, though.

'He's lying, miss and he just called me a fat effin' retard. I wouldn't mind, but he's the one who—'

'That's enough, Ella!' *God give me patience.*

'But I didn't do anything,' the girl whined. 'He's the one who should be getting into trouble, not me. Wioletta has a nut allergy. He could *kill* her.'

Dylan huffed.

'Wioletta's not even in our class. You're such a drama queen, Ella.'

'It doesn't matter whether she's in our class or not,' his classmate continued haughtily, 'nuts are banned in the school. Miss, you should send him down to Mrs Hughes's office.'

'*I'm* the teacher in this classroom, Ella Hogan, not you. Please *do not* tell me how to do my job.'

Ella's eyes went wide; she wasn't used to being spoken to like that by her teacher. Maria was well liked by the kids; she'd hate to be one of those teachers that the children dreaded getting when the new class lists were announced each year. The sharp, shouty ones who didn't seem to like children at all and had clearly chosen the wrong career. They were few and far between these days, thankfully, unlike when Maria herself had been in primary school, but there were still a few who ruled their classrooms with fear. Ella was pouting now; she'd have a face on her for the rest of the day. A right little madam that one was. Give her ten Dylans over one Ella any day of the week, despite all the trouble he caused. Still, she *was* right, as she so often annoyingly was. Nuts were strictly banned in the school.

'Show me your lunch please, Dylan.'

'Sure, miss, no problemo.'

She knew by the smug grin on the boy's face as he handed her his foil-wrapped sandwich that his tattling classmate had just been pranked.

A strong yeasty smell rose from the foil as she opened it. Bovril. Yuck. She hadn't smelled that in years. Her grandad Kenny used to keep a jar of the stuff in the press and she remembered wrinkling her nose in disgust at the smell of the salty meat extract. It was a lot darker than chocolate spread, but she could see how Ella could have been fooled.

'I told you it wasn't Nutella, miss. Ella's just trying to get me in trouble as usual. I'd never tell a lie on me dog's life.'

Judging by the lowered heads and shaking shoulders in Dylan's vicinity, there were a few others in on the joke.

'Funnily enough, I wouldn't have put you down as a Bovril man myself, Dylan O'Leary.'

'No, miss, I wouldn't touch the stuff, it's gross, but me Granda Billy loves it. Mam must have made a mistake this mornin', given me the wrong sambo. She didn't get in 'til very late last night, shur you know yourself.' He gave her a mischievous wink, curling his fingers and pretending to knock back a drink. The whole class erupted in laughter, apart from a red-faced Ella, and Dylan looked delighted with himself.

Maria handed him back his sandwich, stifling a smile herself. It wasn't funny really, because the reality of the child's life was that his mother would always put drink before him, but she couldn't begrudge him the odd moment in the spotlight in his role as class clown.

'What are you going to have for your lunch so?'

'Ara, I made a spare Tayto sandwich, just in case.' Another wink, and more laughs from his audience.

'We're not allowed Taytos. Miss, it's against the healthy eating policy ...' And Ella was off again, clearly not having learnt a thing. They weren't allowed junk food, but if the parent wasn't prepared to abide by the rules, how could she expect the child to? She couldn't let him go hungry.

'That's enough now. Everybody please take out your handwriting books and get started on page fifty-eight.'

She sat back down at her desk and pretended to be immersed in the pile of correcting in front of her. She yawned deeply, setting off a series of yawns that made her eyes water. She'd been awake half the night again, finally giving up on sleep at 5:30 a.m. and going down to the kitchen to make herself a cup of tea. The solicitor's words had kept playing over in her mind.

Biggest issue ... some of what Ms De Marco is saying is true...
You were her teacher ...
You did have a sexual relationship with her ...
You really don't want this to hit the media ...

Tadhg had looked haggard after the solicitor left last night. He hadn't tried to reassure her, as he usually would, that there was nothing to worry about, which made her worry even more. They had agreed not to do anything for now that might antagonise the American woman or draw her on them even further. They had barely spoken after leaving his mother's house. She hadn't known what to say, what to think. She was still struggling to force her mind to bend itself into a shape capable of reconciling *her* Tadhg, the man she had married and loved for almost as long as she could remember, the father of her children, with the man, albeit young and drunk, who had slept with his eighteen-year-old recently graduated student. It was like being asked to believe that black was white or the Earth was flat, that up was down and in was out.

She heard a buzz coming from her bag and checked her phone. It was a voice note. From Justine.

Hi, Maria, sorry to disturb you at work but I can't get hold of Tadhg. I've just come off the phone with Brian Fitzpatrick and I need to talk to you both. There's been a development in relation to Dani De Marco. Can you ask Tadhg not to talk to the guards if they get in touch with him without speaking to me first?

CHAPTER 25

Dani

The owners of the castle were out of the country but when Dani explained who she was to the guy at the ticket kiosk on the way in, he handed her a map of the grounds and waved her through, telling her how sorry he was for her loss. She knew from the cops that the CCTV had shown Jessie buying a hot drink from the cafe close to the entrance to the grounds, before making her way towards the castle to kiss the stone. A staff member had seen her filming in the Poison Garden behind the castle, and she had been caught again on CCTV at 3:34 p.m. walking towards the Rock Close. That was the last known sighting of her daughter alive.

Dani went into the cafe and bought a coffee and a blueberry muffin. She sat at a table outside in her hooded winter parka, the only one braving the cold. It had been snowing heavily in Boston when she left, the temperature minus five. It was minus one here and was doing what the locals called snowing but was really just icy drizzle, melting as soon as it landed.

She took a sip of her coffee, wishing Joe was here beside her as she made this lonely pilgrimage in her daughter's final footsteps. Or somebody at least. Jessie's death had underscored the emptiness of her own life: she didn't have one person close enough to ask to come to Ireland with her. Not one who had offered. Her friends these days were just fair-weather drinking and pot-smoking buddies. Not *friends* in any real sense of the word.

She stretched her shoulders, shrugging off her despondence. Screw the lot of them. She'd come through so much already, she could do this alone. A spark of grit ignited the parched tinder of her rage. She had never expected to see Michael Murphy again, the man who had changed the trajectory of her life the day he walked into her homeroom. Who knew where she'd be now or what she'd be doing if that hadn't happened? If he hadn't sent her down a road of messed-up relationships, booze, drugs and comfort eating? And now Jessie, her beautiful girl, was gone, and it was all because she had come to Blarney to look for him.

Who had she arranged to meet on Thursday? It had to have been him. Nobody else here could have known he was her father.

There was no freakin' way she was getting on a plane out of here until she was completely satisfied that her baby's death had been properly investigated.

She had called her attorney's office first thing this morning, but his secretary had said he was in a meeting, so she'd left a message for him to call her back. Unlike her fiasco of a meeting with the cops, Dani had left his office yesterday feeling she'd really been listened to. He'd agreed to take on her case and to correspond with the Garda Síochána and the city coroner on her behalf, making them aware of her serious concerns about Jessie's death. He had promised to make contact with the Garda yesterday afternoon, but she'd heard nothing from him since. Time was of the essence here and she couldn't expect Joe to fund her stay in Ireland indefinitely while also paying her legal bills and possibly the cost of a private post-mortem.

She looked down at the empty muffin wrapper in her hand. She hadn't tasted a bite of it yet felt an intense craving for another one. Her daughter's face floated into her mind, eyebrows raised, a look that said so much: *Really, Dani? You really think you need another one? Isn't there a healthy option? A piece of fruit, maybe? Or nothing at all, considering you've already had a big breakfast ...* She could picture her healthy-living daughter crunching an apple or nibbling on a handful of sprouted nut medley or wild berry mix – something certified vegan, high in antioxidants, superfood-infused, gluten-free, sustainably sourced, et cetera, et cetera – a dietary insurance policy to protect her from ending up like her mother.

Dani sighed inwardly. She had once been the kind of girl who made heads turn when she walked into a room; now when heads turned her way, it was for all the wrong reasons. She hated being the way she was. Always hungry. For food, for sex, for booze, for anything that might stuff that void inside her. A gnawing, insatiable wanting. Trying to fight the cravings was futile. Her mother and all her aunts were fat – not as big as her, granted, but it was in her genes. It wasn't as if she could go cold turkey, which might have been easier; giving up food simply wasn't an option. And it was probably the only thing stopping her from hopping onto that opioid train with so many other people she knew.

She went back into the cafe and picked up another muffin, chocolate chip this time, and a couple of bars of Dairy Milk, which she stuffed into her purse for later. Then, following her map, she made her way along the pathway that led to the castle, munching as she walked. She had no intention of climbing the spiral stone staircase up five storeys to the top of the tower to kiss the famous stone herself. She wasn't here as a tourist.

She crossed a wooden footbridge, pausing to peer into the gurgling brook that met a narrow river as it gushed past on her right. The riverbed sparkled in the clear winter light and when she looked closer she saw that it was covered in coins, as if a leprechaun had stumbled trying to outrun the troll beneath the bridge and dropped his pot of gold over the side. There was more silver and copper than gold in the water, though; coins of every nationality. Plenty of quarters, dimes and nickels, lots of euro coins and others she didn't recognise. She didn't bother making a wish.

The castle rose formidably above her at the other end of the bridge from a bedrock of solid limestone. She stopped to inhale the earthy, organic smell of ancient stone and moss that had stood in this spot for centuries. Consulting her map again, she followed the path around to the rear of the castle, where a sign directed her to the Poison Garden. She passed a replica of medieval wooden stocks, and she just knew that when she was eventually up to looking through the photos and videos on her daughter's phone, there'd be one of Jessie posing here, her face beaming out from the hole cut into the wood for the unfortunate prisoner's head, hands waggling from the two holes at either end of the diagonal beam. Tears pricked at the back of Dani's eyes, but she blinked them away; plenty of time for that later. She would have the rest of her miserable life to mourn her child.

She kept going, her fleece-lined boots crunching on the gravel path, until she found herself in a garden unlike any she had ever seen before, where some of the plants were so toxic they were encircled by steel cages to prevent people from touching or eating them. The purpose of the garden, according to an information board, was to educate visitors on the positive and negative aspects of the plants grown there, their various uses in today's world and their perceived magical properties from ages gone by. She wandered through the plot, past plants like poison hemlock, European mandrake (so dangerous it was kept behind bars), and *Atropa belladonna*, also known as deadly nightshade – commonly used during the Middle Ages as a powerful defence against witches and spirits, and the primary ingredient in many spells believed to summon second sight.

A gardener passed her on a quad bike, hand raised in greeting, as she left the eerie garden and followed a sign for the Rock Close. As she stood reading about the history of a stone lookout tower that had once been part of the original wall surrounding the estate, she felt the hairs prickle on the back of her neck. She turned to face the castle behind her where, perched on a security camera positioned in one of the window slits, there was a large crow, beady black eyes pinned on her. It struck her that this might be the camera that had picked up the very last image of Jessie.

It felt so surreal. As if any moment now she was going to wake up in her own bed back home, realise this had all been a horrible nightmare, and get up to resume her normal life.

Continuing along the curved path, she came to a narrow stone tunnel set into a high wall. Bending beneath the low ceiling of the dank passage, she emerged at the foot of a set of meandering stone slabs, set into the sloping land to her right. She climbed the steps, puffing slightly as she neared the top.

'Woah.' She found herself standing in what could have been the set of a fantasy drama. 'Man, this is fucking awesome.'

Shafts of light clawed through gaps in the canopy of ancient yew trees, still somehow green and leafy even at this time of year, shadows dancing on the forest floor. It was so still, the only sounds the chattering, chirping chorus of birdsong, the sibilant shushing of the trees and from somewhere not far away, the galloping gush of rushing water. The air seemed different in here, perfumed with an ancient blend of earth, tree and stone. She made her way along the earthen path into the centre of the glade, the otherworldly beauty of the place almost enough to make her forget the reason she was here.

Noelle had told her that this was the oldest part of the estate, the site of a druidic settlement, and many of the huge, strangely shaped rock formations had been here for over 2,000 years. Jessie had come back after her visit 'raving' about it, according to Noelle, and Dani could understand why. A sort of Tolkienesque parallel universe; she had never seen anything quite like it. She almost expected a couple of hobbits or a band of wood elves to pop their heads out from behind a tree or rock.

She trailed her fingers along the rough, weathered surface of a sacrificial altar, stepping into and quickly out of the claustrophobic confines of a hermit's cell. She stood in front of a boulder shaped like the side profile of a witch's face, poking at the random collection of offerings strewn on top, from coins in various nationalities to candy and, weirdly, a Labello lip balm. Legend had it that the witch of Blarney was imprisoned within this stone and could only escape after nightfall. During the night she was said to make her way to the Witch's Kitchen, where she built a fire against the cold, and if you arrived very early in the morning, you might even catch the dying embers of this fire.

Oh, Jessie, baby! You'd have been blown away by this place – it's like stepping into Middle-earth.

She came to a majestic yew tree, its massive roots clinging to the bare rock like the bulging, ropey veins of a varicosal crone. She pressed her forehead against the huge, solid trunk, leeching comfort from its ancient stoic energy. It was darker in here, gloomier, the smell even earthier, the sound of the water cacophonous.

The Wishing Steps lay only feet away, strange claw-shaped rocks guarding the entrance to the uneven, old steps. She wasn't sure now if this had been such a good idea. Would it be too much for her? Should she ask somebody to come back with her – Noelle, maybe?

No! You can do this.

Taking a couple of deep breaths, she walked to the entrance, where she stood and looked down into the stairwell. She had to force herself not to turn and run away from the place where her child had fallen to her death. It was dark in there and smelled of damp and moss, the ceiling and walls on both sides hewn from the rock, a handrail along one side. A sickening shudder tore through her and she felt a fleeting urge to fling herself down the stony staircase. Who would really miss her? Another unwelcome thought crept in ...

Is there any way ...? No, not Jessie ... She'd never have done that to Mamma. No more thinking. Just do this now.

She put one foot on the first uneven step, grasping the icy handrail on her left, and then the next, grateful for the strong grip on the soles of her boots. How the hell did people do this with their eyes closed, some backwards, while thinking only of their wish? You'd wanna be out of your mind.

Jessie would have been hugely entertained by it all, but Dani found it hard to believe that her daughter would have actually made a wish and done the whole blind backwards thing. Although under the spell of this place, maybe that really was what had happened. Maybe she had just slipped, and it had been an accident after all.

She reached the last step, emerging into daylight again and into yet another world, a waterfall racing off the rock face to the left of the steps, dive-bombing into a pond. Another huge boulder stood to her right, a bench in front of it. A bouquet of beautiful wildflowers lay propped against the bench, withering now, and some smaller floral tributes had been placed there too.

She fell to her knees on the grooved wooden boardwalk, where there was nothing apart from the flowers – not a drop of blood on the ground or a scrap of crime-scene tape tied to the railing – to indicate that her daughter had taken her last breath here. Her upper body crumpling onto the ground in front of her, arms outstretched in child's pose, Dani opened her mouth wide and roared. She lay there for some time, keening and wailing, cursing the God who had let this happen to her beautiful girl, oblivious to the cold and the wet that soaked through her pants.

And it was while she lay there, collapsed in a fit of agony, that it happened.

CHAPTER 26

Noelle

'Ah, you're havin' us on now, Mam.'

'I swear to God, Liam,' Noelle said. 'A message from the other side. I'm getting seriously worried about her now.'

Liam and Molly had invited Noelle out for a bite to eat in Christy's Bar at the Woollen Mills Hotel to thank her for all her help with the baby. She'd told them there was no need, that she was delighted to get to spend time with her grandchild. Still, it was nice to be appreciated. Molly was always telling her how lucky they were to have her. Her own mother was worn out looking after her younger siblings, so Molly didn't like to impose on her too often.

Christy's was quiet this evening, apart from the handful of hardy regulars at the bar. Come St Patrick's weekend, the place would be wedged, tour buses lined up in the car park outside and not a room to be had in the village, but on a chilly, midweek evening in January, most people were probably at home by the fire.

'So what was the message she got?' Molly asked as she spooned pureed fruit from a pouch into Leon's open mouth.

'Jesus, Molls, she didn't actually get a message,' Liam said. 'Don't be encouragin' her, Mam. She believes in all that stuff – fortune tellers and tarot cards and that crap.'

'Well, she didn't tell me anyway, just that she knows now what she needs to do. It kind of freaked me out, to be honest. I don't know whether the woman is having some kind of breakdown or whether she's just mad as a box of frogs. Maybe I should have gone with her to the castle, but I had an appointment for my vaccination and she was insisting she had to do it this morning. I can't even imagine how traumatising it must have been for her. I'm half thinking about ringing the brother who booked her in to let him know what's going on – he left me his number in case I needed to contact him.'

'She's not your responsibility, Mam,' Liam said. 'She shouldn't be here on her own in the first place. Imagine if something happened to Holly; there's no way I'd dream of letting you make that trip all alone …'

'Stop, Liam, don't even say that,' Noelle said, wincing, at the same time as Molly elbowed her boyfriend hard in the side, saying, 'Jesus, Liam, have you no cop on?' It was a place Noelle couldn't let her mind go to, or she'd never have a moment's peace thinking of Holly, so far away. He was right, though: the woman might be a bit pushy for her own good, but it was dreadful that she was going through this alone.

'What's the story with … you know, getting her daughter back to Boston?' Molly asked as she wiped orange mush from around the baby's mouth.

'Well, the cremation was supposed to have been today, and I think the plan was for her to fly home with the ashes at the end of the week, but everything seems to have been put on hold.'

'It's hard to believe she's gone, isn't it?' Liam said. 'I mean, I know we didn't know her very long or anything, but one minute she's making all these plans to start a new life over here and the next minute, her feckin' funeral's being planned. It's mental.'

'It is, love, and it really puts things into perspective. We should all be trying to make the most of every day. Life's short and you just never know … Anyway, enough of the morbid talk. Oh, here comes our food, good timing.'

As Liam fell on his chicken wings like a starving lion on a felled wildebeest, and Molly said – as she did every time they came here – how much she loved the coleslaw, Noelle felt a warm sense of gratitude for all she had been blessed with. Sure life had been shit for a while, but everybody had their ups and downs, and now look at her. It felt like only yesterday that it had been Liam in the high chair, shoving rusks into his mouth, and now here he was a grown man, one she was immensely proud of, and a father himself. And Molly, who was nearly as besotted with Liam as she was with their beautiful baby, had turned out to be a wonderful addition to their little family. Who'd ever have thought that one day she'd consider herself fortunate to welcome one of the Mad Macks as a potential daughter-in-law?

She leaned in to give her grandson a kiss on his fuzzy head and he grabbed her hair with one of his mush-coated hands.

'Uh-oh, here comes trouble,' Molly said, getting to her feet as Darren McCarthy, one of Liam's oldest friends, wove an unsteady path towards their table. 'My cue to head to the loo. State of him on a work night. Make sure the dope doesn't fall in on top of the baby,' she warned Liam.

'Liam, aul buddy, how's tricks? And Mrs Kiely, looking lovely as ever. I'd swear you haven't aged a day since we was in juniors.'

Noelle and Liam rolled their eyes in synchrony.

'Christ, boy, what are you doing out on the lash on a Wednesday night?' Liam said.

'Ah shur I was at a funeral, one of the lads I work with, his granda died. Cancer of the testicles, the poor fucker, 'scuse the French, Mrs K. I went for a couple a scoops after the graveyard and sure you know yourself, bud, best intentions and all that ...' He chuckled. 'How's the young fella? Jaysus, boy, you didn't get a look in there at all. Are you sure he's yours?'

'Excuse me, Darren McCarthy,' Noelle said. 'You must need glasses. He's the cut out of Liam when he was that age.'

'Ah I donno, Mrs K, I'd be hunting down the milkman if it was me like.'

'You're fuckin' hilarious, boy,' Liam replied dryly. 'If you had two brains, you'd be twice as stupid.'

'Where were you last week anyway, Liamo? You missed a great night at Deano's gaff. Sloppy brought the decks and all.'

'Ah, somethin' came up last minute. Have you work in the morning, O'Sullivan? Would you not want to be headin' home?'

'Stop, boy, don't fuckin' talk to me. I'm on me final warning. Didn't wake 'til lunchtime last Friday after Deano's party, the boss lost the plot.'

'Well, if I was you,' Liam said, 'I'd head straight home to bed. You've a cushy enough number in Carroll's, it'll be hard for you to get another gig like that if you fuck this up.'

'You're right, boy,' Darren said, clapping Liam soundly on the back. 'A rock of sense, he is, Mrs K, a rock of sense. One for the road now and I'll be gone.' Her son's friend staggered back towards the bar, just missing Molly by seconds.

As Liam busied himself lifting Leon out of his high chair, saying they should probably be thinking about making shapes themselves, Noelle wondered why he had lied to her about where he had been last Thursday night. Her earlier sense of contentment was suddenly overshadowed by a dark, prickling unease.

CHAPTER 27

Maria
Thursday, 18 January

She had been checking her phone incessantly all morning in class, something she normally never did unless one of the kids was home sick from school, but she was anxious to find out if Justine had managed to get an appointment for Tadhg with the guards today.

The solicitor had informed them yesterday that the gardaí had agreed to make enquiries into Jessie De Marco's movements in the days leading up to her death. A contact of Justine's, a senior officer at Divisional HQ in Anglesea Street, had given her the inside track, telling her the order had come from high up. 'The super inside is in line for the chief's role when the current chief super retires later this year,' she had said. 'Probably doesn't want any negative publicity affecting his promotion, so he's making sure all i's and t's are dotted and crossed. I don't think it's anything to worry about.'

It was impossible not to worry, though. She couldn't focus on work, her mind spiralling, a constant sick feeling in her stomach. She probably should have taken another day off – it wasn't fair on the children – but she couldn't bear the thought of being at home all day with nothing to do.

She reached into the bag under her desk now and sneaked another peek at her phone. Her heart skipped when she saw she had one new message. She had to lean closer to her phone for it to recognise her face.

Tadhg.

Call me asap

Her heart thudded. She checked the time he had sent it. Midday. Nearly half an hour ago.

This couldn't be good.

The viper coiled itself around her bowel and began to squeeze. She looked down at the children, heads bent, pens skittering across pages. Sophie O'Connell whispered something into Eabha Power's ear and they both sniggered. Through the window, the sky was a dull whitish grey. The radiator at the back of the classroom gurgled and clanked and she could hear Karen Madden's shrill voice through the wall, reprimanding one of her pupils. A door closed further along the corridor, muffled voices moving away.

'I must go on a quick message, everyone. Keep going with your writing and I'll be back in a minute. Silence while I'm gone, please, or Miss Madden will be in to you.'

She speed-walked to the staff toilets, hoping she'd get some privacy in there. One of the fourth-class SNAs was using the hand dryer, but otherwise it was empty. Maria waited until the door had closed behind the special needs assistant before calling her husband.

It rang out.

Shit.

Maybe he's had to go into a meeting and he's turned his phone off.

Oh God, what if the school has got wind of what's going on?

What if Dani has contacted them herself before Tadhg has had a chance to talk to anybody?

What if he's in with the board of management right now?

Her phone vibrated in her hand; she was so twittery she nearly dropped it into the sink.

'Is everything okay?' Her voice echoed off the concrete block walls of the bathroom.

'Jesus, Maria. She's after putting all this mad stuff up on Facebook. It's on her Instagram as well, and Twitter or X whatever the fuck it's called now …'

'Tadhg, slow down. What are you talking about?' The panic in her husband's tone was triggering alarm bells all along her own sympathetic nervous system.

'It's Dani – she's set up an online campaign. Justice for Jessie. She's making all kinds of allegations about me … I've just left a message for Justine; she's in court today, but I've asked her to contact me urgently. I'm going to have to let the school know what's going on before they hear it from someone else.'

'Oh my God, Tadhg. Surely, this can't be legal. She can't just—'

'I don't know. Jesus, Maria. The things she's saying. It was Cathal who gave me the heads-up. He got an email from her last night, asking him to help publicise her campaign in the *North Cork News* and he rang me straightaway.'

Jesus Christ. The *North Cork News* was the local freesheet, Tadhg's friend Cathal Cronin its owner and editor. The paper's

Facebook page was an active and reliable source of local community information, whether you needed a plumber, lost your cat or wanted information on a power cut in your area. Cathal had run the original interview with Jessie about her search for her father, the interview that had brought her story to the attention of the local and national media.

'And has she named you?'

'No, but it's pretty obvious it's me she's talking about after the show she made of herself in the hotel. Look, I need to go; I want to send Justine a text message in case she checks her phone while she's in court. I'll let you know as soon as I hear anything.'

She had never heard her husband's voice sound like that. Scared.

Hands shaking, she opened the browser on her phone and typed in Justice for Jessie. There was a series of links to a story about a family in New Zealand fighting for compensation for their son who had been left with catastrophic injuries after a hit and run. That poor family. Now that was a real problem.

She went back into the search bar and added the words Blarney and Facebook. It popped up straightaway. The public group page Dani had set up for her daughter. The cover photo across the banner was of a smiling Jessie: her luminous skin, those haunting eyes. As she read down through the pinned post, Maria lowered herself heavily onto the toilet seat behind her. Somewhere, from what sounded very far away, the bell went for lunch and a crescendo of chattering children rose up.

CHAPTER 28

Dani

Brian Fitzpatrick was not a happy camper. He had texted Dani earlier this morning, asking her to contact him asap. She had known he probably wouldn't be too keen on her going off on a solo run, which is why she hadn't told him in advance, but it had been two days since he'd contacted the cops on her behalf and although he had been assured by a senior officer that they would be making enquiries, there was no indication that any kind of official investigation into her daughter's death was being opened. Brian had been in touch with the city coroner, who had agreed to hold onto Jessie's remains for five more working days to facilitate a second post-mortem. Dani had been hoping the authorities might cover the cost, under the circumstances, but there was no sign of that happening. The private pathologist Brian normally used from Northern Ireland was unavailable and it would be next Tuesday morning before the guy he had contacted in the UK could fly over to do it.

Dani had spoken to the very nice man in the undertaker's to let him know the situation and he said he'd get onto the crematorium for her. The cremation would be a simple service when it did take place. The family would want to give Jessie a proper Catholic funeral with all the pomp and ritual that entailed when Dani brought her home. She couldn't allow herself to think about that right now, didn't want to think about back home at all.

Yesterday's message from her mother had been a real kick in the teeth. 'Fr Paolo called to visit today. He said he's praying for us all but I told him not to waste his prayers on you because you're cursed. Since the day you came into this world, you've been—' She'd stopped it there, deleted it like all the others. Joe had told her not to listen to any of them, that Mamma was so out of it on meds at the moment, she didn't know what she was saying. But for some reason, Dani felt compelled to hear them, like a child irresistibly drawn to touch a naked, dancing flame.

It was a week – either today or in the early hours of tomorrow – since her baby had fallen to her death, and she couldn't just sit around and do nothing while the cops retracted their fingers from their butts at sloth speed.

What had happened yesterday at the Wishing Steps had been the strangest experience she'd ever had, which was saying something for a woman who'd lost count of the number of K holes she'd fallen into over the years. She had been lying on the freezing ground, shivering uncontrollably, when she'd felt the air shift around her and the light had started to shimmer, kind of like a migraine aura without the nausea, and then the shimmering had intensified and the leaden weight of her physical body seemed to just whoosh right out of her, and an energy of pure lightness, like no high she'd ever felt before, rushed in to fill every space. As she had lain there, no longer feeling cold or grief or fear, she had been vaguely aware that the energy inside her was at one with the energy all around her, with the trees and the water and the ancient stone.

It was then that the message had come to her. Not spoken or received in the normal way, but somehow transmitted through this field of lucent resonating light. How long she remained in this state she had no idea at the time; it felt like seconds and it felt like years but turned out to be mere minutes. When she did emerge, it was to a physical body that felt colder and heavier than ever, a dead weight hitching her back to Earth, but it was also to a strong sense of conviction. She knew now what she had to do.

She had marched straight back to her room at the B&B, dropped her sodden clothing to the floor and cranked the temperature of the shower as high as she could bear it, thawing her frozen feet and limbs. Then she had opened her phone and got to work. A quick Google search seemed to suggest that Facebook might be the best platform for what she needed and setting up the group couldn't have been easier. She had spent a couple of hours after that writing and perfecting her first post before she uploaded it; it was important she got it right.

> My beloved 22-year-old daughter Jessie Doyle De Marco died in a fall down a flight of steps in the grounds of Blarney Castle, Cork some time between last Thursday afternoon and the early hours of Friday morning. Within a matter of hours, the local cops came to the conclusion that her death was the result of a tragic accident, and so, incredible as it is to believe, that was the end of the police investigation.

Some of This Is True

Jessie had come to Cork in search of her birth father ten days prior to her death. All she knew about him apart from his name (which I can't mention here in case I get sued) was that he came from a village in north Cork with a castle. She shared the story of her search extensively via social media and the local media in Cork, but as far as anybody knew, Jessie never found her father or at least if she did, she never told anybody about it before her death. So you can imagine my shock when the day after I arrived in Ireland to identify my beautiful baby's body, I bumped into the man I knew to be her father.

What are the chances that Jessie, after publicly highlighting her search for her father, had not met him in the ten days she had spent in Blarney, if I was only in the village for one day and I met him? Coincidence much?

I had already raised my serious concerns about the investigation (or lack of) into Jessie's death with the Garda when two days ago, I found out something that shocked me even more. I discovered that Jessie had messaged a friend to say she was meeting somebody last Thursday, the day she died, who might know who her dad was. Those were her final words. I want to know if that meeting took place and if so, who did she meet that day and what did they tell her?

You might be interested to know that today, Jessie's father is married with two children and works in a position of authority in Blarney. Or that 23 years ago, this 'pillar of the local community' was my English teacher at Holy Cross High School in South Dorchester, Boston. Or that I was barely 17 years old when I became pregnant with his child.

From the moment I set eyes on that man again, I had a strong sense that there was something not right going on here. I believe my daughter's death was NOT an accident, and that is why I have set up this campaign and why I WILL NOT STOP until I get JUSTICE FOR JESSIE!!

If anybody has any information about my daughter's search or who she met last Thursday afternoon before her fatal 'fall', please DM me here. I have engaged the services of an attorney who is liaising with the Garda in order to have a proper investigation opened into the circumstances of her death and we are also in the process of arranging a second post-mortem privately. Please please support #JUSTICEFORJESSIE

Dani had sent invites to all of her Facebook friends, asking them to share the post as widely as possible, and already thirty of her friends had joined the group, but they were all on the far side of the Atlantic, which wasn't much use to her. In an effort to get more local traction, she had emailed the editor of the *North Cork News*, asking him to post the details of her campaign on his Facebook page and run the story in his paper. He had over 20,000 followers and Jessie's original story had garnered a lot of activity there, with hundreds of likes, comments and shares. He hadn't replied to her email. Nor had he put anything up on the Facebook page yet. She tried the mobile number listed on the page. No answer. She was going to have to physically track this Cathal Cronin guy down.

Noelle hadn't been at all helpful this morning when Dani asked her if the paper had an office locally, explaining that she needed to speak to the editor urgently. The temperature outside might be rising as the icy spell was replaced with a dismal mizzle, but her hostess's attitude towards her was becoming frostier by the day. She knew that Noelle, though invariably polite, would be a lot happier if she was staying elsewhere, but Dani wasn't budging. She got that it was awkward for Noelle, that this was a small, tight-knit village, but surely the woman couldn't condone what her friend's husband had done? Surely she must feel some sense of responsibility towards Dani, given the circumstances that had brought her to this village and to her guesthouse in particular?

Noelle had rushed off again this morning – her excuse this time that she was going into the English Market in the city centre to buy fresh fish – leaving Dani alone in the breakfast room when she really could have done with someone to talk to. She thrummed her fingers on the table now. She needed to make a list, to keep moving things along. She went back into the final YouTube video Jessie had posted. She couldn't bring herself to watch it yet, but she had been keeping an eye on the comments underneath.

At the top of the thread was a long string of condolences.

So sorry to hear this terrible news. Such a tragedy. May she rest in peace.

Simpaties to the famly of this gorjus girl.

Ah God help her, I was really hoping she'd find her father. What a sad end to this story. RIP Jessie.

On and on they went in this manner.

What Dani needed to do now was follow in her daughter's digital footsteps.

She had watched Jessie and her friends record enough clips for TikTok to know what to do.

She set up in the same spot in front of the entrance to the Woollen Mills shop where Jessie had recorded her last video, her phone connected to her daughter's tripod. She was going to post it on Jessie's account, to harness the support of all her followers. While she didn't have access to Jessie's phone, as her property had not yet been returned to her by the guards, her daughter had left her iPad in the room. Dani had been able to get into her YouTube account with the password her daughter had used for years and never changed: Bruno2002##, the name of her beloved Bichon Frise, who had been hit by a car when Jessie was fifteen, and her year of birth.

Apart from a few curious looks from people going in and out of the shop and from an older man nursing a takeaway cup at an outside table, his dog on a lead beside him, she was left to her own devices.

She pressed the clicker and, hoping it was recording, began to speak to the camera on her phone. 'Hi folks, I'm Jessie's Mom, Dani. I wanted to come on here to thank you all for your messages and to let you know that they are ... um ... giving me so much comfort during this—'

She swallowed.

'This isn't an easy thing for me to do,' she said, clearing her throat and biting back tears. 'I'm heartbroken over the loss of my beautiful baby girl here in Blarney, but it's real important that I get this message out, 'cos I am *seriously* concerned that my daughter's death may not have been an accident and I cannot understand why the Garda have not launched an urgent official investigation into her death in light of the new information I provided them with this week. I have evidence that on the day of her death, Jessie was plannin' to meet with somebody who claimed to have information about the father she came here to try to find. Whether they're just blinkered, downright incompetent or if there's something shady going on here, I don't know, but what I do know is that I'm not prepared to just sit back and do nothin'.

'So I've set up my own Justice for Jessie campaign to try to get some answers and to fund a private autopsy. I'll be refusing to allow my daughter's body to be moved from the morgue at Cork University Hospital until this happens. Please support this campaign for Jessie and help me spread the word. Hashtag justiceforjessie.'

After checking her phone to make sure it had recorded, Dani went into the hotel bar for lunch. While she was waiting for her food, she decided to bite the bullet and call Brian back.

He answered straightaway, clearly not in the mood for pleasantries.

'You need to take that post down off Facebook immediately unless you want to be sued for slander, although it may already be too late: half of Cork has probably seen it by now.'

'How can I slander the man if I didn't specifically identify him?' She knew she had gone close to the bone, but everybody knew Jessie was looking for a Michael Murphy. Dani hadn't mentioned that he was known as Tadhg and was principal of the local secondary school, much as she'd been tempted to.

'And what I'm sayin' is true.' She wasn't about to mention the YouTube video that was uploading as they spoke.

'You don't have to name somebody to identify them; all it takes is for somebody to infer from what you've written that it's him for it to be slanderous. Defamation law is very strict here compared to the US; it gives strong protection to a person's right to a good name or reputation in the community. It's pretty clear who you're writing about here: I mean, you alleged the man was Jessie's father in front of half the village on Sunday evening by the sound of it. And accusing the gardaí of incompetence, you simply cannot—'

'But they *are* incompetent. I'm just trying to light a bit of a fire under their asses, get them to do their job.'

'Look, Dani,' the attorney said, slowing his speech now as if he was speaking to some kind of imbecile, 'I understand you're impatient and you want things to move faster, but you need to remove that post right now. I know what I'm doing – this isn't my first rodeo. The sergeant at Gurranabraher was onto me first thing this morning looking for a meeting with us both; it'll have to be tomorrow now because I'm tied up all afternoon. You need to try to be patient and let this matter proceed through the proper channels.'

'I already met that guy. On Monday. We've given him all the information we have. What's the point in another meeting? He should be out there banging on Tadhg Murphy's front door.' Why could nobody else see where she was coming from?

'I assume that will be happening as part of their enquiries, if it hasn't already. He'll update us in the morning. You just need to take that post down right away, okay?'

She barely acknowledged the waiter who brought her soup

and sandwich. It was positive that the sergeant had contacted Brian, but things were still moving far too slowly. She could feel the adrenalin-fuelled energy that had been powering her since she got back from the castle yesterday being sucked out of her body, like a deflating electric air mattress. Could what she had thought was some kind of psychic connection with her dead daughter in fact have been some kind of psychotic episode? Was she losing her fucking mind? Her crazy brain turning on her, making her believe she was some sort of spirit medium now?

Tears pricked at her eyes. Joe would bust a gasket if she had to ask him to pay for her defence in a defamation case on top of all her other mounting costs. Her brother had been surprisingly noncommittal and distracted when she had spoken to him yesterday about her extended stay and her need to pay the attorney a retainer, but the baby was still in the NICU undergoing tests. She would have to cut him a bit of slack. Joe had never let her down before and Brian wasn't chasing her for the cash, not yet anyhow. She said a prayer every night that the baby would be okay. She was sure she would. Two of her nephews had spent time in neonatal and they were fine now.

She'd better delete the video first, before Brian got wind of it. She clicked back into YouTube, where it had finished uploading, and was surprised to see that there was already a comment under it.

Paddyislangers: 'Hey Jessie's Mom. Sorry 4 ur loss, terrible sad. Shared with all my friends & told them to share. U need to get on2 Benny Mac on Rebel FM, de Irish version of Howard Stern. He not be long callin' out those useless fn shades for not doing their jobs.'

She googled Benny Mac, Rebel FM. By the time she had done that and taken a screen shot of his contact email, there were two more comments under the YouTube video.

She put her hands over her heart, instantly re-inflated.

Thank you, baby, for sending this sign.

CHAPTER 29

Maria

Maria stared at her phone, willing it to ring. She had gone straight into Essie's after school, and they were both waiting anxiously to hear how Tadhg had got on with the guards. He had insisted on going into the station at Gurranabraher to talk to them, despite Justine saying there was no obligation for him to do so. There was no talking to Tadhg once he made his mind up about something, and he felt it was best to be proactive and 'get out in front of this thing', especially in light of Dani's social media 'campaign'.

Tadhg had pointed out that he had a strong alibi for the day of Jessie's death, having been in school until about six – which could be easily confirmed by CCTV – and then at home with Maria all evening, apart from an hour or so when he had been in next door with his mother. He felt it was important to be upfront about the fact that he had slept with Dani, while stressing that he was categorically not the girl's father. He also wanted to make the gardaí aware of his own concerns about the insidious and very damaging rumours that the American woman was spreading about him in person and online, although he was holding back from making any kind of formal complaint at this point. While Dani hadn't mentioned his real name in her posts, he had been 'outed' in some of the comments.

Having to sit Eva and Ben down last night and explain that their father had had a very brief and inappropriate relationship with Dani months after she graduated had been excruciating, but they'd had no choice. They had to warn their children about the allegations the woman was making about Tadhg before they heard them elsewhere. Ben hadn't said a word, making Maria wonder if he had even taken it in, while Eva had been hotly indignant on her father's behalf. It wasn't the reaction that Maria would have expected from a Gen Z kid, growing up in an era where it seemed that every second week another powerful man was being outed for abusing his power, but Eva couldn't see beyond the fact that the father she adored was under attack. She clearly wasn't thinking, as Maria was, of how horrified her parents would be if they found out *she* was in a sexual relationship with a male teacher seven or eight years older than her, mere months after she did her Leaving. 'What a freak, like who would do that?' was her only response when she heard about Dani's online campaign. Maria had gone up to them both later to see if they wanted to talk about it, but Eva was yapping away on the phone and seemed fine and Ben barely lifted one of his headphones. She had been halfway out the door when he called her back.

'Mom?'

'Yes, love?'

'Why would she say Dad's that girl's father if it's not true?' He still had his back to her, facing his screen.

'I don't know, Ben. She's just lost her only child; she's over here away from home and probably still in shock.' She had stood talking to his back, thinking of that article she'd read lately, advising the parents of teenagers, especially boys, that it was better to have difficult conversations when they were in the car or somewhere where they weren't face-to-face. 'I'd probably be losing it too if I was her. I know it's not nice, the things she's saying, but hopefully she'll be gone soon.'

'K.'

'Is there anything else on your mind, love?'

'Nope.'

'You do know, don't you, that if there's ever—'

'*Yes*, Mom.'

And now they were going to have to sit down with them again this evening and tell them about the woman's online campaign, because there was no way they weren't going to hear about that in school. The whole village was probably abuzz with it right now.

She pounced on her phone when Tadhg finally rang, putting it on speaker so Essie could hear.

'I'm just on my way home. I'm glad I went in: I feel it was the right thing to do, so they can see I've nothing to hide.'

'What did they say?'

'They said they're talking to anyone who had any kind of contact with Jessie in the days leading up to her death to try and piece together her final movements. I told them I was at school all day and home all evening with you—'

'And will they be contacting me to confirm that?'

'They didn't say anything about that – they seemed happy

enough that I have a strong alibi. I knew one of them; his brother played for Cork with me at one stage, so we were chatting about that as he walked us out afterwards. It was all very informal and friendly.'

'And what about clearing your name, love? Can they do anything at all to make her take that stuff down off the internet? Surely she can't be let just leave it up there?' Essie said.

Justine had reported the defamatory posts and comments to Facebook and YouTube on Tadhg's behalf, but she wasn't holding out much hope that they would be removed swiftly, if at all.

'There's nothing the guards can do about it, unbelievably. Justine is drafting a cease-and-desist letter – that's a formal demand that Dani remove the defamatory allegations and not repeat them in future. She's going to contact Dani's solicitor first, though, and give her the chance to take it down before we send her the letter, because she doesn't want to antagonise her, given the type of character we're dealing with.'

'And what happens if she has to send the letter and Dani doesn't comply with it?' Maria asked.

'Well, then we'd have to apply to the High Court for an interim or pre-trial injunction, pending a defamation trial, but that's the last thing we want and she says it's highly unlikely it will end up in court. The threat of it should hopefully be enough to make that mad woman stop what she's doing.'

Maria hoped to God it was, because the image of her son's tracksuit drying in her utility room was stuck in her mind like a fishbone in the throat.

She and Tadhg had been at home last Thursday night and Eva had been upstairs studying, but she had no idea where Ben had been or what he had been doing. He'd been allowed down to the village to meet the lads for a couple of hours, which, now that she thought of it, had been the last night he'd asked to go out. Hopefully it was a sign things were cooling with Harry Ahern and that gang. Having the wrong kind of friends could be worse than having no friends at all.

He couldn't have known who the girl was, though, or what her mother would claim in the wake of her tragic death. How could he?

CHAPTER 30

Ben

He wished he'd never set eyes on Harry fucking Ahern. If it wasn't for Harry putting him under pressure to rob drink, he'd never have been in the sitting room that night and he'd never have heard what he heard.

It was a Monday night, a few nights before the protest at the hotel. A few nights before Jessie died.

He'd waited until he was sure everyone was asleep and then a bit longer before he snuck back downstairs and into the sitting room. The drinks cabinet was full to the gills after Christmas 'cos his dad got given loads of bottles as presents, but he didn't want to chance taking a full one so he was using a plastic funnel one of the lads had stolen from the chemistry lab to pour vodka into an empty water bottle. His plan was to top up the vodka bottle with water so his parents would be none the wiser.

Dad would go nuts if he caught him drinking, would probably ground him for the rest of secondary school or confiscate his PlayStation for ever. He was so fucking sick of all his rules and regulations. And even sicker of being mocked all the time just for being his son, his old 'friends' dropping him like a hot snot once they started at St Vincent's in case the stink of being the principal's son rubbed off on them.

He didn't even like the taste of drink. Beer wasn't too bad, but vodka tasted like piss. But anyway, thanks to Harry, there he'd been, on his knees on the carpet in front of the drinks cabinet, when he heard a creak from above his head and stopped to listen. His parents' room was right above the sitting room but he wasn't too worried, because it was probably just one of them turning in the bed. But then it happened again and this time, it was right above his head, closer to the door of their room.

He had stiffened, listening, trying not to breathe. There it was again. Definitely floorboards. Shit, was somebody up? It was 2:13 a.m. for fuck's sake. The whole house was usually fast asleep at this time on a school night.

He had screwed the lid loosely back onto the vodka just in case and shoved it into the cabinet, stashing his water bottle and funnel in behind it before closing the door quietly. Then he'd turned his torch off and listened again. All had seemed quiet then; it must have just been the house settling.

He'd had his hand on the knob of the cabinet door, ready to get back to his task, when he heard a sound that made his heart stop.

Fuck!

There was someone at the door of the sitting room. Making himself as small as possible, he had rolled as close to the back of the sofa as he could, heart pounding. The door opened slowly, the only sound the carpet catching slightly underneath it.

Fuck, fuck, fuck!

First time he'd ever tried to rob drink and fucking typical, he was going to get caught.

He had waited for the light to flick on, for his father to let out a roar, but neither of those things happened.

Instead the door had closed again just as slowly, as soundlessly.

Phew! Maybe it was Mom just up for a glass of water, but then why open the … Shit, there's somebody in here.

Heavy breathing.

It's Dad.

He had covered his mouth with his hand, taken tiny breaths in and prayed he didn't need to sneeze.

What the hell is Dad doing up? Just my luck.

'You're not going to fucking believe this.'

What the … Who's he talking to?

'Remember … mad Italian one … Holy Cross?' Dad was on the phone. Speaking just above a loud whisper. It had been hard to hear him.

'You do. One … dropped … that clinic.'

'Yeah … her daughter … Blarney … looking for father.'

'I'm serious, Scott, listen to me. This isn't a joke.'

Shit.

His father had moved closer to him, and sat on the sofa. If he stood up, he'd see him curled in a ball on the ground.

'It looks like that crazy bitch told her that I'm her fucking father. She's here in the village right now looking for a Michael Murphy.'

What?

'No, not Daniela – the daughter. She's twenty-two. Her name is Jessie De Marco and she's over here looking for her father, whose name is Michael Murphy.'

Silence for a few moments.

'I know they add up, but I knew that baby wasn't mine, for fuck's sake. I only slept with her that one night and used a johnny each time, God only knows how many lads she was sleeping with at the time; she was all over me like a rash. I only brought her to the clinic to stop the mad bitch from blackening my name. If it had come out that I'd been with her, that would have been the end of my teaching career.'

He had pressed his hand tighter against his mouth, swallowing the gasp of horror back down his throat where it had nearly got stuck halfway. He'd stifled a cough, barely breathing now.

'I don't fucking know! She said she took the pill in the clinic. I waited outside for her, dropped her home afterwards. She told me it was just like a really bad period. Either she was lying or it didn't work.'

His father was on his feet again, moving away from the sofa, towards the window.

'Jesus Christ ... email ... Boston back in ...'

Silence again while he'd listened to what Scott, whoever he was, was saying.

'Just found out, apparently. Piece in the local paper ... photo of her ... the daughter ... could be her at that age ... nearly fucking died ... all over social media too.'

His dad had paced closer again.

'Exactly. Why wait so long to tell her I'm her father if it was true? ... What the fuck am I going to do? How do I fix this without anybody finding out what happened in Boston?'

His father sounded panicked now, his voice rising again.

'Yeah, you're right. I'm going to have to try and brazen it out. I just want to make sure we're both singing from the same hymn *sheet okay? Daniela was my student, end of, and if anybody asks you, we knew nothing about any baby.'*

Then his Dad had slithered out of the sitting room as quietly as he had slithered in. Once Ben had heard the toilet flush upstairs and the bed springs settle above his head, he'd taken out his phone and googled Jessie De Marco Blarney.

CHAPTER 31

Noelle

'You're going to have to ask her to leave, Mam.'

Liam speared a flaky chunk of hake, the prongs of his fork sliding easily into the succulent white flesh. Noelle – and Liam, by dint of the fact that she shopped and cooked for him – had started a new healthy-eating lifestyle, *not* a diet, after Noelle woke up one morning last year to find that her waist had disappeared.

She usually bought her fish from the fishmonger who plied his wares from a van outside the village post office twice a week, cooking it the day she bought it because she couldn't stick the smell of it in the fridge. Today, however, she'd gone into town, needing to escape the house and Dani for a few hours.

Just as Noelle was leaving the English Market with two lovely pieces of fresh hake from O'Connell's, Maria had called her in a state, asking if she had seen the Facebook post the American woman was after posting online. She hadn't, but Maria sent her the link and Noelle had stood leaning against the window of the health food shop in the middle of Patrick's Street as she read in horror.

'Mam?' Liam was looking at her across the table.

'Sorry, love, I'm totally distracted with everything that's going on.'

'I'm not surprised, it's crazy stuff. I know her daughter just died, like, but putting that shit up online is fuckin' nuts. Everyone knows it's Tadhg she's on about.'

'I know. Poor Maria's in bits. I wish I'd never have taken that girl's booking in the first place and then none of this would have come to our door. Tadhg was in with the guards today: he wanted to let them know he has an alibi for the time they think she might have died. Apparently, they're going to be talking to everybody who had contact with her in the days leading up to last Thursday. Which includes us.'

He piled his fork with food, peas diving off the side as he lifted it to his mouth. He didn't seem particularly fazed by the idea of the guards sniffing around. Showed none of the uneasiness his mother was feeling.

'Surely their solicitor has to be able to do something. Make her take that post down for a start. I mean, okay, Tadhg fucked up big time by having anything to do with a young one like that, even if she had finished school, but that was nothing compared to that *Teacher's Pet* shit that was going on in Australia back in the eighties. You should listen to the podcast. All these teachers from high schools in this one area of New South Wales were sleeping with their students, and not just male teachers either. It was insane – all these kids being groomed by their teachers, basically a sex ring, and nothing was ever done about it. Or not until it all came out in the podcast that one of the teachers was accused of killing his wife. He'd become obsessed with his teenage girlfriend. The wife disappeared off the face of the Earth and two days later he moved the girlfriend, who had been his pupil, into his bed. The craziest part is that he'd have got away with it, they all would, if it wasn't for this podcast. I mean, you couldn't make that shit up.'

'That sounds like the last thing I need to listen to right now, Liam. I just hope to God nothing else comes out about Tadhg. That no more women come out of the woodwork, like. I know everyone thinks the sun shines out of his arse, but that can go to a lad's head. He wasn't always the angel that Maria thinks he is.'

Maria hadn't known Tadhg when they were in school, apart from to admire from a distance like a lot of girls, but Noelle had. She'd grown up three doors down from the Murphys on Willow Grove, before they moved up to Castleview, although even as kids, she'd preferred hanging around with his brother Gavin. He was a much nicer kid than Tadhg, who always wanted to be in charge of whatever game they were all playing. It couldn't have been easy for Gav, growing up in such a staunch GAA family, with his father heavily involved in the local club and his older brother winning medals and trophies left, right and centre. It wasn't the sport for such a soft, gentle boy: the bigger, tougher kids barged right through him. His father had hoped it would toughen Gav up a bit, but Essie had finally put her foot down one day when he was about twelve – yet again rolling around on the pitch, howling in pain after getting a belt of a hurley across his fingers while his team-mates and coaches rolled their eyes – and had taken him out of the sport. She'd put him into tennis instead, a sport he excelled at and where he found a great group of friends.

It was hardly surprising that having been hero worshipped from a young age, Tadhg's head had swelled, although he kept it well hidden most of the time under his Mr Nice Guy cap. Noelle had been one of a small minority of girls in her year who hadn't had a crush on him, one of the few who had seen his cap slip over the years and knew he wasn't as perfect as everyone seemed to think.

When they were in sixth year, he had gone out with a fourth-year girl from one of the private schools in the city; she was three years younger than him, a big age difference at the time. Noelle had played camogie with her older sister Orla, who despised Tadhg because of the way she said he'd treated her fifteen-year-old sister, dumping her because she wouldn't 'go all the way' with him. Noelle hadn't heard any other stories about him perving on younger girls or pressuring them to have sex, but maybe that's because most girls had been only too willing to give Tadhg Murphy what he wanted. She really hoped for Maria's sake that there weren't any more Danis out there.

Things were so different now to how they were when Noelle was growing up. It was like another world. Back then, if a lad grabbed your arse in a night club, you'd give him a slap or tell him to fuck off; now a boy could find himself up for sexual assault for something like that.

She took a deep breath and turned to Liam, affecting a casual tone. 'By the way, where were you on—'

He put up his hand. 'Shush, Mam, I think that's Dani now.'

The front door banged shut and they listened for the sound of their guest on the stairs going back up to her room. Instead, her footsteps padded down the hallway and there was a brisk knock at the kitchen door before it opened and she came in, a huge pizza box in her arms, another smaller one on top.

'Hi, guys,' she said, a wide smile on her face. 'I bought an extra-large pizza, thought you might like to share it. And I got some garlic bread with cheese too.' She placed the two cardboard boxes on the table and opened the lids, releasing a pungent scent of garlic and spicy pepperoni into the air.

'You're grand, Dani, we've just eaten, thanks,' Noelle said.

'That's no problem. You don't mind if I eat it here, do you? Don't want it stinking up my room.' Dani gave a girlish giggle, seating herself at the table and pulling back the tab on a can of Coke, cool as a breeze. As if she hadn't just lit the fuse of a depth charge underneath Noelle's best friend's life.

Noelle stared at her.

Is she actually for real?

She felt the blood pump faster through her veins, flushing her cheeks. She had to say something; she couldn't just sit here playing happy housemates, as if everything was normal.

'Dani. We need to talk.'

'Oh. Sure,' Dani said, folding a slice of pizza over and taking a bite. 'You don't mind if I eat, do you?' She put her hand in front of her mouth while she chewed.

'No, of course not. Look, we understand you're going through an awful lot at the moment and we're really sorry, but it's just all this stuff about Tadhg ... It's gone too far now. Clearly what happened between the two of you back in Boston was totally inappropriate and wrong, and please don't think we're condoning that for one moment, but all this stuff you're saying about him ... It's just ... you just can't say things like that ...'

Dani put her pizza slice back in the box and took a deep breath. She took a deep breath. 'Look, Noelle, I get that this is a tricky situation for you. He's your friend's husband and I'm sure she's probably very upset about all of this ...'

'He's not just my friend's husband. I've known his family all my life; I grew up a few doors down from them. These are good people we're taking about here.'

Good might have been stretching it a bit for Tadhg, but so was bad – and as for a murderer, well, that was just ridiculous.

'Which makes it hard for you to believe that he might not be the person you all think he is,' Dani said, nodding sympathetically. 'And I get that, but—'

Noelle felt her blood begin to boil. 'Actually no, Dani. What is hard for me to believe is that you could say those awful things about Tadhg, despite having no proof whatsoever that he's Jessie's father, or that he ever met her ...'

The other woman opened her mouth to interrupt, her eyes flashing, not so cool now.

'No, please, let me finish,' Noelle said. 'You go and put it up online for everyone to see without any thought at all for the impact it might have on Tadhg and his family. You do realise they have two teenage kids in the school where he teaches? Have you stopped to think for one minute about the impact of all this on them? And on Maria and Essie? Two kinder people you couldn't meet.'

Dani looked at her in horror, crossing her hands dramatically over her heart.

'The impact on him? Oh my God! I'm the one who has just lost a child. I'm the one in a strange country trying to— Jesus Christ, you people think I'm making this all up, don't you?'

'We just think that maybe the shock of what you've gone through—'

'So you think this is all in my head, that I'm crazy? Is that it?' Her eyes were welling up.

'No, Dani, of course not,' Liam said softly, leaning forward towards her. 'But this isn't America. You could get yourself sued over here for the kind of stuff you're saying about Tadhg and that's the last thing you need right now. What happened to Jessie was awful, but it was an accident. It's time to bring her home now. It's the right thing to do. For her. And for you and the rest of your family. And if you don't stop, well then, I'm sorry but we're going to have to ask you to find somewhere else to stay. It's not fair on Mam, being stuck in the middle of this. She's had enough stress in her life; she doesn't need any more.'

Dani slumped back in her chair, silent now, just nodding and staring sadly at the table in front of her where oily orange pools had started to congeal on the cooling pizza.

Noelle felt a swelling of sympathy for her then, this broken-hearted mother who had probably been clawing for any distraction from her pain, no matter how ill-conceived or destructive. At the same time, though, she was hopeful that her son might have got through to her. She wanted Dani gone from under her roof.

The last thing they needed was the guards putting two and two together and making a potential line of inquiry.

CHAPTER 32

Maria
Friday, 19 January

Maria was in the staffroom on small break, pretending to listen to Emma Buckley wittering on about her wedding plans, when her phone rang. The younger teacher was showing her the Pinterest board she'd created, Maria 'oohing' and 'ahhing' in what she hoped were the right places, remembering when she'd been like that. Full of hopes and dreams. And she had been fortunate in life up until now, despite feeling a bit stuck in a rut this past while.

She had slept a bit better last night after Noelle's call. Her friend seemed to think she and Liam had got through to Dani, that she might stop all this madness now.

When she saw Noelle calling now, she interrupted Emma mid-flow, saying, 'Sorry, I have to take this,' and rushing from the room, down the corridor and outside into the front portico of the building. Noelle never rang her during school hours. Hopefully, it was good news.

Kids ran up and down the puddle-pocked yard, chasing each other and squealing. Others stood in smaller groups chattering intently, as if they were solving world peace. Mr Hurley and Mandy, one of her favourite SNAs, walked up and down between them, deep in conversation. Outside the main gate cars swooshed past, spraying water from their tyres, and a woman in a petrol-blue hat walked a big brown dog.

'... hear me? Maria?'

'Yes, is everything okay?'

'I'm so sorry. We were so sure she listened to us yesterday ... that she was going to stop ...'

Her heart began to pick up speed.

'Tadhg needs to get on to his solicitor right away.'

Maria felt her mouth dry up, ice running through her veins, at the alarm in her friend's voice. She leant against the wall behind her for support. 'Why? What has she done now?'

'She's on the radio, on Rebel FM.'

'What?'

'She's on with Benny Mac.'

She sank down onto the cold concrete steps.

'Maria? Are you okay?'

'Wha ... what's she saying?' Her mouth was so dry now that the words were sticking to her tongue.

'All the same stuff she put up online. You need to hang up now and call Tadhg right away, tell him to ring the solicitor. There has to be something she can do to stop this.'

'Okay.'

'If you need me to come down to you, I can be there in five minutes, okay?'

Maria walked around the side of the building to the car park. It was quieter here, nobody around. She opened her browser and did a search for Rebel FM. She clicked onto the station's link and tapped the 'Listen Live' button, holding the phone to her ear so it looked like she was on a call.

'I know. You couldn't make it up, right, Benny?' It was *her*, speaking to the presenter as if they'd known each other for years.

'Wow, Dani, what are the chances of you bumping into this guy so many years later?'

'Pretty darn low I guess, even though Blarney's very small and everybody seems to know everybody and this man ... I know I can't identify him for *legal reasons*, but suffice it to say, he's a well-respected member of the local community in a position of authority who ...'

'I'll stop you there, Dani, just in case. I can feel our own legal advisors squirming in their seats as we speak.' The presenter was chuckling away as if this was all a joke to him. 'Let's go back a bit. You say you were only seventeen when you began your sexual relationship with this older man, and not long out of high school.'

'Yes, that's right but, Benny, as an adult, I can see that the relationship had started before that, emotionally, ya know? I mean, grooming wasn't even a word back then, least not one I'd ever heard about, but looking back now, I can see that's what that man was doing, almost from the first moment he set eyes on me.'

No. Please, God, no!

'The way he always singled me out for special attention, asking me to stay back after class to discuss my work. The way he brushed up against me all the time, trailing his hand along my back when no-one else was looking. So many tiny, subtle things that you'd never pick up on as a kid but now ...'

'Yeah. That behaviour certainly does sound like it bears all the hallmarks of a groomer,' Benny said knowingly, as if he had a PhD in child sexual abuse. 'What age were you when that started, Dani?'

'Um, let me think. I wanna say sixteen? Yeah, I was sixteen when I switched into his class ... when we first met.'

Maria nearly dropped the phone, her palms sweaty.

'Only sixteen? Still a child. Wow ...' He made a sound of disgust. 'Do you think you were this teacher's only victim?'

'Gosh, I never really thought about that, to be honest. I don't know, is the answer. I mean, I never saw him pay particular attention to any of the other girls, not the way he was with me anyway, but then nobody saw anything going on between us either, so who knows, right?'

'You were seventeen when you got pregnant and eighteen when you gave birth to Jessie, Dani. Did this man ever support you in any way?'

'No, Benny, he did not. His reaction when I told him I was pregnant was to try to make me get rid of our baby and to tell nobody. He made an appointment for me at Planned Parenthood and dropped me off, at seventeen years of age, to get the abortion pill. He waited outside for me and dropped me home afterwards to wait alone while my baby died. Only I never went ahead with it – I just couldn't – so it would have been a huge shock for him to find out that not only had I had the baby, but that she had come to Ireland all these years later to look for him.'

'Well, you've come on here today with us to raise awareness of a new campaign you've set up to try and get justice for your daughter. Tell us a bit about this, Dani.'

'I will, Benny, and thanks for giving me this opportunity. I've set up a Justice for Jessie campaign group on Facebook and I'm publicly calling on the Irish police to open a full investigation into my daughter's death. I'd like to appeal to all your listeners to join my campaign and to like and share my posts because I really need to spread the word about this as far and wide as I can.'

'And I'm sure they will too, Dani. Our listeners here on *The Benny Mac Show* are a great bunch. Can you tell us why it is you are so convinced there's more to your daughter's death than meets the eye?'

'Well firstly, Benny, there's the fact that, as I already told you, within a day of arriving in Blarney, I discovered that Jessie's father, the man she had come here looking for, was living here. And I find it very hard to believe that he was – as he claimed to be – totally unaware of her presence in the village and her search for her father. If he was, then he must have been one of the only people in the village who hadn't heard about it.

'Then I became aware of a message Jessie had sent to a close friend, saying she'd arranged to meet somebody on the day of her death who knew her dad and that she hoped to have found him by the time she messaged again. I informed the guards of this and yet they are no closer to finding out who Jessie met with that day. I believe this person may know something about her death and may even have been involved. They're pretty strong grounds for suspicion in my book.'

'They'd be pretty strong grounds in anybody's book in fairness, Dani. And I believe you're also calling for a second post-mortem to be carried out on your daughter?'

'Yes, otherwise I'm goin' to have to fly a guy in from London at my own expense and, you know, these things cost a lot of money. I rang the morgue at Cork University Hospital to tell them my daughter won't be going anywhere until I get a second autopsy and I was shocked to find out that under the law here, unless the guards direct otherwise, the coroner can arrange for her to be buried if I don't collect her by next Wednesday.'

'No way? That can't be right, surely?'

'I know, I couldn't believe it myself, but my attorney says it is. Shortage of space in the morgue, if you can believe that.'

'God, Dani, I really am so sorry. Fair play to you for finding the strength to set up this campaign and come on here with me today when you must be going through such unimaginable pain at the moment.'

'Thanks, Benny,' Dani said. 'And as if things weren't awful enough already, the lady who owns the B&B where I'm staying, her and her son, have threatened to throw me out unless I shut my mouth because they're close friends of Ti— of him, my former teacher, and his family. And ...' she whimpered, 'the only reason I booked in there is because it's where Jessie was staying and I'm sleeping in the bed she slept in before—' Her voice broke. 'I'm ... sorry.' She was crying harder now.

Benny Mac stayed silent for a few moments; the only sound in the studio was Dani's agonised sobs.

Maria crouched onto her hunkers, the phone pressed painfully to the side of her head.

'Well, Dani, I can't tell you how shocked and sorry we all are here at Rebel FM to hear this, and I know our listeners will feel the same. What you've been going through at the hands of our gardaí and so-called justice system, and now these B&B owners ... It's just appalling. As a proud Corkonian myself, I'm ashamed of the way you've been treated and I can guarantee you that if we put an appeal out right now, you'd be inundated with offers of accommodation for the rest of your stay in Cork. I'd be more than happy to name and shame that B&B too.'

'Thank you, Benny. It means so much to me just to feel somebody here is finally listening. I've felt so alone. And thank you, but I need to stay where I am for now. I feel close to Jessie there.'

'You're one brave woman, Dani De Marco. Thanks for coming on with us today and for sharing your story, although it occurs to me that if this guy is so sure he's not the dad, there's one way of finding out, isn't there? I'd be calling on him to have a paternity test if I was you. Anyway, you have the full support of the show and my team here at Rebel FM in your campaign and I'm sure many of our listeners will jump on board too. You keep fighting the good fight. And now we're going to take a quick break for—'

Maria stumbled to her feet, moving through the car park and out the gate, leaving her bag behind her in the staffroom, telling nobody she was going.

CHAPTER 33

Dani

The adrenalin was coursing through her bloodstream like an Oxy rush as she left the studio. She hadn't planned on saying any of that stuff about the grooming, but once she started talking to the radio presenter, it just came out. It wasn't until Jessie had reached sixteen or seventeen that it had hit home with Dani what had actually been going on between her and Michael while he was her teacher.

She had dug out her high school yearbook a few years ago from under a pile of old photo albums at the top of her closet, flicking through the pages until she found his photo, her treacherous heart skittering as she took in his handsome features, that smile that used to light her up. The years hadn't dampened her physical attraction to him; he had been so fucking hot. And she, so desperate for attention, had been such an easy target; he'd made her feel sexy and grown-up, desirable. Until he flicked her away like a cigarette butt.

She had leafed back through the book until she found her own photo, the air whistling through her teeth as she sucked it in. Christ, she had been so young, so beautiful – just like her Jessie was. *Most likely to: Win an Oscar someday!* She remembered being upset by that, the bitchy girls on the student council sneering at her with no clue that her bolshy bravado was all a front. That behind it she was drowning. A desperately lonely girl who needed support and guidance from her teacher, not to be groomed, fucked and dumped. A girl that, looking back all those years later, Dani could see had been a victim.

She'd been all fired up when she'd gone out that night after work, but when she told her female friends about Michael, they'd said what had happened to her was tame in comparison to some of the stories they'd heard. He hadn't forced her to do anything she didn't want to; after all, he hadn't touched her 'til she'd graduated, they'd pointed out. One of the women, Tammy, said she'd been groped by her swim coach when she was thirteen and told nobody, just never went near the pool again, while another told them about a kid in her school who'd been raped and murdered by her own stepfather. Their reaction had made her think that maybe what had happened between her and Michael hadn't been that bad after all. But the reality was that her English teacher had spotted the surface swirls of her pain and vulnerability beneath her mouthy front and cast his line. Reeling her in slowly and keeping her wriggling on his hook until she was done with school.

Maybe now that she'd gone on the radio, the cops might finally sit up and take some notice of her, realise she wasn't going nowhere. That the more people tried to silence her, the harder she would bang her drum, louder and louder, until she was satisfied that her daughter's death had been treated with the gravity it deserved.

She'd been crushed by the way Liam and Noelle had spoken

to her last night. Bad enough that they clearly thought she was making all of this up, though she could understand that to some extent. They didn't want to believe ill of their friend. But to tell her to bring her child home and get out of their lives, and then to threaten to throw her out of their house, had been downright cruel. She had wanted to tell them about Michael pressuring her to get rid of their baby, dropping her at the clinic, but the words had congealed in a painful lump in her throat and got stuck there.

She had left the kitchen, taking her pizza up to her room, her tears salting the slices of pie as she ate. Her baby girl was gone and she was trying to find answers about how she had fallen down those steps, but nobody seemed to give a damn. There seemed to be no sense of urgency at all. All she heard from her solicitor was what she couldn't and shouldn't be doing. The private pathologist, Professor Malcolm Russell, was booked to fly in to do the second autopsy on Tuesday, but there was no sign of the Garda footing the bill for it. And the cremation had been rescheduled for Wednesday afternoon. The clock was ticking.

She had called Joe, desperate to talk to the one person in the world who had her back, crying into the phone, but as he tried to console her, Mamma had pulled the phone off him and started shrieking at her. He must have called into the apartment to check on her.

'You need to bring my Jessie home where she belongs. Why are you torturing me like this? I don't even have a grave to visit. If you don't get on a plane back here asap, I'm sending Joe over to get you.'

'Mamma, I'm just trying to—'

'I don't care what you're trying to do, Daniela. I want my baby back.' Her mother was sobbing. 'My heart can't take much more of this: I'm old and sick and I'm not going to be around much longer, I can feel it. Do the decent thing and bring her back, for God's sake.'

She had fallen, fully dressed, into a deep, exhausted sleep after that, waking with a start at 3:29 a.m. Something had felt different, her daughter's scent stronger. The hairs on her arms stood to attention in a field of goosebumps, but she felt no cold, no fear. And then it happened. That beautiful presence, energy, whatever it was, was in the room with her. There was no shimmering this time, no aura, but she could feel the air shift around her. She had held her breath, afraid to move in case she broke the spell. And then, as quickly as it had come, it was gone and the cold had bitten into her, causing her to shiver uncontrollably, her teeth rattling. She'd changed into her PJs, pulled her fleece top on over them and got back into bed, pulling the covers tight around her.

Her daughter had been trying to send her another message. Of that she felt sure. It hadn't been as clear this time, not like at the Wishing Steps. She hadn't heard or received any instructions, but she felt ... different. Strong, resolute. Maybe this time it hadn't actually been a message; perhaps Jessie had simply sent her the courage she needed to keep going. She had vowed not to let them stand in her way, not her attorney, nor Noelle or Liam, nor Mamma, whose messages she was going to ignore from now on. Not any of them.

Wide awake at that point, she had reached for her phone, opened Facebook and gone into the Justice for Jessie group, which she hadn't taken down despite her promise to Brian, ignoring his calls yesterday afternoon. If Tadhg sued her for defamation, it'd be his own stained laundry he'd be pulling out in public; shit, that might actually be a good thing for her campaign, she'd figured.

The Facebook group had still had only forty-three members, most of them in the US, although her YouTube video had got a good few shares and some really supportive comments. As she closed the apps, she'd noticed that she had three new emails. Two were spam, but the third was from a researcher at Rebel FM, replying to an email Dani had fired off earlier and saying they'd love to have her on *The Benny Mac Show* the following morning if she was free.

Jen, the researcher, had ordered a taxi to bring her back to Blarney after the show, compliments of Rebel FM. Dani asked the driver to bring her straight to the Gab. She had been too nervous to eat breakfast before her interview and was now ravenous. She was too wired to go back to the guesthouse and the inevitable showdown with Noelle and Liam. They weren't going to be happy with her for calling out their shitty behaviour on local radio, but they were the ones in the wrong, not her.

She asked the driver, a thin man with skin like a walnut who reeked of smoke, if he could turn on Rebel FM.

'No bother at all, at all,' was his chirpy reply.

Benny had moved onto another item now. The arson of a hotel near Blarney. Dani had heard about this from Noelle; it had happened the same night Jessie died.

'Well Benny, if they're going to start bringing unvetted child molesters in here from other countries, somebody has to stand up and protect our children.'

The taxi driver tutted loudly.

'I understand that, Gerry, but the HSE have denied they had any intention of moving anybody with a criminal—'

'Ah, shur, they're hardly goin' to admit it now like, are they? I can tell you for a fact, Benny, that they were moving a lad in there who raped not only a six-year-old girl but also a woman in her eighties back in Nigeria.'

'He knows for a fact', the taxi driver scoffed, turning the sound down a notch. 'It'd be more in that lad's line to go out and get a job for himself instead of spreadin' lies and inciting people to burn down property. It'd make you sick the way the likes of him goes on, so it would.'

'What if it's true, though?' Dani asked. 'Why would he make it up if he didn't think it was?'

'It's not feckin' true, girl. It's a way of getting attention for himself and the gowls who follow him, all those far-right crackpots. Most of the young fellas at that fire in Blarney last week believe all this crap, that's what's so dangerous about it. Easy to rile up a bunch of young lads high on drugs and drink and—'

'Could you turn it up again?'

Benny had finished up the interview with Gerry and was reading out messages from listeners in response to other items on the show. 'There's been a huge reaction to the interview I did earlier with Dani De Marco, the lovely lady from Boston who's trying to get an investigation opened into the tragic death of her daughter at Blarney Castle last week. The text line is hopping here, loads of people wanting to show their support for Dani.'

Dani felt her spirits rise on a surge of elation at his words.

'Maura in Fairhill has texted in to say: "Fair play to that woman. It's an absolute disgrace she has to go on the radio to get the cops to do their job." You're dead right there, Maura.'

'And Damo in Blarney has texted: "I'm shocked to hear this happening in our village. Dani should set up a GoFundMe campaign, I'd definitely donate." Thanks for that, Damo, that is a good idea. Now, there's loads more in that vein, but I'm afraid I don't have time to read them all out. Make sure to check out the Justice for Jessie Facebook group if you want to show your support for Dani and her daughter. The link is on our website. We're going to take a short break and then the news, and then I'll be back to tell you about the thief who bit off a bit more than he could chew when he tried to steal Coco, the not so cuddly Cavapoo from Bishopstown.' The presenter's hearty laughter faded into an ad for a local locksmith service.

GoFundMe. She'd never have thought of that, but what a great idea. If she could raise enough money, that would take the financial pressure off her. She wouldn't have to bum off Joe and wouldn't be in any rush to go back home. It wasn't as if there was anything good waiting for her in Boston.

The guy behind the bar in the Gab gave her a big wave when she went in. She wasn't sure if he recognised her from when she'd been in earlier in the week or if he was this friendly to everyone. She settled herself at a table and ordered a full Irish and a double-shot Americano. Tea just didn't do it for her. She couldn't understand the Irish obsession with the bland beverage.

As she sipped her coffee and waited for her food, she noticed a group in the corner glancing in her direction. Ignoring them, she took her phone out to check the Facebook group and see if she had any new followers or comments.

'Ah sorry, love?' A short man with a buzz cut stood beside her table. He had been sitting with the group in the corner. 'I hope you don't mind me comin' over, but I heard you on the radio earlier and I just wanted to say well done. That can't have been an easy thing to do.'

'No, no, of course I don't mind. Thank you, that means so much,' she said, surfing another wave of elation. As he walked back to his group, they all smiled and waved over at Dani, an older man giving her a thumbs-up and shouting, 'Good on ya, girl.' She grinned gratefully back at them, feeling buoyed by all the support she had received in the last couple of hours from complete strangers. She had felt so utterly alone after that nasty scene in the kitchen last night. Thank God Jessie had given her the strength to keep going.

She turned back to her phone and opened Facebook.

'Holy shit!' she whispered.

The group had ninety-seven join requests. Things were starting to happen.

CHAPTER 34

Noelle

'Where is she now?'

Maria gestured upstairs. 'She's in her room. I told her I'd be up to her in a few minutes, but what am I supposed to say to her? I can't cope, Noelle. It's one awful thing after another.'

'What did she say was written on the door?'

'"Mr Murphy is a paedo." It was in the boys' toilets at lunchtime, in one of the cubicles. The caretaker covered it up, but there's photos of it going round the whole school. It's all because of the radio interview – everyone knows it's Tadhg she was talking about.'

'Nobody who knows Tadhg will believe a word out of her mouth, Maria.'

'I don't know. Betty heard it on the radio while she was up in Perfect Cuts. She told Essie the whole place was talking about it. They even got Nuala to turn the volume up so they could hear it over the dryers.'

'Ah, for fuck's sake.' Noelle frowned. 'Betty should know better than to be telling ye that, the stupid cow.'

'It's not her fault, though. It's that woman's. How can she go on radio and say this stuff? Tadhg was horrified when he heard what she was accusing him of. They had a brief fling over twenty years ago and she's never tried to contact him since. Why does she hate him so much? Why is she so fixated on him now? I just don't understand.'

Maria's eyes were filled with confusion and dismay. What a bloody nightmare! Noelle had no idea what to say or do to make her feel better. This was such a horrible situation they had all found themselves in the middle of. She'd nearly died when she'd heard Dani tell Benny Mac she was threatening to throw her out of the B&B, so she could only imagine how poor Maria must have felt. Her friend had called her after the interview, practically hyperventilating, saying she'd walked out of the school. Noelle had told her to go straight home and said she'd meet her there. She had contacted Jackie the school secretary to say Maria had been called away on a personal emergency; they'd all know about it soon enough if they didn't already.

Essie had been in with Maria when Noelle arrived, bustling around making tea and arranging biscuits that nobody had any mind for on a plate. Trying to pretend she wasn't going out of her own mind with worry. Noelle was mad about Essie. She was so lovely. Just as Tadhg's father, Jim, had been too. You wouldn't hear many people with a bad word to say about the Murphys. Growing up, the kids on their street had always been in and out of each other's houses. You could always count on Essie to have a packet of Cadbury's fingers in the cupboard, a jug of MiWadi in the fridge and Chilly Willies in the freezer. Unlike Noelle's house, where her mother would run them soon as look at them if they came near her in between meal times. Or worse, dared to bring a friend in with them.

Only minutes later, Tadhg had called to say that Jack O'Flynn, the chair of the board of management, wanted to see him before he went home that day. A number of parents had called the school on the back of the Rebel FM interview and Jack knew the board members would be on to him as well, wanting to know what was going on. And Maria had barely put the phone down on that call when it rang again. This time it had been the secretary's office at the secondary school, asking her if she could come and collect Eva as she was a bit upset. Maria had instantly pulled herself together at the thought of her daughter needing her.

Noelle had driven her to the school to collect her daughter and the tears Eva had been holding back had burst through their floodgates as soon as she saw her mother. Noelle blinked back her own tears as through her rearview mirror she watched her friend hold her daughter in her arms, rubbing her arm and telling her it would all be okay.

The whole thing was such a bloody mess. Tadhg had admitted sleeping with Dani, so it certainly wasn't beyond the realms of possibility that he had got her pregnant. And if that was true, convincing her to have an abortion and keep it quiet would be just the kind of thing a man like him would do. A man who, even though he hid it well most of the time, undoubtedly considered himself a step above the rest. She remembered that day in the hotel when he saw Dani, the flash in his eyes she wasn't sure she had imagined. That had been real, she realised now. He must have been horrified and yet, he'd acted as if he had never laid eyes on her.

Noelle had no idea why Dani would accuse him of grooming her if it wasn't true, although she could see why a man in his position would want to deny it. Things may have been very different nearly a quarter of a century ago, but every day now there were women coming forward with stories of things that happened to them long ago. These kinds of suppurating boils had a habit of coming to a head eventually. She hoped to Christ for Maria's sake that the grooming story wasn't true, but she was probably one of the few who wouldn't be completely shocked if it was.

CHAPTER 35

Maria

She felt now that she was in the vortex of a tornado, the air spinning violently around her. Every hour bringing a fresh shock.

The radio interview had been a punch to the stomach and now here was another one, no chance to catch her breath between blows. She was sitting in the sunroom with Noelle, trying to steel herself to go up to talk to Eva, when her friend's phone beeped with a message. Maria could tell by Noelle's face that it was bad. That just when she'd thought things couldn't get any worse, they already had.

Liam had forwarded Noelle a link to an article on the *Examiner* website. Her breath had caught in her chest and Noelle had squeezed her hand as they both stared in horror. Under the heading 'Mother of Tragic Blarney Castle Fall Victim Calls for Investigation into Daughter's Death' was a large photo of a radiant, smiling Jessie. It was a report of the Rebel FM interview, highlighting the 'grief-stricken mother's call for a proper investigation and a second autopsy', and including details of the Justice for Jessie Facebook group.

'At least it doesn't say anything about the grooming or the other stuff she said about Tadhg,' Noelle said gently.

'Oh God, Noelle, if it's online today, it'll probably be in the actual paper tomorrow and then all the other papers will pick up on it ... Oh Jesus, what if the tabloids get hold of this? They might even mention the grooming accusation. They might name Tadhg.'

Her daughter, who should have been studying for her exams, was upstairs in her room, her eyes red and swollen from crying, saying her father was now the butt of paedophile memes and jokes and there was no way she could go into school next week. Meanwhile her husband was waiting to find out whether he still had a job to go to on Monday.

Even Essie wasn't able to hide her worry: her face had crumpled as they read the article out to her from Noelle's phone. Far from going away, this thing was mutating, metastasising now beyond social media into the newspaper that Jim, when he was alive, used to have delivered to the door every morning.

After Noelle left, Maria was heading up the stairs with a can of Coke and a packet of crisps for Eva when she heard a key turn in the front door lock. Her breath catching in her throat, she turned to greet her husband. But it wasn't Tadhg; it was her son, banging the door behind him and storming past her up the stairs.

'Ben, love, what—' She checked her watch. It wasn't even three p.m. School didn't finish for another half an hour.

Oh God, he must have heard about the graffiti too, maybe even seen it. She should have collected him when she got Eva, made up some excuse. The staff were probably all talking about it anyway.

She was on her way up again when the front door opened a second time. This time it *was* Tadhg who came in. He closed the door behind him and stood with his back pressed against it, covering his face with his hands, breathing heavily through his nostrils. He hadn't noticed her on the staircase.

'Tadhg?'

He started, looked up. He looked sick, as if all the blood had been drained from his face. 'Sorry, love. I didn't see you there.'

'What's happened? Why is Ben home early?'

'He punched Jamie O'Sullivan in the face.'

She gaped at him.

'What?'

Ben had been best friends with Jamie through most of primary school but they had drifted apart when they started secondary, along with the rest of that group of friends.

'Apparently, he asked Ben if I had the hots for any of the girls in particular, said there were a few "nice juicy" first years that would be right up my alley.'

Tadhg sounded shattered. 'A few of the other lads joined in and they all started laughing, and Ben just lost it and thumped Jamie. Felt like thumping the little prick myself when I heard, after we were always so good to him.'

'Oh Jesus Christ. I better go up to him.' She wondered what Jamie's parents – Caroline, quiet and a bit standoffish and Tommy, one of the coaches for Blarney GAA and the complete opposite of his wife – would make of all this.

'No, wait,' Tadhg said. 'I need to talk to you inside first.' He nodded his head towards the kitchen.

As she followed him through the hall – with its elegant wood panelling, the walls painted a warm oatmeal colour, the smiling faces of her family framed in happier times – Maria thought of how much she wished she could rewind time. To before Jessie De Marco booked that flight to come to Cork to find her father. Or back further, to before that woman in that bar in Boston told the girl her father was not who she thought he was. She wondered if that woman, whoever she was, was aware of the awful consequences of the bombshell she had dropped on Jessie that day. But no, she needed to rewind even further: back, back, back to that weekend when Tadhg had made the biggest mistake of his life. Or back to the fateful day when he had decided to go to Boston in the first place. She wished he had stayed at home, got a job locally and never set eyes on Dani De Marco. Too late for that now, though. There was no way of turning the clock back.

Tadhg stood leaning against the breakfast bar, rubbing his eyes with his knuckles. 'I spoke to Jack, explained my side of things. I admitted what happened between me and Daniela, but I also told him that I wasn't the father of her child and there was categorically no grooming involved. Christ, even the idea of it makes me sick.'

Justine had explained that even if the grooming allegation had been true, it would have been outside the jurisdiction of the Irish police and probably well outside the statute of limitations for taking a criminal or civil case, even in the US. While it was certainly a relief to know that, it was still dreadful that the seeds of such a horrible rumour had been planted in people's minds; and it was probably spreading like Japanese knotweed.

'So what happens now?'

'Well, the board are meeting on Monday night – they were due to meet anyway – and Jack's going to prepare something brief to read out to them. He was very nice about it, in fairness; he could see how upset I am over it. It's an awful position for him to be in too.'

Jack O'Flynn was a real community man, involved in Blarney Tidy Towns and the local Meals on Wheels. He'd want to believe the best in Tadhg, knew the Murphy family well, but he'd also be acutely aware that so-called 'pillars of the community' were toppled from their pedestals all the time. Anybody who read a newspaper or listened to the radio would know that. Schoolteachers and swim coaches, scout leaders and even the St John Ambulance. Anywhere evil men had access to vulnerable, defenceless children. Groomers and predators and abusers who joined forces with other monsters just like themselves to prey on the boys and girls in their charge. There would be plenty of people out there who'd sniff the smoke swirling around Tadhg and jump to the conclusion that there had to be fire beneath it.

'Nothing like this has ever happened before, so it's not like there's any protocol,' he explained. 'I haven't committed any crime. I was worried about it being referred to the investigations committee of the Teaching Council, but Jack doesn't think there's any grounds for that. It's basically up to the board of the school as my employer to decide what, if any, action should be taken.'

'Oh thank God, Tadhg. I was so worried they were going to suspend you.' She felt her carriage steady on its tracks again.

'No, we don't have to worry about *me* being suspended, not as things stand, anyway. But I'm afraid Ben is another story.'

And off she went, hurtling down another steep slope on the big dipper of anxiety, powerless to stop.

'Oh God, no!'

'I'm sorry, love, we have a very strict policy on physical aggression. It's set out very clearly in our code of behaviour. And I, of all people, can't be seen to show favouritism, certainly not now. He struck another child; he's facing a one-day suspension, probably next Tuesday. He's lucky he didn't break Jamie's nose, or it would be even more serious.'

'But he's never done anything like this before; he's never been in any kind of trouble. And he was totally provoked by that little shit, by the sounds of it. I'm telling you, if I get my hands on that—'

'Look, I know it seems unfair, love, but Ben hit out. He was in the wrong and he has to face the consequences now.'

Maria felt a hot surge of anger flood her chest. None of this was her son's fault. He had only been defending his father against disgusting comments that would never have been made if Tadhg hadn't slept with that girl in the first place.

'None of this is fair though, is it, on any of us?' she said.

Something in her tone made him look at her, wondering perhaps if she was including him in that. Or blaming him for bringing this mess to their door. And who could fault her if she was? You'd have to be a saint not to.

'You do believe me, don't you, Maria?' She'd never seen her husband so unsure of himself, so … needy. There was an unfamiliar, plaintive note in his tone, almost pleading. 'You know I'd never have done what she's saying. I know I fucked up ... but I'd never ...'

'I know that. Of course I do.'

And she did, didn't she? Although, two weeks ago, she'd never have dreamt that even as a young man he could have slept with a girl he'd taught only months earlier. Was it that much of a stretch to ...? But surely, if there was even an iota of truth in what Dani was now saying, she'd have gone to the police in Boston long ago.

'Did you manage to get hold of Justine?' she asked.

'Yes, she's gone ahead with the cease-and-desist letter. It's probably being hand-delivered to the B&B as we speak. She's hoping this might stop that woman from doing any more interviews or repeating her lies online. She's sending one to Benny Mac as well. There's nothing we can do about this morning's interview – the horse has well and truly bolted on that. We just have to try to prevent any more. She's had no luck yet with Facebook or YouTube, but she says they're notoriously difficult to deal with. They don't seem to care if people are being defamed on their platforms, if their lives are ruined, as long as they're making money.'

They should have sent the cease-and-desist letter yesterday, straight after the YouTube video went up. Holding off had been a big mistake, but Noelle had really believed they'd got through to the woman.

'Oh God, Tadhg, what if she doesn't stop even after she gets Justine's letter? What if she gets onto RTÉ or Newstalk? What if—'

'We just have to hold tough like Justine said, love, and hope that this time next week, she'll be gone out of our lives for good. There's nothing else we can do now but wait.'

'There is, though.'

They both turned their heads in the direction of their son's voice. Ben was standing in the doorway, his lips curling, as if there was a rotten smell in the kitchen. 'Sorry, love?' Maria asked.

'There is something else he can do, isn't there?' He wouldn't even look at his father. 'He could prove he's not the father if he's so sure, like that guy on the radio said. It's not rocket science, is it?'

CHAPTER 36

Dani

Things were really taking off now. The #justiceforjessie campaign wasn't quite trending yet, but word was spreading fast. Benny Mac had shared a number of clips of her interview on his own Insta and TikTok accounts and they'd already got hundreds of likes and shares. Her Facebook group now had nearly 200 new members, all actively engaging with her posts and video; still too few to put much pressure on the Garda, but she was only getting started. If one interview on a small local radio station could have this impact, imagine what an interview on national radio could do.

She had been thrilled when Jen from Rebel FM had WhatsApped her a link to an article in the *Examiner*. She hadn't even needed to contact them; they had simply reported on her interview with Benny, although a far tamer version. That guy in the *North Cork News* who had been ignoring all her emails and messages could get stuffed if he came knocking on her door now.

She could hear Noelle in the kitchen below, speaking in that silly voice she used for the baby. 'Where's my best boy? Where is he? Oh, there he is.' She could hear the rumble of Liam's deeper voice too, and another female voice. Probably Molly. Silverware clinked, water gushed from a tap and something metal clattered: the sounds of supper being prepared, the table set. No invite for her, unsurprisingly. She didn't care; she'd order some Chinese takeout, eat it in her room.

She sprayed some of Jessie's Victoria's Secret body mist around the room, closing her eyes as she inhaled the familiar sweet scent of coconut and vanilla. She took another deep breath and sat at the bureau, hoping that if she was still enough, quiet enough, she could somehow summon her daughter back. The intrusive, high-pitched chime of the doorbell caused her to flinch, eyes blinking open.

The kitchen door opened, footsteps in the hall. Somebody opened the front door. Noelle's voice. Then a male voice she didn't recognise. A brief conversation. The door closed again. Silence for a few moments. Then the tread of footsteps on the stairs. Dani's chest tightened.

There was a sharp tap on her door. When she opened it, a sour-faced Noelle handed her a white envelope.

'This just came for you,' she said, in a clipped tone. 'Hand-delivered.'

Dani looked at the envelope. Her name was printed on it, c/o Avalon Bed and Breakfast, Station Road, Blarney.

'Thank you.'

Noelle opened her mouth as if she was going to say something else, but then turned away. Dani closed the door behind her and sat back down. She turned the envelope over. No return address. Maybe somebody had sent her a cheque for her GoFundMe: it wasn't live yet, but she had posted in the group earlier that she was in the process of setting one up. She hadn't given out her address, but this village was so small, it wouldn't be hard to find out where she was staying.

She tore along the seal of the envelope and pulled out the sheet of paper inside. She froze when she read the sender's address at the top of the page. O'Connor McInerney Solicitors, South Mall, Cork. She skimmed the letter quickly, words hopping from the page.

My client Tadhg Murphy …

… cease and desist …

… any further false statements defaming my client …

… Defamation Act 2009 …

… damage to good character and reputation …

… malicious intent …

… reasonable inference drawn by listeners …

… Failure to adhere … relied on in court … fix the cost of such proceedings on you …

Fuck!

Joe would lose his shit if she got herself into any more trouble, especially now, when he had so much on his plate with the baby.

She settled herself at the same table in the Gab as earlier, near the door, and ordered a club sandwich with fries. She hadn't eaten since brunch and stress always made her extra hungry.

Brian had let her have it with both barrels when she'd called to tell him about the letter, asking her what she expected after 'attacking the man's reputation over the airwaves'. He was furious that she'd ignored not only his advice but also his calls, warning that he wouldn't be able to continue to act for her if she didn't stop her 'invasive and counter-productive activities' immediately. When she argued that she hadn't specifically identified Tadhg on the radio, Brian pointed out that, as he'd already warned her, she didn't have to name him for it to constitute defamation.

'And as he has been named on Facebook and YouTube and who knows where else, it's quite clear who you were talking about. As it stands, the man has a strong case against you if he decides to take it and the onus would be on you to prove that the allegations you've been making about him are true. I just hope for your sake his solicitor advises him to hold off for now, because the national media would have a field day with that story if they got hold of it.'

She had felt pretty crap after coming off the call, and with the walls of her room starting to close in on her, she'd decided to come to the Gab. At least people were friendly to her in here; the owner had even given her brunch on the house earlier. She eyed up the dessert menu while she waited for her food, sipping on a glass of surprisingly good Chianti Classico, as good as anything they served in the restaurant at home. Ooh, they had Toblerone cheesecake. Her mouth watered at the thought of it. Where the hell were they with her food? It seemed to be taking for ever. She took another sip of her wine and tried to distract herself from her gnawing belly.

What would she be doing if she were at home right now? She checked the time on her phone. It was 8:05 p.m. here, which made it – she counted the hours backwards on her fingers – around three p.m. in Boston. She'd probably be hanging around the apartment watching mindless afternoon TV shows, biding time until her shift in the restaurant started. And after work, going to a bar and drinking too much. Maybe hooking up with some random guy. Waking up the next morning feeling and looking like shit, gathering up her clothes and wondering where the hell her life had gone wrong. None of those guys ever offered her breakfast or asked for her number.

She looked around her now. The bar was busy, but not overly so. A waitress was heading in her direction with a tray of food. *Please let this be mine.*

'BLT with chips?'

'Yeah, that's me. Thank you so much. Could I get another glass of the Chianti, please?'

As she dug into her food, her ears tuned in to the conversation going on at the table beside her, where a group of people had just sat down. Two men and three women, about her age or a bit older.

'Ah, shur she got no time at all, God love her,' one of the women was saying.

'Shockin' how they missed it when she was complainin' of pain for months,' another woman said. 'She was only diagnosed three weeks before she died.'

They all shook their heads.

'The family have a case there, I'd say,' one of the men said, lifting his pint to his lips.

'And what do ye think about Tadhg Murphy?' the second man in the group asked now. Dani stopped chewing, leaning closer on the pretext of fishing her purse from the floor with her foot. 'Did ye hear the American girl's mother on with Benny Mac this morning?'

'No,' the first woman said, 'but Maura told me about it and I listened back to it this afternoon. I was in shock, to tell you the truth. The Murphys was always lovely people and Tadhg never seemed the pervy type.'

'Well, the girl'd hardly make it up, now, would she, Carol?' a third woman said hotly.

'I dunno,' said the man who had brought the topic up. 'Why did it take her so long to say anythin' about it if it was true, like? Why didn't she make a complaint to the police over in Boston before now? Why wait twenty-odd years?'

'D'you know, this is exactly why she probably didn't make a complaint back then, Noel,' the third woman spat. 'Because of this kind of attitude. It'd sicken you. Girls who speak up about bein' groomed and abused made to feel like they're the ones in the wrong. That it's their fault for wearin' short skirts or skimpy tops, because they were askin' for it. That's why so few sexual assault cases go to court in this country, and I'm sure things are no better in the States. Worse, probably.'

'I dunno know though, Ger,' the woman called Carol said. 'I knows Tadhg with years – he used to pal around with our Dean when they were kids. He was always sound enough—'

'Ah would you fuckin' stop,' the other man said. 'Sound, me arse. That lad thinks his shit don't stink, sitting up in his big house on the hill looking down on the rest of us. Big man up at the school, holdin' a fuckin' welcome night for all the new Ukrainian students when me cousin Marty's young fella couldn't even get in.'

'Sure he doesn't even live in the catchment area, Rory, he lives out in feckin' Dripsey,' Carol said, laughing.

'Yeah well,' Ger said, 'I believe the mother and I'd do exactly the same if 'twas my child, God forbid. Sounds like she's well able to go, too, can't see her backing down too easily.'

Dani couldn't keep her mouth shut any longer. 'Excuse me, I hope you don't mind ... It's not that I've been listenin' in, but I couldn't help overhearin' and um ... I'm Jessie's mom. The one who was on the radio? And I just want to say *thank you*' – she looked at the woman called Ger – 'for believin' me, because you're right, it's not easy to speak up about this stuff and ...' She swallowed hard. 'Um ...'

'Oh God. Dani, isn't it? I'm so sorry for what you're goin' through, God love you,' said Ger, sincerity spilling from her eyes. The man and woman who had defended the Murphys didn't know where to look, him settling on staring into his pint, her at her feet.

'There's plenty people round here who believe you, love,' the man called Rory said. 'The whole place is talkin' about it. Your daughter was very well got here, it's fuckin' terrible what happened to her. It's not surprisin', though, the cops in this country are useless. Too busy scratching their holes, more interested in fuckin' protectin' the paedos our government's bringin' into this country than doing the job they should be doin'.'

Ger bobbed her head in agreement, while the couple who had defended the Murphys said it was time they 'made a move', put their coats on and headed out, leaving their unfinished drinks behind them.

'Gosh I hope they didn't leave because of me ... I'll leave you in peace now, I just wanted to say thanks,' Dani said. 'I got a letter from Tadhg Murphy's attorney this evening that really upset me, but hearin' what you said about me not backin' down easily, well, it's made me feel a lot better.'

'Ah no, that's awful. Look, d'you want to join us if you're on your own, hun?' Ger asked.

'Are you sure? I wouldn't want to interrupt—'

'Not at all, girl,' Rory said. 'You're more than welcome. Sit yourself in here now and tell us about this letter.'

Rather than tell them about it, she let them read it for themselves, not allowing herself to think of Brian Fitzpatrick's reaction if he heard she was showing a confidential legal letter to random strangers in a bar. The more of the locals she could get on her side, the better for her campaign.

Rory and Ger scanned the letter, their faces curling in disgust.

'Typical bleedin' bully-boy tactics,' Ger said, handing the letter back to Dani. 'Trying to buy himself out of trouble, hidin' behind solicitors.'

'D'you know what I'd do with that letter if I was you, love?' Rory said, jabbing at the table with his index finger. 'I'd go off and make a video about it and tell everyone that Tadhg Murphy and his legal team are tryin' to shut me up but that it won't work! And I'd say I'm prepared to go to jail if I fuckin' have to, to get justice for me daughter.'

CHAPTER 37

Noelle
Saturday, 20 January

Maria had called her first thing, so upset Noelle could barely make out what was after happening now between her friend's shuddery breaths.

It turned out that having cried herself to sleep last night over everything that was going on, Maria had been woken this morning by Ted Hickey from across the road, telling her someone had sprayed 'PAEDO' in red paint across their gate during the night. He had spotted two young lads in hoodies acting suspiciously from his bedroom window when he was going to bed – he stayed up until all hours every night watching the telly – and let a roar at them. He hadn't wanted to wake them at that hour, but he'd brought over a tin of black paint so that he could cover over the graffiti for them.

Noelle had promised she'd be there as soon as she'd served breakfast to the woman who was the cause of all this trouble. She had all but slammed Dani's eggs and toast down in front of her, not even able to stomach looking at her, never mind speaking to her. She didn't care anymore that she'd just lost her child or that maybe she'd been driven mad with grief. She was sick of the sight of the woman.

They were sitting in Maria's kitchen now, her friend looking as if there had just been a death in *her* family. Ashen and shell-shocked. Still in her pyjamas, puffy purple pouches under her eyes, her hair stuck to her head. Tadhg had gone down to the GAA pitch as he did every Saturday morning, not wanting to give people even more to talk about if he didn't turn up.

'I don't know how he was able to face going over there this morning, Noelle. There's no way I could do it. I don't want to leave the house. It's not even just *her* anymore – it feels like we're under attack from all sides. Even in here. I can't believe this is happening to us.'

'God, Maria, ye don't deserve any of this, but the gougers who did that last night do not represent the majority of people. It's like that crowd protesting against the asylum seekers, a noisy, pig-ignorant minority. You're always going to have people like that, but there's plenty more out there who *are* on your side. I meant to tell you, Noreen Heaslip rang me yesterday asking me to let her know if there was anything she could do for you.'

Maria looked like she hadn't heard a word Noelle said, her pink bloodshot eyes welling up again. 'Every morning I wake up with this sick feeling in my stomach and then it hits me all over again. If Tadhg loses his job over this, how will we pay the mortgage on my salary alone? And the car loans. I don't know how Eva's going to sit her exams with all this going on or even study, when it's such an important year for her. They're refusing to go into school on Monday and how can we possibly make them? I don't know if they're ever going to be able to go back there.'

Her friend looked at her from desperate eyes. Noelle put her arm around her and held her, feeling the tension humming through her body.

'That sounds like pure anxiety, Maria. Have you a Xanax or a Valium or anything like that?' Noelle had needed to take a sedative for a short while herself, along with an antidepressant, to get through her marriage breakup and what had come after. Those little white pills that her GP had doled out so stingily, with warnings of how highly addictive they were, had offered her respite at that time.

Maria shook her head listlessly. 'No, I've never needed anything like that before. I think Essie might have some for flying, though.'

'I'll pop into her to see if I can get you something to help relax you a bit and then on Monday I think you should make an appointment to see your GP. If you ring first thing and tell them it's urgent, you might get one for that day. I'll be back to you in two minutes.'

She went out to Essie's, tapping on the window before she opened the door and stepped inside. The kitchen was empty, a half-drunk cup of tea on the table, a breakfast-show cookery segment playing on the wall-mounted TV.

'Essie,' she called.

'In here.' The older woman came through the double doors that led to her sitting room, a can of Mr Sheen and a yellow dustcloth in her hand.

'Ah, Noelle love.'

She put the polish and cloth down on the table. 'Is everything okay?'

'I was just in with Maria and she's not in a great way at all this morning, very panicky and anxious. She said you might have something you take for flying that would help calm her a bit.'

'Ah God,' Essie said, her face creasing in concern. 'I'll have a look; hopefully I might have a couple left. I'm not sure, though.' She stood on a small step and began to pull a large plastic tub from a top cupboard.

As Essie rummaged through the box, pulling out packets and bottles, plasters and bandages, Noelle felt her heart go out to her. She was such a lovely person; she didn't deserve this. She was clearly doing her best to stay strong for everyone, but it must be soul-destroying for her to see her son publicly accused of such terrible things. Noelle had always envied Maria her close relationship with her mother-in-law; she had never been close to Kevin's mother Nuala, a right auld witch if ever there was one, or any of his family for that matter.

'Ah, here it is.' Essie held up a tiny transparent bag with a pharmacy label on it, a small blister pack inside.

'There's only a few in it, but they'll be enough to keep her going anyway. I'll come in with you now and we'll get her sorted.'

Noelle felt her phone vibrating in her pocket. 'Hang on, Essie, it's Liam. I'll take this quickly in case it's about your one.'

'Hi, love, I'm just—'

'Have you seen what that mad bitch is after doing now, Mam?'

Her heart sank. *Oh no.*

'No, what?'

'She's after posting a video about the letter she got from

Tadhg's solicitor. Mackie just sent it to me. I'll forward you the link.' Noelle heard a voice in the background on Liam's end. 'Oh yeah, Molly is just saying that one of her buddies was in the Gab last night, and Dani was telling anyone who'd listen that Tadhg Murphy was trying to shut her up. She was drinking with Rory Ahern and some of his buddies.'

'Oh my God, surely she can't get away with this? How is she not worried about being sued? And what the hell was she doing with Rory bloody Ahern of all people?'

The Aherns had been trouble going back years, and it seemed to be worse they were getting. She remembered her own father saying that Rory's father Bobby would 'take the eye out of your head and come back for the lashes'.

'She doesn't give a shit, Mam – the woman is a fucking law unto herself. We need to get her out of our house.'

'But we can't bloody well do that, can we, Liam? She'll get straight back onto Benny Mac or the papers and maybe even name us next time.' They had already been named in some of the comments on social media. Noelle had put her heart and soul into the B&B and she relied heavily on the American market. It was far too easy to destroy somebody's reputation these days.

'I know, I know, but she can't keep getting away with this. God knows what the fuck she'll do next. Watch that video.'

'Alright, love, but I don't want you saying anything to her. We'll talk later, okay?'

'What's she after doing now, Noelle?' Essie asked. Shaking her head, Noelle opened the link Liam had sent her, holding her phone up between the two of them.

On the screen, Dani was sitting on the sofa in the guest

sitting room of the B&B, her face solemn and unsmiling, as if she were about to deliver a state-of-the-nation speech.

'That's my house, the cheeky bitch.'

'So, guys, I promised to keep you all updated on my journey to get justice for Jessie and I need to let you all know about somethin' that happened yesterday evening.'

The two women huddled together, staring at the screen.

Dani was holding up the letter. 'This was hand-delivered yesterday evening to the door of the B&B where I'm staying in Blarney, the same place where for those of you who don't know, Jessie was staying up until her death. It's a letter from O'Connor McInerney Solicitors on the South Mall in Cork city, which I'm going to read now for you.'

'Is she for feckin' real?' Noelle muttered.

On the screen Dani was reading the letter out, stopping at intervals to take a deep breath before resuming. When she had finished, she took another deep dramatic sniff in through her nose, and looked straight at the camera, her brown eyes glistening. 'I will admit that I was shaken when I got this letter, shaken and scared, and I thought maybe I'm not strong enough to do this, maybe I should just give up trying to fight for a proper investigation into my baby's death ...' She released a fragile sob, swallowed hard and continued. 'Because it's so damn hard and I'm so alone ... But then I went to a local bar here in Blarney called the Gab where I met some kind, wonderful people who reached a hand out to me and told me that I am not alone, and that there are plenty more like them who support me and Jessie.'

She jabbed the air with her finger as she spoke. 'I'm a mother looking for answers and I will not be silenced by bully-boy gagging tactics.' She held up the letter in both hands and ripped it down the middle. 'I WILL NOT SHUT UP. I WILL NOT BE SILENCED! I am prepared to go to jail if I have to for my daughter. Justice for Jessie!'

'Oh Lord,' Essie said.

The kitchen was empty when they went back in to Maria's house, the hall door open, the sound of voices in the hall. Maria was standing at the front door, talking to somebody. As Noelle and Essie came into the hall, she turned towards them, her face a rigid rictus of shock.

'Who is it, love?' Essie moved forward.

Maria took a couple of steps towards her mother-in-law, holding on to the wall with one hand as if to steady herself, and two people, a tall man and a shorter woman in that distinctive navy and yellow uniform, came through the open door behind her.

Fuck.

CHAPTER 38

Maria

She sat on a chair in the kitchen breathing in and out of a paper sandwich bag, her relief that she wasn't having a heart attack after all tempered by the presence of the gardaí. The only time a guard ever came to their house was when Pádraig, the community garda, came to talk to Tadhg about school-related business; he usually stayed for a chat and a cup of tea with them afterwards.

A panic attack, the nice young guard with the red hair had told her – Amy, she said her name was. Maria had an aunt who'd suffered from them for years, but she'd never experienced one herself. Never experienced anything like it: such utter certainty that she was going to die, such intense, choking terror.

She had grabbed Essie's arm, her eyes bulging, unable to speak, to tell her she was having difficulty breathing. Her erratic heart beating so fast she feared it was going to break loose from its moorings, rip free from its anchor of blood vessels.

Hunkering down beside Maria, the guard had got her to hold the bag over her mouth and nose and take in twelve normal breaths, then to remove the bag and take a few more breaths. She told her there was nothing wrong with her, that her breathing would settle in a couple of minutes. Maria had wanted to tell her that no, no, there was something very, very wrong and beg her to call an ambulance, but she couldn't get air in, never mind words out.

The guard had been right, though. After another few rounds of breathing into the bag, the pounding in her ears had started to ease and although her heart was still racing, the strong sense of impending death had dissipated.

'Oh God, the kids. Essie, will you go up and see if they're alright?' she asked her mother-in-law.

While Noelle had been in with Essie, asking her if she had any sedatives, Maria had heard her daughter wail from upstairs.

'Mommm!'

She had run straight up to see what was wrong, bumping into Ben at the door of Eva's bedroom. Eva had been standing at her window, looking out onto the road where a squad car had pulled up and two uniformed gardaí were getting out.

'They're probably just here about the graffiti,' Maria had said, trying to fake nonchalance. 'Nothing for you to worry about.' They hadn't even reported last night's incident to the guards yet, but the kids didn't know that.

The doorbell had rung and she'd tramped back down the stairs. Through the opaque glass, the two figures outside were wavy and blurred.

She couldn't for the life of her remember now what the guards had said to her at the door or what she had said to them. And now Tadhg was beside her, holding her hand. Where had he suddenly appeared from?

'I will, love, in a minute,' Essie said before she turned to the young guard again. 'I was just about to give her something to help relax her when you came to the door, garda. She's been under an awful lot of strain with all of this, we all have. The whole thing is a nightmare, and it's really taking its toll on Maria.'

'Of course, Mrs Murphy. We understand this isn't an easy situation for anybody involved. We can come back later, if that'd be better. Let Maria try and get a bit of a rest first, maybe.'

'No, please,' Maria said. 'I need to know ... What's going on? Is Tadhg being arrested?'

'No, no, not at all, Maria. We're not here to arrest anyone, as Donal was just explaining to your husband.' She nodded towards her colleague.

Thank God for that ... but then why are they here?

Essie handed her a tiny white tablet and a glass of water and went to check on the kids. Maria put the tablet under her tongue and washed it down her throat with a mouthful of water. She usually didn't even like taking paracetamol, but she'd swallow a whole box of these if they could take away this horrible feeling of her skin being too tight for her body.

The male garda came over and sat at the other end of the table from her.

'We're just continuing with our enquiries into the death of Jessie De Marco, Mrs Murphy, trying to build up a picture of her last few days. We were on to your husband earlier and he arranged to meet us here ...'

'I rang you to tell you, love, but you didn't answer your phone,' Tadhg said. 'I didn't want them coming over to the pitch – there's enough talk about me as it is.'

She had no idea where her phone even was. She must have left it upstairs after she rang Noelle earlier.

'My husband is not a groomer. That woman ... We don't know why she's saying those things,' she cried. 'Tadhg would never—'

'Look, that's not what we're here about. Our tech guys have examined Jessie De Marco's phone and they've found a number of communications sent in the days before she died that we're just following up on.'

'But what has that got to do with Tadhg?' She looked at her husband, her diaphragm tightening.

'It's nothing to worry about, love; I'll explain after,' he said. 'I had nothing to do with that girl's death. They've already confirmed my alibi for that day.'

She started breathing in and out of the bag again, trying her best not to vomit into it. It wasn't his alibi she was worried about.

CHAPTER 39

Maria
Sunday, 21 January

'I've gone to mass every Sunday morning for longer than I remember and I'm not going to stop now,' Essie said, stoutly. 'There's not a man nor woman sitting inside in that church, the ones up at the altar and the ones handing out communion included, who hasn't made a mistake in their lives. If we *don't* go, it'll look like we're too ashamed to show our faces.'

Which would, of course, be true.

Her mother-in-law had washed and blow-dried her hair, put her makeup on and was dressed in her good coat and boots. As if this was a Sunday morning like any other. Maria was wearing the joggers and baggy sweater she had worn yesterday, not intending to set foot outside the door for the day, and Tadhg was still in the Grinch pyjamas Eva had given him for Christmas.

'We'll go next week, Mam, just not today.' Tadhg was on the sofa in the sitting room, the Sunday papers fanned out around him on the seat and the floor. He had already been up when Maria had woken after another night of broken sleep. The papers had barely hit the mat in the porch when he had grabbed them, bringing them into the sitting room and flicking frenziedly through the pages, throwing the weekend supplements to one side before sinking back against the cushions in relief. Neither of the papers they had delivered every week – the Sunday Indo or the *Business Post* – had picked up on yesterday's story in the *Examiner*. Not yet, anyway. There, it had been the main story on page three, accompanied by a large photo of a mournful Dani holding up a picture of Jessie.

'If you don't go today, it'll be even harder next week, love,' Essie said to her son, as if she were talking to a teenager who didn't want to go to school.

'It's too late, shur,' said Tadhg. 'There's not enough time to get ready.'

'You've plenty of time yet, it's not even half ten.' She turned to Maria, who was standing at the door. 'I think it's important we all go today.'

Maria couldn't think of anything she wanted to do less this morning than walk into that church, all eyes on them, tongues wagging, but she knew Essie was right. They'd be far more conspicuous by their absence. They didn't force the kids to go to mass every week anymore, but as teachers who lived and worked in the local community, Tadhg and Maria tried to make the effort.

'Your mother's right, love. We should go. Run up and have a quick shower. I'll get changed quickly, throw on a bit of makeup.'

Tadhg nodded dully, lacking the energy to put up any more of a fight. He looked like a man who hadn't slept in weeks, his eyes sinking into their sockets.

They made it to the church with minutes to spare, Maria's face burning as they walked up the centre aisle to find a seat around the middle where they usually sat. Her ears felt red-hot as she imagined the nudges and whispers, the Mexican wave of raised eyebrows behind them. She wanted to shrug her jacket off, but it was too awkward in the tight space, so she unbuttoned it. She tried to steady her breathing as her chest squeezed tighter and a wave of dizziness washed over her.

Oh God, please don't let me faint.

Thinking of the 54321 exercise she did with the kids in school, she dragged as much air as she could in through her nose, exhaling slowly through her mouth.

Five things you can see.

The tiles under her feet, the polished pew, the back of the man's head in front of her, a radiator on the wall, stained-glass windows.

Four things you can touch.

The hard bench beneath her, Tadhg's warm hand, the tissue in her pocket, the soft leather of her bag.

A deep breath in, that's better now, starting to slow.

Three things you can hear.

The drone of the priest's voice as he started the mass, a barking cough behind her, the rattle of the radiator.

Another deep breath in, right down to your tummy now.

Two things you can smell.

Burning candles, the crisp woody scent of Tadhg's new Christmas aftershave.

One thing you can taste.

Coffee breath.

Her breathing had eased, the anxiety loosening its grip a bit, and she allowed her shoulders to drop. This place was so familiar to her. It was where her own parents had brought her to mass as a child, where she had been christened and made her communion and confirmation. It was where she and Tadhg had got married and where their own children had received the same sacraments, where they had attended so many weddings and funerals. The stone walls, the soaring, wood beamed ceilings, the thick pillars, the dark confessionals, all standing solid down through the years while people prayed and confessed their sins, celebrated and mourned, lit candles and found comfort.

She knelt and stood and responded by rote as Fr Dennehy moved through the rites of the mass, and then it was time for the first reading and it was the one about the woman who had committed adultery, the one where Jesus said 'Let he who is without sin among you cast the first stone', and she felt Tadhg stiffen beside her as the heat rushed back into her cheeks and her ears and fear dug its claws back into her chest.

What will the new week bring?

And next week?

And the week after?

How long is this going to go on?

She had been stunned when the guards had left yesterday and Tadhg had come into the kitchen, where she and Essie were waiting anxiously.

'It looks like Jessie had googled Michael Murphy Blarney and emailed all of the ones she could find an address for,' he had explained. 'She said she was looking for her father and asked if they had been in Boston around the time she would have been conceived – and if they ever had any kind of relationship with her mother. She got a few replies back, all saying they weren't the man she was looking for.'

'But what has that to do with you, love? Shur you didn't get one.'

Tadhg had visibly squirmed. 'Well, actually I did. My name must have come up somewhere as Tadhg Michael Murphy and she contacted me in case I was related to the man she was looking for.'

'What? But ... how the hell could you not have mentioned this?'

What the fuck?

'I know, I should have, but to be honest, I just ignored it initially. I thought it was just another American searching for her roots. I thought nothing of it until Dani arrived here and I realised who she was. I went back then and read the email properly, and got an awful shock. I didn't say anything about it because I knew it would look like I'd known who the girl was all along and it wasn't like that.'

'So you lied to us?'

'It wasn't a lie, love. I just—'

'And what did the guards say about it?' Essie asked.

'They wanted to know if I'd made contact with her after I read it and I told them I hadn't. They knew I hadn't replied to the email; they have her phone. They're just talking to everyone she contacted, probably to try and find out if they were connected to the person she was meeting the day she died, or maybe even was that person. All I know is that it wasn't me.'

Maria hadn't even had a moment to digest the fact that her husband had hidden the existence of this email from her for days, when Eva came downstairs to tell them about the latest video that mad woman had posted. They had been sure the cease-and-desist letter would stop her from causing any more damage, but instead, it seemed to have riled her up even more. And after they had watched the video, Maria saw something in her husband's eyes that she had never seen before. Pure fear.

Every shred of sympathy Maria had felt for the woman when she first came to the village had evaporated in the face of the devastation she was wreaking on her family. The things she had accused Tadhg of on the radio. He had seemed to be as horrified and bewildered as Maria was, pacing up and down as he tried to make sense of why this was happening.

'She even has me questioning myself now ... trying to figure out is there any way she could have picked up the wrong signals, misinterpreted innocent comments? But I genuinely don't think there is. She was only in my class for a year and I never treated her any differently to the others, apart from trying to encourage her in her writing. What are we going to do, Maria?'

The problem solver in their family was looking to her for answers and she had none to give him. All she could do was look into his eyes and promise him that she believed him. And she did. There was no way her Tadhg would ever have preyed on a teenage student, just no way.

They had had to sit down with the kids yet again and assure them that the awful things Dani was saying about him grooming her were not true. He'd told them that he had made a terrible mistake, that he was ashamed of himself and very sorry for what they were both going through now as a consequence of his actions. He had reiterated that nothing happened between him and Dani while he was still her teacher, and that he knew he wasn't Jessie's father: he had been meticulous about using contraception, ever since one of the lads got a girl pregnant on a one-night stand when he was nineteen.

Ben, who had barely said a word since dropping his paternity test bombshell on Friday night, retreated to his bedroom as soon as the conversation was over. Maria had gone up a short while later and had tried talking to him again. But he was glued to his TV screen, where a man was being dragged out of a car and shot in the head, blood and gore splattering around him while the carjacker drove off at speed. They had held off as long as they could on letting Ben get GTA, but when he hit sixteen he had finally worn them down.

Before leaving Ben's room, she had picked up some clothes from the floor, sighing internally at the fact that neither of her kids, no matter how many times she asked, made use of the laundry basket in their room. She bent down, scooping up socks, boxers, t-shirts and two tracksuit bottoms. She checked the laundry basket; predictably, it was almost empty, apart from one black hoodie. Reaching in to add it to her pile, she realised it was his new Jordan top, the one Essie had washed for him the night this whole nightmare had been set in motion.

'Ben?'

He hadn't answered, his fingers frantically thumbing the controls, his gaze locked on the screen as if under a hypnotic spell.

She'd moved closer to him, tapped his arm.

'Yeah?' He didn't shift his gaze from the screen, didn't stop moving his thumbs and index fingers.

She held the hoodie out. 'Why did Essie wash this for you last week?' She hadn't had a chance to ask her mother-in-law, with all that was going on.

He barely glanced at the top. Shrugged. Muttered, 'Dunno,' and continued with his game.

She felt every eye in the church tracking them as they stood in the line for communion. She stared straight ahead, imagining the muttering going on behind her: 'Hasn't yer man some neck going up for communion?' ... 'The poor wife must be morto' ...

'Body of Christ.'

Fr Dennehy placed the thin wafer into her cupped hands. She wondered if he'd heard about Dani and her campaign. He surely had. What must he be making of the whole thing?

'Amen,' she croaked. As she turned to walk away, he reached his hand out and pressed her shoulder gently, before moving on to the next person in line.

She felt heartened by the unexpected gesture of kindness from the gruff old priest. As she edged her way back into her pew, she looked up and caught the eye of a woman a few rows back, who smiled warmly at her. Agnieszka Wozniak. Her daughter Kasia was in her class. She smiled back.

When they left the church at the end of mass, Kieran Hayes, one of Tadhg's fellow GAA coaches, came up and gave him a hearty slap on the back, the universal sign of male solidarity, and began chatting away to him about the previous day's Man U match – as if everything was normal and Tadhg wasn't standing in the eye of one of the biggest scandal storms ever to hit the village. Kieran's wife, Claire, came over then and gave Maria a hug, saying in a low aside that she was thinking of them all and hoped they were doing okay. Claire's brother, Niall, was a close friend of Tadhg's; he had probably told her that the American woman had added arms and legs to what had really gone on.

'There'll always be the ones who love to kick people when they're down, but their opinions aren't worth bothering your heads about.'

Maria thanked her and tried not to care about the people who walked past them with their heads down, pretending they didn't see them. People like Anne Sheehan, the receptionist from the GP surgery, and Della Cleary from the dry cleaners, and the woman with the Oompa Loompa tan and the cartoon lips who threw Tadhg a filthy look from under her heavy fake lashes, muttering something vulgar-sounding as she passed.

She was glad Essie had pushed them to go to mass, though. It had been the right thing to do. She felt a tiny bit better as they walked back up the hill towards home, thought she might even drive over to SuperValu in Tower and pick up a nice bit of sirloin to roast for dinner.

But then they got to the house and Eva was waiting for them at the window and then she was at the front door. She was trembling, her face red and tear-stained, crying, 'Why didn't you answer your phones? I've been calling and calling,' and they said they had put their phones on silent in the church and Maria thought *Please, God, I can't take any more.*

CHAPTER 40

Noelle

The sight of the guards at the Murphys' front door yesterday had given her a right jolt; for a split second, she'd thought it was her they were looking for and she'd made herself scarce pretty quickly. It was inevitable that they would come back sniffing around her door now, though, and she needed to talk to her son before that happened. In private. She had hoped the gardaí were just plámásing Dani with their questions because of all the negative publicity she was creating, but the way this bloody thing was going, there was every chance of it turning into a full-blown murder investigation.

When she had heard the knock on the door earlier and glimpsed the flash of neon yellow through the hall glass, she had thrown a coat and scarf on, making it look as if she was on her way out. The lie had glided off her tongue. Visiting her mother before mass. She couldn't remember the last time she'd gone to mass, but that's what had come out of her mouth. They wouldn't suspect a decent mass-going woman of anything bad, would they? They'd agreed to come back this evening, when they could talk to herself and Liam together. *Just making enquiries, a couple of questions, all very informal.* She had watched them go back down her driveway and get into their car as she got into hers to drive to her mother's, in case they were watching her, and wondered what they were saying. *Bit of a coincidence, isn't it? The ex-husband and the guest? Both meeting their death in the same way ...*

She'd give anything to be able to confide in Maria, to have shared her fears with her earlier when they spoke on the phone, but Noelle couldn't talk to anybody about it. Just as she hadn't been able to after Kevin's death. And her friend was in no shape to help anybody else at the moment; she needed Noelle to be there for her. Tadhg had a strong alibi for the period during which Jessie was supposed to have died, but the fact that he had received an email from her and mentioned it to nobody had to be a major red flag for the guards. Could he have got somebody else to ...? No, that was just ridiculous. He might think his balls were hand-stitched, but she really didn't think he'd ever harm anybody, especially a young person who may or may not have been his daughter.

I guess you never know what people are capable of when they're pushed far enough, though.

Dani had been as high as a kite when she came down for breakfast this morning, thrilled to have heard from her solicitor that the guards had called to the Murphys' yesterday, and no doubt equally thrilled about her campaign, which seemed to be really picking up momentum. It was all Noelle could do to be civil to the woman at this stage. She'd happily pay for a return flight to Boston, even drive her up to Shannon Airport, to get her out of everyone's hair. One thing was sure: she'd never be taking a booking from her again.

She checked the kitchen clock. *Where the hell was Liam?*

He had left the house at eight this morning to do a foxer over in Clogheen, but had told her he'd be back by now. She wanted to speak to him in private before Molly came over later. She had just picked up her phone to call him when she heard the scrape of his key in the front door. He padded into the kitchen in his thick work socks, his dirty boots left in the porch.

'Hiya, Mam. Is the kettle on? I'm gaspin'.'

As she filled the kettle from the tap, she gazed out the back window at the smart new decking Liam had put down for her last spring. He had refused to take a penny for his labour and insisted on going halves for the materials. He knew how tight things were for her, making sure he paid for his keep, always throwing her a few bob extra to 'treat yourself to somethin' nice' when he did a cash-in-hand job like today. He was a good lad at heart. But that didn't mean he wasn't capable of making bad decisions, as she knew only too well.

She took a couple of deep breaths, steeling herself for the conversation she needed to have with her son, before turning to put the kettle back on its base and flick it on.

'What's the big emergency, anyway?' Liam asked, taking the milk from the fridge. She never asked him to come home when he was out working, but she'd told him it couldn't wait.

The kettle seemed to take an interminable time to bubble to the boil while she tried to figure out how to broach the subject. There was no taking this back if she was wrong. And dear God, how she hoped she was. But just in case there was the slightest chance, she had to know, had to warn him. Either way, they had to get their stories straight.

'Mam? Are you deaf?'

She rushed the tea, making it far too weak, bringing the mugs over to the table and sitting across from her son. He had his legs out in front of him, crossed at the ankles, showing no inkling that he was in any way concerned.

'The guards were here earlier; they're coming back this evening to talk to us both. About Jessie and her final days in the village.'

He still didn't look the slightest bit alarmed.

'Grand, I've no plans anyway. I'll be here,' he said. 'Have we any biscuits?' He got up and opened the treat press. There were slim pickings in it these days, ever since Noelle had started her new healthy regime, but it would always be known as the treat press.

'Ah, happy days.' He brought a packet of Jaffa Cakes back to the table and opened it, offering it to her. She waved it away. They were the only biscuits she bought anymore, because she knew that no matter how desperate she got, she'd never be tempted by those rotten yokes. Liam swallowed one in two bites.

'They'll probably want to talk to *you* about being with her in the Gab the night before she died.'

'Right, yeah.' He shoved another biscuit into his mouth.

'And your whereabouts around the time of her death. Between three p.m. on Thursday afternoon and three a.m. on Friday.'

Liam picked up the Jaffa Cakes and stared intently at the list of ingredients on the back of the packet. He had uncrossed his feet, stiffened in the chair.

Jesus. She really didn't want to do this, but she had to.

'Where *were* you that night, Liam? You never came home and I know you weren't with Molly.'

He looked at her, dumbfounded.

'Surely you don't think I … *Jesus Christ, Mam! For fuck's sake.*'

'No, of course not, but I need to know *where* you were so we're on the same page for the guards. I heard you telling Molly you went to that party at Deano's with the lads, but you didn't go, did you? Darren dropped you in it rightly that evening in Christy's; you were haunted that Molly didn't hear him. So if you weren't at that party and you weren't with Molly and you weren't here, where the hell were you?'

He leaned forward and grabbed her hands across the table, his eyes wild, pleading. 'I swear on Leon's life I was nowhere near that girl that day. Or that night, Mam. You have to believe me. This isn't like Dad, if that's what you're thinking. I can't tell you where I was, but I wasn't near her or the castle – and Mam, I need you to tell the cops I was here all night.'

CHAPTER 41

Dani

'Dani! C'mere, girl. Have you seen this?'

Howls of laughter erupted from the high table where Rory was sitting in the middle of a group of men of varying ages, sizes and shapes. All drinking pints and looking at their phones.

'Hop up there, love. Ger'll be along in a while.' He pushed a free stool towards her. She perched uncomfortably on it; she hated stools, especially ones like this with no back. She had a profound fear of toppling over and ending up sprawled on the floor on the flat of her back.

'What'll you have?' Rory asked.

'Um, just a coffee thanks. I want to order some food.' This was her third evening in a row in the Gab; she had met up with Rory and Ger and their friends last night and they'd invited her to join them again this evening. It was far better to be out than stuck in the B&B, where she was persona non grata, but she needed to take it easy on the alcohol. She'd been pretty hammered last night.

'Ara, you'll have something stronger than that. I'll call you a Bud, will I? It's probably a bit early to start on the hard stuff.

You were fairly knocking the JD and Cokes back last night,' he said, smiling and winking at her.

'Okay, I'll take a bottle of Bud, thanks.' She really needed to order food soon, didn't want to start drinking on an empty belly. She'd gone back to bed for a nap after breakfast – having been up until after two a.m. reading comments and emails when she got home last night – and then fallen into a deep sleep, missing lunch.

'Davey, bottle of Bud, buddy, and same again,' he said, indicating the group with a twirl of his finger.

The other guys were still looking at their phone, whooping and shouting things like 'This is fuckin' hilarious, boy' and 'Fuckin' class'.

'You have to see this, girl. Poor aul Mr Murphy is goin' to lose his shit,' Rory said, handing her his phone. It was open on a website called thetouchyteacher.info: she was looking at a photo of Tadhg Murphy, dressed smartly in a jacket and chinos, the school in the background. Imposed over the image was a logo in the school colours. *The* in grey, *Touchy* in maroon and *Teacher* in white.

The caption on the photo read: *'Principal of St Vincent's Secondary School, Blarney, Tadhg Murphy, prides himself on his hands-on approach to education, especially when it comes to his female students.'*

Dani felt a swell of disquiet in her empty stomach. She scrolled down.

The always impeccably groomed Mr Murphy has a real good feel for his female students and can smell what they really want deep down. So dedicated is he to his job that he likes to bring his work home with him, not even switching off in bed.

A bottle of Bud was placed in front of her and she put it to her lips.

'Keep scrolling down,' Rory said. 'It gets even better.'

There was a series of photos of Tadhg at various school events, one where he had an arm around a student, his hand cupping a breast, another where he was groping the ass of a girl in a cheerleader's skirt and another of him with his hand up a girl's skirt. The videos and images had clearly been doctored, the faces of the girls pixellated to make them unidentifiable.

It was repulsive. She felt the blood pounding in her temples, sweat breaking out all over her body.

'Who did this?' she asked.

'I dunno, probably some kids from the school,' Rory said. 'They'd buy and sell us when it comes to this kind of stuff. Brilliant, isn't it?'

She took another drink, spluttering as it went down the wrong way.

'D'you not think it's funny?' Rory asked.

'No, I really don't.'

'Why not? He deserves it after what he did to you, shur. You shouldn't feel a bit bad for the dirty fucker.'

'It's not … It's … What he did to me was real, okay? This' – she nodded at the phone – 'is just making a joke out of it. And it's revolting. Those photos … He's got kids in that school who could see this.'

'Don't you be feeling sorry for that fucker, Dani, after what he did to you, takin' advantage of you and you only a child. I know what I'd fuckin' do to him if he went near a kid of mine. I'd rip the cunt's balls off him.'

She winced. She was used to guys like Rory from the bars back home, all talk when they had booze in them, but he was getting so worked up, as if it had been his own child Tadhg Murphy had groomed and fucked – even though as far as she knew, he didn't even have kids.

'Rory, this makes him look like a total pervert. It wasn't like that. He did lead me on; he did … groom me …' That word still felt uncomfortable to say. 'But he never actually touched me in that way while I was in school and I never heard about him bein' with any of the other girls. It was just me.'

'Sorry to tell you, love, but it's highly unlikely you were his only victim. Guys like that, they're fuckin' predators. Evil they are, scum.'

Dani scrolled further down, fanning her flaming cheeks with a laminated menu. An accusation by Dani De Marco of a sexual assault against her in Boston in 2001, which resulted in a pregnancy. Claims of Mr Murphy's touchy-feely style of teaching were *corroborated* by a number of people, including his wife, Mrs Murphy, a teacher herself, who agreed that she was 'far too old to satisfy her husband's needs but happy for him to throw himself fully into his female students', and a number of former students who all claimed to have been impregnated by him. There were photos of girls in their school uniforms, faces blurred again, with photoshopped pregnancy bumps.

Jesus Christ. This was taking things way too far.

'Oh, and Dani.' Rory whispered into her ear, his wet lips grazing her skin, making her flinch. 'That business we were talkin' about last night – it's been taken care of, girl.'

Business? Fuck. That had just been drunk talk; she didn't think they were actually going to …

She knocked back the rest of her beer and started on another bottle that had appeared on the table in front of her. She needed to relax, to drown out the voice telling her she was starting to lose her grip on things. She couldn't do anything about it, anyway. That site was nothing to do with her. And she hadn't given Rory and Ger the go-ahead for anything; whatever they had done was on them.

The conversation around her had moved on to soccer and then a story about some guy they knew who had shifted – which Rory, seeing her confused face, said meant making out – a man dressed as a woman who 'you'd want to have been blind not to realise was a man', and then they were on to Boston and they all seemed to have an uncle or a cousin or some sort of relative living there. Somebody else handed her a beer, and her tension started to ease and she joined in the laughter. A couple of the guys left over the course of the evening and Ger arrived, grabbing her in a hug as if they were long-lost friends. At some point, she ordered a burger and chips – nobody else seemed to have any interest in food – and, too full to keep drinking beer after that, she switched to bourbon.

As she weaved her way to the restroom at the back of the bar, she thought of how at home Jessie must have felt here. Being made to feel so welcome by people, as if they had known her for years. Sure, the sparkle would probably have worn off a bit over time, but her daughter could have been really happy here. And maybe she could be too. After all, it wasn't as if there was anything or anyone waiting for her at home.

She was on her way back to her new friends when Mark, the

owner of the bar who had given her the complimentary meal the first day she went in, approached her. 'Sorry Dani, could I have a quick word?' He guided her into a private alcove under the stairs out of view of the front bar.

'I hope you don't think I'm oversteppin' the mark here or anything, but I just wanted to ...' He looked intensely awkward. 'Look, I just think you should know that those lads you're with, Rory Ahern and that lot ... Well, I wouldn't be taking too much heed of any advice they might be giving you.'

'What do you mean?'

'Look, they're good customers and they don't cause me too much trouble, but they're neck-deep in all the anti-immigrant protests goin' on over here at the moment. Rory's got totally carried away with it. And you didn't hear this from me, now, but he and one of his nephews were arrested and questioned over the arson of a hotel up the Kerry Road last week.'

'No way! I heard about that on the radio.'

'Yeah, well, he was apparently one of the organisers. Goadin' young lads full of drink and God knows what else into flingin' bottles at the gardaí and firemen up there. A security guard was taken to hospital with injuries and a squad car was set on fire, a grand hotel burnt to the ground. It was lucky somebody wasn't seriously hurt. So I just wanted to mark your card for you. I know you're goin' through a tough aul time yourself and I just ... well, maybe they're not the best people to be surroundin' yourself with at the moment.'

It felt as if he had stuck a pin in her, bursting the warm, floaty bubble of her delusion, leaving her on her own again. Out in the cold. What the hell was it about her that attracted people like this to her? What kind of weird vibes did she give off? Why was she such a shitty judge of character?

'I'm sorry, now. I hope I haven't upset you, but ...'

'No, no. You were right to tell me, I appreciate it. Could you get my bill ready for me, please?'

She walked back to the table and, fake-yawning, picked up her jacket.

'Time to call it a night, I'm afraid, gentlemen. I've hit a wall.'

'Ah, Dani, you'll have one more. I never even got a chance to talk to you about your campaign. I've a few ideas about—'

'Another time, Rory, when I've less alcohol on board,' she said, forcing a smile onto her shaky lips.

One of the younger bar staff dropped her food bill off as he was passing and said he'd be back with a card reader. Rory wanted to take care of it, but she insisted there was no need. She pulled her coat on after paying and eventually managed to get away, after having to repeat a number of times that she really didn't want 'one for the road'.

Outside, it was dark and miserable, spitting rain.

Shit.

She had left her scarf inside. She really didn't want to go back in and have to go through another long rigmarole of goodbyes, but it was the Burberry cashmere one she had bought on sale at Neiman Marcus. She was standing in the entrance porch, wondering what the chances were that Rory or one of his friends would hand the scarf in behind the bar if they noticed it, when she heard her phone ring.

It was after eleven. Who'd be calling her at this time of night?

Shit. It must be someone from home.

She rooted around in her purse for the phone, but by the time she found it in her pocket, it had stopped. She was alarmed to see she had four missed calls from Joe. And a message in capital letters. ANSWER YOUR GODDAMN PHONE!!

Oh God. The baby.

A cold, sickening dread gripped her insides.

Something must have happened. Her chilled older brother would never send a message like that if it wasn't serious. He'd messaged her yesterday to say they were due to bring the baby home from hospital today, that she was doing good.

Mamma.

The dread squeezed tighter.

She called her brother back, begging God not to have let anything bad happen to the baby. Or to Mamma without her getting to say goodbye. Despite everything, she couldn't bear it if she didn't get to say goodbye. What if the shock of losing Jessie so suddenly had caused her to have a heart attack or a stroke or something?

The call connected.

'Joe. What's wrong? Is everything okay?'

'Why the hell haven't you been answerin' your phone, Dani? I've been tryin' to get hold of you for hours. I called the B&B and the lady there said you left hours ago and she didn't know where you were.'

'I'm sorry, I went out for dinner and stayed on for a couple of beers.' She tried to sound sober. 'What's happened? Is the baby okay?'

'The baby's fine. What I want to know is what the hell is going on over there? I had some guy call me earlier from IrishCentral lookin' for your number and when I asked him why, he said he was doing a story about your campaign for Jessie. I told him I'd have to call him back, then when I couldn't get you, I googled it and found a big article about you and your *campaign* on the *Irish Examiner.* What the fuck, Dani? What the hell are you up to now?'

CHAPTER 42

Maria
Monday, 22 January

How had this happened to them? This time two weeks ago, they'd been living their normal lives, sweating the small stuff, completely oblivious to the tornado that was tracking its way towards them. What she'd give now to wedge herself back into that safe, boring rut she'd been whining about, to teleport out of this hellish reality they found themselves in. Her children couldn't go to school, and she couldn't even go to the shop for milk, never mind work, in case she bumped into somebody she knew.

Even trapped within their own four walls, they weren't safe from the hatred of the vile, disgusting trolls and the poisonous darts shot from the cesspits of their monstrous minds. The only troll Maria had feared as a child was the one who lived under the bridge and who drowned at the end of the fairytale, leaving the three Billy Goats Gruff free to eat grass on the other side of the bridge and live happily ever after. The trolls that lived in her children's world, though, weren't quite so easy to get rid of. She had warned the kids not to look at the stuff that was being posted and shared about their father, tried to get them to stay off social media for the time being, but asking this generation's teenagers to stay off TikTok and Snapchat was almost like asking them to cut off their oxygen supply.

She had heard a psychologist on radio saying one of the worst things you could do to your teenage child was take their phone away: in doing so, you were taking away their whole ecosystem and friend network. While she could quite happily come off all social media and ignore the online world herself, asking digital natives like Eva and Ben to do that would be like asking them to move to another planet.

She kept hoping that they were in the eye of the storm now, that there wasn't still worse to come, and tried to focus on the people who had gathered around them, the ones who couldn't do enough for them. The ones who really mattered, as Essie would always say. The ones who were on to her constantly, letting her know they'd be there at the drop of a hat if she needed them. Like Fiona, who yesterday had dropped in some fruit and a loaf of her lovely homemade brown bread, along with a box of cupcakes for the kids. And Lorraine, who'd told her she'd pick up anything they needed from the shops, even offering to do a full grocery shop for her. Tadhg's closest friends too, most of them going back years, had rallied around him, a few of them calling over last night for a few beers. They'd been unable to convince him to show his face in his local this weekend, Casey's bar being the place where this had all started, when Dani had first set eyes on him again.

Maria was aware she needed to push her own fears aside now and find out what the hell was going on with Ben, because she could no longer ignore the fact that there was clearly something. It seemed to go much deeper than disgust at his father for sleeping with a former student, almost as if he somehow knew something the rest of them didn't.

She would never be able to shake the image of her son flying down the stairs into the hall after mass yesterday when they were consoling Eva over that stomach-turning website, his face beetroot-red, eyes spitting fire. His fury aimed not at Dani, as Maria had anticipated, but his father.

'This is all your fault. I fucking hate you!' They had all looked at Ben in shock, never having heard him raise his voice or swear at his father like that before.

'Ben,' Essie had said sharply, the rest of them rendered mute. 'We know this is really hard on you, but that doesn't mean it's alright to talk to your daddy like that. We need to stick together as a family, not let that woman's lies start tear—'

'But they're not lies,' Ben shouted, crying now. 'Are they? *Dad?* Go on, tell them. Why don't you?'

Tadhg, grey-faced, had rocked on his heels, his mouth hanging open as if it were broken at the hinges.

'That's enough, Ben,' Maria had said, tears spilling uncontrollably down her cheeks. What was happening to them? 'Please, go back up to your room. I'll be up to you when you've had time to calm down.' He was probably just overwrought by everything that was going on, the photoshopped images of his father sleazing all over teenage school girls the final straw. Please let that be what this was.

Ben had looked his father in the eye and, quieter now, his voice shaking, said: 'Get a paternity test so and we'll see who's lying and who's telling the truth.' Then he had turned on his heels and gone back up the stairs.

Tadhg had stared after him in shocked confusion, saying nothing.

When Maria went up to Ben half an hour later, after she'd finally managed to get Eva to stop crying, he had refused to talk about it – had refused even to come out from under the covers, where she knew he was only pretending to be asleep.

She had left him alone, and was planning to try again today. After she spoke to her mother-in-law.

'I'm just going to pop into your mum to see how she's doing,' she said now to Tadhg, who was tapping away at his laptop on the island.

'I can do that, love, if you like,' he said. 'I'm just checking emails.'

'She shook her head. 'No, you stay there. I need to get out of the house, even if it's only just next-door.'

As she picked up her phone to take with her, afraid to be parted from it in case something else happened, it beeped. Her gut clenched, as it did any time her phone made a sound now, her adrenal system stuck on red alert.

Please let it be a message from Noelle or one of the girls just checking in.

It was a WhatsApp message. From Eva.

Oh God!

A screenshot.

Comments from a Reddit thread about 'The Touchy Teacher'.

Her phone buzzed again.

Another screenshot, more comments.

Her bowel muscles squeezed tighter as she read.

Rebelyeller23 Dat daughter of his is a fine bit a stuff, wonder if he's had a go off of her yet

Queenofsorrows_99 Hear he's been suspended. Shd be fired. No way that yoke shd be let anywhere near young girls. Wonder how many more baby mamas going to come out of the woodwork now!

She forced herself to keep reading, needing to know what her daughter had seen, trying to breathe deeply to ward off another panic attack.

Bawlsofsteel Judges in Ireland far to easy on pedo scum, why viglanties has to take matters into der own hands

Sliotarhead Those bleedin vigilante groups do more harm than good. They've made loads of wrong calls, harassed innocent people online and reported their names and addresses and made them targets

Maria dropped her phone and leant forward, dry-heaving.
'What is it, love?' Tadhg asked.
She shook her head, unable to talk, handing him her phone. No matter what happened now, every word of this was out there for ever. Their kids exposed to the vile, disgusting content of some truly warped winds. Tadhg had been named on TikTok and Snapchat and there were fake videos of him circulating. He had been moaning in his sleep last night; she'd had to wake him to tell him he was dreaming. His pillow was soaked this morning, and the sheets beneath him. This was the

stuff suicides were made of. If he didn't drop dead of a heart attack first. He had always been a strong, fit man but this kind of relentless stress, day after day, was brutal.

'Jesus Christ,' he said. 'How the hell do we make this stop?'

'There might be a way.' It had been playing on her mind since that radio interview on Friday, and then Ben had brought it up again last night. 'How are you so sure that Jessie wasn't yours?'

'Because we were only together that one night, love, and I used protection, and a girl like Dani, well, you can be sure I wasn't the only one she was sleeping with. She was pretty wild.'

'Even if you only did it once, Tadhg, and she'd been sleeping all round Boston, there could still be a chance it was yours.'

'It wasn't, Maria. You saw her photo. That girl looks nothing like me, nothing like any of my family. There's no resemblance whatsoever.'

'Well then, maybe Ben is right.'

'What?'

'Maybe you should get a paternity test. The only way to make this stop is to prove to them that you're not Jessie's father.'

She needed to divert the guards away from her family. Just in case the awful thing she was thinking was true.

CHAPTER 43

Dani
Can you please answer your phone? I just need to run through the schedule for the PM tomorrow.

She was in Casey's hotel having coffee, avoiding the Gab and her new *friends*, when she got the message from her attorney.

She had been dodging his calls again, knowing he'd more than likely be losing his shit over her YouTube post about the cease-and-desist letter and was probably calling to tell her he could no longer represent her. She couldn't afford, quite literally, to just sit on her ass and do nothing. Her request for a second autopsy having been completely disregarded, she was going to have to foot the bill herself.

On a more positive note, the word was really starting to spread about her campaign now. Benny Mac had shared clips of her interview on his own Insta and TikTok accounts and they'd already had hundreds of shares. Her Facebook group had jumped to over 1,000 new members over the weekend, #justiceforjessie was being shared across all platforms and her GoFundMe had raised nearly €5,000.

She should have been thrilled at this success. Instead, she'd spent a restless and fretful night, her brother's furious words going round and round in her head.

'You need to get your ass back over here,' Joe had spat, 'and bring Jessie's ashes with you so we can commemorate her where she rightly belongs and start to grieve for her. If you're not back here by the end of the week, Daniela, so help me God, I'll come over there and drag you back myself. But if you make me leave Laurie and the baby to come and pull you out of another fuckin' mess, I'll be even more pissed than I already am. Ya got me?'

She had tried to protest, to say this wasn't like the last time, that she was telling the truth, but he wouldn't listen.

'I don't care, Daniela. You're a forty-year-old woman, for cryin' out loud. You ain't a kid no more. You need to get your goddamn life together and stop your crap, before you put Mamma into an early grave.'

He had hung up on her then, left her standing outside the pub in tears. Joe had never spoken to her like that before. He'd always been the one who had her back, even when the other boys and their snooty wives had turned their backs on her. No matter how many times this had happened to her before though, she had always been able to run to Joe. Steady, solid Joe. The eternal bachelor. Until Laurie had swept the legs out from under him, surprising nobody more than himself. And now he was a father and it looked like he too was turning on her. Story of her life. Being dumped on the scrap heap.

She had walked back to the B&B, barely able to see the sidewalk in front of her through her tears. Incapable of understanding how he could be so cruel at the lowest point of her life, when she had never needed him more.

She had texted him in the early hours of the morning, too distressed to sleep.

I can't believe you could be so cruel when I've just lost my baby girl. I'm so crushed

He had sent a terse, cold reply.

Get some sleep and we'll talk tomorrow about making arrangements to get you home.

She had known her brother wouldn't be too happy about the media publicity around her campaign, which was why she hadn't planned on telling him until she'd achieved a positive result. She'd never thought the media back home would have picked up on the story; she just hoped they didn't start digging any further. All she wanted was answers about her daughter's death.

What if I'm wrong, though, and it wasn't Tadhg Murphy Jessie was planning to meet that day?

What if it was just an accident?

What if the Globe *drags all that other shit up again?*

No! She couldn't allow these doubts to unnerve her now. Couldn't even entertain the idea that she might be in the middle of the biggest fuck-up of her life – and God knows, that would be saying something.

She dialled the attorney's number back.

'Dani.'

'Hi, Brian, sorry I've—'

'Look, I'm just going into a meeting here, but I wanted to let you know that Mr Russell is planning to start the post-mortem at eleven tomorrow and should be finished up around two, all going according to plan. He'll send me a short preliminary report afterwards and his full report by the end of next week, along with his invoice.'

'Great, thanks.'

'Also, I just had a call before lunch from a Sergeant Ryan at Gurranabraher station. You wouldn't know anything about an anonymous call to the gardaí yesterday making some very serious allegations about Tadhg Murphy?'

'An anonymous call? No. What kind of allegations?' She was glad they were speaking on the phone because her face, flooding with blood, would have ratted her out.

'The sergeant said he wasn't at liberty to disclose any details at this time, apart from the fact it was made by a woman. I just wanted to check if you had any knowledge of the call. Just in case.'

In case of what?

She wanted to ask him if they could trace it but didn't want to raise his suspicions and couldn't trust her voice to come out right.

What the hell had Rory and Ger done?

They were the ones who had suggested that maybe it was time for more of Tadhg's *victims* to come out of the woodwork. It was nothing to do with her.

'He mentioned there's been some pretty vicious trolling of Mr Murphy and his family as a result of your *campaign*,' Brian said sharply, 'and some nasty graffiti outside their home.'

She felt bad about the trolling. Tadhg's wife and kids were total innocents. She'd had a taste of it herself and it wasn't nice. It wasn't her fault that some people were turning #justiceforjessie into a Tadhg Murphy witch hunt, though. That had never been her intention. All she wanted was to get to the truth about what had happened to her child. She had been forced to go public – and okay, maybe stretch things just a teensy bit – to get people to listen to her. She had no control over the trolls of this world.

The pathologist would be in Cork tomorrow to do the second post-mortem and she was hopeful that he would find something to validate her concerns. It wasn't that she wanted anything bad to have happened to Jessie, of course not, but if it had, she had to ensure the perpetrator didn't get away with it. Whether that was Tadhg Murphy or not.

CHAPTER 44

Noelle

She really should have offered to call over to Maria. If it had been the other way around, her friend would have been banging her door down, but after the conversation with Liam yesterday, Noelle was afraid she wouldn't be able to hide her own worry from her friend.

Her son's words kept replaying in her mind, a horrible skipping record.

... I'm sorry, Mam. I've fucked up ...

... real bad ...

... need you to tell the cops I was here all night ...

... swear on Leon's life I was nowhere near that girl that day ...

The blast of déjà vu that had hit her as she looked into his frantic eyes had been so strong it made her head spin.

Bringing her back, back ...

Back to the day of her former husband's death, and the last time Liam had asked her to lie about his whereabouts.

That had been an accident too. Kevin had been pissed out of his mind, nothing new there. Had lost his footing at the top of the stairs outside the rented kip of a flat he had ended up in after his last lady friend got sense and threw him out.

Her Liam was a good lad; he wouldn't harm a fly. He had only been watching out for her.

She had been inconsolable after Kevin's visit earlier that day. The callous way in which her estranged husband had sat in her kitchen, sober as a judge although his breath still reeked from the previous night's drink, and told her he wanted his half of the value of the house. It was an eventuality she hadn't even allowed herself to think about, otherwise she wouldn't have been able to keep going day after day, struggling to pull herself out of the pit he'd left her in.

They had taken out a joint mortgage on the house initially, but they had been forced to remortgage: although she had worked her arse off in the B&B, they couldn't meet the repayments on the income she made while her husband drank and whored his way around the village.

'But I can't afford ... Where do you expect me to get that kind of money?' She had been gobsmacked at the casual way he had made his request, as if he was looking for her to go halves on a lawnmower or something. Not her beloved home, her livelihood, their children's inheritance.

The B&B had just about been washing its own face over the last couple of years, with enough on top of the monthly mortgage payments to support her and the kids. She had tried to put a bit extra aside every month, but it was inevitably eaten up by some unforeseen expense; the washing machine packed up or the car broke down or the electric shower in one of the guest rooms needed to be replaced.

She had been the sole breadwinner in the house for years. Kevin, when he had lived there, had been too unreliable to hold down any kind of meaningful employment. Such a sad waste of potential. He had been a talented sportsman in his youth, skilled at whatever he put his hand or foot to. Hurling, football, soccer, basketball. The life and soul of every party with his cheeky grin and loud, hearty laugh.

Noelle had been stone mad about him back then. She had asked him to her debs and he had said yes and they had been a couple after that. He got a bit messy the night of the debs but he certainly wasn't the only one. They were all big drinkers, the lads he hung around with. Many, like him, were chippies and brickies, sparkies and plumbers. They all liked to party, and indeed so had Noelle and the rest of the girlfriends, but while most of the other lads had settled down over the years as they got married and started families, Kevin had never really grown up. Noelle blamed his mother. As far as she was concerned, her son could do no wrong, not even when she caught him as a grown man, with two children of his own, riffling through her purse for money to squander on booze.

'Maybe you could release some equity, or remortgage or something?' he had suggested. 'Or sell the place and buy somewhere smaller? It's far too big for just you and Liam now. He shouldn't be still livin' at home at his age anyway.'

She had stared at him in utter disgust. This sorry sack of shit who cared about nobody but himself – and who would piss away every last cent of any money he got out of her – had the cheek to cast aspersions on their son, who despite not having had a father in any real sense of the word, had turned out a hardworking, decent young man.

'This is my livelihood. How the hell do you expect me to survive if I sell the B&B? This place needs so much work ... I wouldn't be able to afford to buy anywhere else, not even an apartment, with what we'd get for it.'

'You'd get a job in Centra no problem sure, or one of the hotels.'

'Jesus Christ, Kevin, you can't do this. After everything you've put me through, me *and* the kids, you can't take the roof from over our heads. I've worked myself to the bone to make this place work, not just for myself but for the kids. I've pretty much reared Liam and Holly alone, while supporting us all. Please, I'm begging you, don't do this.'

'Look, Noelle, I'm not trying to take the roof from over your head,' he said, scratching a knot in the wood of the table, 'but I'm entitled to it. Rory Ahern's cousin's a family law solicitor and he was sayin'—'

'Rory fuckin' Ahern! You've got to be kiddin'. Have you gone that low that you're taking advice from that scumbag? He's been trouble his whole life, just like his father and his brothers and their kids now too. All that conspiracy theory crap they were spouting during Covid—'

'Ah, stop would you, Rory's sound out like. He's only tryin' to help—'

'Get out.' She couldn't even look at him.

'Look, Noelle, we need to—'

She stood up and shoved her chair back, its legs screeching against the tiles, and pointed her finger at him.

'Get the fuck out of this house and don't ever come back here again!' she roared.

He had left with his tail between his legs, but she knew she hadn't heard the end of the matter. He might not have the balls to come back himself, but if he had a family law solicitor advising him, it was only a matter of time before some sort of legal letter came in her door. The law didn't give a shit whether you stuck to your marriage vows or not; after all, you could still murder your wife in this country and profit from her death at that stage.

She had been sitting at the table with her head in her hands when Liam arrived in a few moments later and found her. He had met his father in the driveway, ignoring him as he had done ever since the day he'd found out about Kevin's cheating.

'What's wrong, Mam? What's he done now?'

So she told him.

Her son had been like a bull, unsurprisingly. He had called to his father that night, determined to have it out with him. Kevin hadn't been there when Liam arrived, so he had waited around the side of the large, rundown house that had been converted into a number of makeshift bedsits and rented out to men like his father. Men with addictions and mental illness and anger issues, who had pushed their families beyond breaking point and been thrown out of their homes.

Liam told her he had waited in the shadows for his father to root around in his pockets for the key, make a number of attempts to get it into the lock and then finally open the door. Then he had pushed his way into the flat behind him, shoving his father up against the wall and warning him to stay the fuck away from his mother and their home or he would 'do time' for him. Kevin, the big man when he was full of drink, had followed his son out onto the landing, roaring slurred gibberish after him about his rights and who the hell did he think he was talking to him like that.

Liam was at the front door when he heard the thump and turned to see his father tumbling arse over head down the bare wooden stairs. He landed sideways on the bottom step with his neck twisted at an angle that no human neck had any business being at. Liam had stood there for a few seconds, checking to make sure he was dead, before he turned towards the door again and left as quietly as he had arrived. 'Even if I hadn't been sure, I wouldn't have called an ambulance for the cunt,' he had told her when he got home.

Noelle would have lied to the guards for her son, but when they called to her door later that night, it wasn't to talk to Liam, but to impart the sad news of the demise of her former husband. She acted suitably upset – not overly so, they were going through a separation, after all – and said she would break it to the kids herself. She and Liam had waited anxiously for the guards to come back asking questions about a row outside Kevin's flat that night, and had their stories well-rehearsed, but it never happened. Maybe the other men in the house hadn't heard anything, maybe they didn't want to get involved or maybe they thought Kevin had been ráiméising with the drink again. The verdict at the inquest was death by misadventure; Kevin's alcohol levels had been three times the legal driving limit. There was never any doubt it was anything other than a fall.

Herself and Liam began to breathe easy again.

Some time after that, she had been watching an American true-crime documentary on TV one night with Liam and Holly. The pathologist and detective were standing in the morgue discussing the cause of death of the body on the slab.

'Could he have been pushed?' the detective had asked, in a strong New York drawl. 'He and his wife had a rocky relationship.'

'Sure he could have, but good luck proving it,' the female pathologist had replied. 'A push is one of the hardest crimes to solve, as you well know.'

Noelle had believed her son when he told her his father's fall was an accident, and even if he had pushed Kevin, she'd have stood by him. But now Liam had asked her to lie for him again. And this time was different. This time an innocent young woman with her whole life ahead of her was dead.

Had her son been involved with Jessie? Had she threatened to expose their relationship to Molly?

He loved Molly, adored Leon. He wouldn't want anything to put that at risk. He'd never have deliberately set out to hurt the girl, but what if it had been an accident? What if he had grabbed her or pushed her without meaning for her to fall down those steps?

Surely, though, if Liam had been responsible for a young woman's death, he wouldn't have been able to hide that from her? He hadn't been acting any differently since Jessie's death, had been showing no sign at all that he was unduly upset or feeling guilty about anything. And he wouldn't have sworn on his baby's life if he had been lying, would he?

She had told her son she was prepared to tell the guards he'd been at home with her on the night of Jessie's death, but only if he told her the truth about where he had actually been. He just kept saying he was sorry, that he'd fucked up, and then he'd said something that made her blood run cold.

'If Molly found out, Mam, she'd never let me see Leon again.'

So when the guards had called yesterday evening, of course she'd lied for him.

CHAPTER 45

Maria
Tuesday, 23 January

She stood at her bedroom window looking down over the village, where life was going on as normal for everybody else while she and her children were prisoners in their own home and her husband had had to force himself to go into work. Could it really have been less than two weeks ago that she had stood in this spot on a beautiful winter's morning, watching all the activity going on around the castle and hoping nobody they knew had been hurt?

It was a miserable morning out, raincoat and wellies weather. A faded white sky draped low over the castle, the hills shrouded in fog. Lashing rain was being driven sideways by a heavy wind, the trees at the back of the church swaying and bending beneath its force. A woman dashed from her car to the supermarket with a shopping bag over her head; another battled with an inside-out umbrella she'd been foolish enough to try to put up. Everybody else was in their cars, wipers flicking back and forth. Even Billy Walsh was nowhere to be seen; he must be taking shelter in the bookie's while he waited for the pub to open.

It was 10:40. Small break would just be over. The children hated days like this when it was too wet to go outside. Poor Dylan would be like a caged animal. She hoped her substitute would be patient with him; there hadn't been time to do a proper handover and his new SNA wasn't hectic. Maria would have to email her stand-in a more detailed list of instructions. It was very important that Dylan be brought for a time-out break at least once every two hours, especially if they were stuck inside at break time. To 'say it, write it and repeat it' when giving him an oral instruction, and to encourage him to complete whatever he was doing. He was a child who thrived on praise and positive language, like many kids with his issues.

She had almost envied Tadhg going off to work this morning although it wouldn't be easy having to endure the sniggering looks and whispers of hundreds of smart-arsed teenagers. Sitting at home waiting for the next axe to fall on them was pure torture too, but she couldn't leave Eva and Ben, not in the state they were in at the moment. They needed her at home for the rest of the week at least, and after that, who knew what was going to happen? The kids couldn't stay off school indefinitely; she couldn't stay off work. The uncertainly about what was going to happen was a killer.

The kids hadn't surfaced yet, although she had heard sounds of activity from Eva's room. There was silence from Ben's room, which could mean he was still asleep or that he was awake and plugged into some device or another. Today was his suspension day. He wouldn't have gone in anyway, but it would be on his record now.

Tadhg still hadn't done anything about the paternity test. He needed to get Justine to contact Dani's solicitor for permission to take a swab from the body. Maria had googled it: it was just like doing a Covid test. She was going to insist he asked for it today, and hope to God it wouldn't backfire on them. If Dani refused to agree to it, that would tell a lot in itself. Maybe there was some way of forcing her to cooperate, given the allegations she was making against Tadhg. They'd have to check with Justine.

She was at the top of the stairs when the doorbell rang, freezing her in her tracks.

Please don't let it be the guards back again.

She quickly checked the Ring app on her phone, and released her breath. A Tesco van was parked on the road outside their gate, a delivery driver lifting a blue crate out the side of it.

She had never been so grateful for something to keep her busy as she unpacked the shopping and put the groceries in their allotted spots in the fridge and the freezer and the cupboards. She preferred going to the supermarket herself, hand-picking the fruit and veg to make sure it was fresh and selecting the meat with the longest use-by dates, but right now, she couldn't imagine being able to do anything as normal as grocery shopping again.

That job done and her email about Dylan winging its way to the school, she picked up her phone to ring Noelle. She hadn't heard from her since yesterday afternoon, which was strange. Her friend knew how upset she had been over the vile trolling. She would normally at the very least have called back, and more than likely would have offered to call round to her for tea and sympathy. Maybe the stress of having Dani under her roof, while at the same time witnessing the devastation she was wreaking on Maria and her family, was taking its toll on her. Maybe Maria was leaning on her too much. But she needed to unburden herself to somebody outside the family and Noelle had always been that person. Lorraine and Fiona were great too, but Noelle was the only one who knew her nearly as well as she knew herself. She couldn't tell Noelle about the worst of her fears at the moment, though – couldn't talk to anybody about that until after she'd spoken to Essie. Betty had been in with her mother-in-law yesterday when Maria had called in, so she hadn't yet had a chance to ask her about the day the American girl had died.

Unable to put it off any longer, she made herself a mug of coffee and brought it in next door with her, along with a couple of tubs of fresh berries she had ordered for Essie. Her mother-in-law was at the sink, up to her elbows in suds, scrubbing at one of the glass shelves from her fridge – clearly trying to keep herself distracted as well.

She was some woman really. When Tadhg's father Jim died suddenly of a massive stroke only a year after he'd retired as manager of the local credit union, it had come as a complete shock to them all. He had given up smoking twenty years earlier, wasn't a big drinker and walked for an hour every day unless it was bucketing down. Once she'd done her grieving, Essie had picked herself up and got on with things, filling the absence left by her husband with outings with friends, an annual trip to see Gavin in New York and personal training sessions in a local gym, after she'd read that lifting weights for a year in your mid-sixties could preserve the strength of your leg muscles for years to come. She exercised every second day now, using a resistance band at home and putting Maria, whose only exercise was the short walk to and from school every day, to shame.

'Well, love, any news?' she asked, rinsing the suds off her hands and wiping them on her apron.

'No. The kids are still in bed and Tadhg's gone into work. I'm just so worried about what might happen next, Essie.'

She didn't want to offload on Tadhg's mother again, but she'd go insane if she didn't talk to somebody. 'I'm trying not to look at the stuff that's being posted online, especially the really bad stuff, but one woman who has a daughter in St Vincent's is calling for a protest at the school and another couple of parents have said they'd support her. And if that happens, how can Tadhg keep going in and—'

'Of course you're worried, love,' Essie said, gripping her hands. 'We all are, but you'll be no good to anybody if you let people like that into your head. No matter what happens, Maria, we'll get through this together.'

'How are we ever going to be able to move on from it though, even if the guards are satisfied it was an accident? The rumours and the gossip will never go away; all that awful stuff on the internet will be out there for ever.'

'When you get to my age, Maria, you tend to care a lot less about people's opinions. At the end of the day, the only people we need to worry about are the ones closest to us – our family and friends – and the ones who aren't even that close to us but who've shown us such kindness over the last couple of weeks. Like Lucy Daly from the florist, who arrived at my door yesterday with that beautiful bunch of lilies, and that girl who sent you the lovely message.' Maria had received a text message from the mother of a friend of Eva's who she didn't know very well, saying she was thinking of her and offering to have Eva over to their house any time.

'I know it's not easy,' Essie continued, 'but as I keep reminding myself, nobody has died and nobody is seriously ill. Did I tell you I got a call yesterday from a woman I know who lost two sons in the last seven years to suicide, and *she* wanted to know how *I* was doing? Life hands us all crosses to bear. I'd far rather carry this one than the loss of any of my children or grandchildren.'

Her mother-in-law was right. If anything ever happened to Eva or Ben, they'd never get over it.

'Essie, I need to ask you something.'

'What is it, love?'

'You know that Thursday night that Ben stayed here? The night Jessie died. He'd gone out somewhere: he didn't answer his phone when I tried to get hold of him and then he sent me a message to say he was staying with you.'

Essie nodded.

'I saw his tracksuit on the clothes horse and I was wondering why you washed it.'

Dread filled every fibre of her being as she watched her mother-in-law pull two chairs out from the table and sit on one of them. Maria sat on the other.

Essie let out a small sigh. 'Look, I only agreed to cover for him on the condition that he promised to have nothing more to do with those blaggards he was hanging out with. He was in such a state when he came into me that night, near hysterical. Shaking and crying. Saying his dad would kill him if he found out. I know it was wrong to keep it from you, but I'd never seen the child so upset, so I gave him my word. I thought it was worth it to get him away from that gang.'

That gang. Harry Ahern and them. What the hell had they got her son involved in? 'Oh God, Essie. What did he do?'

'You know that fire up at the Lodge? Well, Ben was up there that night with those lads. He said they'd all been drinking, including him. Their older brothers and uncles were all involved in the 'protest', as they called it – I think one of them was one of the organisers. Ben said he was in total shock when he saw the hotel going up in flames; he'd had no idea what they were planning. One of the lads he was with threw a lit bottle at a patrol car and he was terrified someone was going to get killed.

'He turned around and ran the whole way back down the Kerry Road and then walked the rest of the way home, about an hour it took him. He was totally sober by the time he got here, and absolutely petrified that the guards were going to come looking for him. That's why he's barely left the house since. He's been getting a load of abuse from the lads since for *ghosting* them, as they call it. They have a video that shows Ben was there that night and they've warned him that if he tells anybody, they'll send the video to the guards. I've told him they're not going to do that. They wouldn't take the chance that he'd land them all in it, but he's still worried about it. Anyway, he reeked of smoke when he arrived into me. That's why I washed his clothes.'

'Oh thank God, Essie,' she said, her shoulders slumping back against the hard wooden chair in relief. 'I was so … I didn't want to think … I just didn't know …'

'Well, I certainly wasn't expecting that reaction. I thought you'd murder him and me for not telling you, but I told him I couldn't lie outright to you if you asked me about that night.'

'I thought ... God, it's just with everything that's happened and that night ... It was the night Jessie fell and Ben has been so angry with Tadhg ... But what kind of a mother am I that I could think that my own child could ever ...?' She put her head on Essie's table and started to cry.

Her mother-in-law patted her back as she sobbed. 'You're a great mother, Maria Murphy, the best mother those two children could ask for. It's no wonder your brain got carried away, with all the stress you've been under.'

Two weeks ago, she and Tadhg would have come down on Ben like a ton of bricks for being so stupid and irresponsible. Getting himself involved with a crowd of racist thugs and being at the scene of a vicious attack on gardaí who were trying to do their job would have seemed like a major crisis for their family. Yet now, compared with the alternative scenario that had been lurking on the curtilage of her mind, it was a far sweeter pill to swallow.

CHAPTER 46

Dani

'It's just his preliminary finding, as I said – his full written report is to follow – but from his examination, he's satisfied Jessie's injuries are consistent with a fall from a height down a flight of stone steps and he found no sign of foul play being involved.'

'Okay. Thanks, Brian.' Her phone started to buzz, an incoming call that she ignored.

'That should hopefully give you some peace of mind, anyway. He did a very thorough exam and is confident she wasn't assaulted before her death.'

'Is he confident she wasn't pushed, though?'

'Well, there's no indication of that, but in the absence of eye witnesses, I don't think any pathologist could be fully confident that somebody wasn't pushed.'

Her phone began buzzing in her ear again, another incoming call. It was very distracting. She hoped it wasn't Joe calling to give her another ear-bashing or wanting to confirm that the cremation was going ahead tomorrow, because it wasn't.

'... given the icy steps and the pattern of bruising, that the cause of death was traumatic brain injury, consistent with an accidental fall.'

The awful feeling of apprehension that had stayed with her since Joe's call on Sunday evening had begun to whisk itself into a horrible, unsettling agitation as she got off the call with the attorney. It wasn't that she had wanted to be told her daughter had been beaten or attacked, that her last moments on this earth had been filled with terror or pain, but she'd been so sure ... She didn't know what you'd call it. Maybe not mother's instinct – she'd never experienced much, if any, of that – just this niggle that wouldn't go away, and then there'd been those messages from her daughter. At least that's what she'd thought they were, but what if they had come from inside her own fucked-up head and ...? NO! She knew what she had felt.

She was just stressing now because of Joe turning on her and that fucking false accusation Rory and Ger had made and that article on IrishCentral yesterday. It had focused mainly on her campaign and hadn't mentioned anything about the grooming, but it was still worrying. What if the Boston press picked up on it? The last thing she needed was for all that to be dragged up again, for the Irish cops to allow it to colour their attitude towards her. Because this was different. This time she was telling the truth. Mostly.

She checked her phone to see who had been trying to get through to her while she'd been on to Brian. It hadn't been Joe, to her relief. She had two missed calls, one from Jen at Rebel FM and one from a Boston number she didn't recognise. Jen had WhatsApped her asking her to 'give her a shout'. She smiled at the quaint Irishism, imagining herself bellowing down the line at the baffled researcher. She knew Benny wanted her to go back on his show to update him on how her campaign was going, but she was reluctant to do any more media interviews at the moment.

The Boston caller had left a voice message. She decided to listen to it in case it was another one of Jessie's friends with some new information, even though kids these days didn't really do voicemail.

It wasn't.

Sweat broke out all over her body, the soup and sandwich she'd had for lunch threatening to make a reappearance.

This was bad. Real bad. Joe was going to go apeshit.

CHAPTER 47

Maria
Wednesday, 24 January

It was like waking up from a nightmare and feeling that intense relief that it was over, but your body hadn't got the memo.

They'd been in their room getting ready for bed, exhausted and drained, when Tadhg saw the message. It had been delivered a few hours earlier but he'd been trying to stay off his phone, to resist the temptation to check what people were saying about him. Digital torture.

It had turned out to be from a reporter from an Irish tabloid, looking for a comment about an article that had appeared in that day's *Boston Globe*.

'Is this some kind of ... Where did they get *my* number?' he'd said when he listened to it the first time.

What now? She'd tried to brace herself for whatever bad news was coming.

'I don't fucking believe ... This is ...' He still had the phone pressed to his ear.

'Tadhg? Who is it?'

'Two seconds.' The phone was in his hand now and he was tapping it frantically.

'Is it something bad? Please, tell me. You're really worrying me now.' She stood facing him, on the other side of their king-size bed, in her pyjamas.

'No love, if this is true, I think it might be good news.' His eyes flicked back and forth across his screen like wipers in heavy rain. 'Jesus Christ, Maria, you are not going to believe this.'

He came around the bed, holding the phone out to her. It was open on an article on the *Boston Globe* website. The words of the heading jumped out at her and the photo underneath.

Has the Boston babysitter stalker struck again?

It was *her*, Dani.

Tadhg tried to scroll down, but was stymied by a paywall. A tab popped up telling him he'd been selected to get unlimited access for $1 for the rest of the year. He didn't even bother reading the small print, just clicked on 'Get Access' and tried to sign up, but he kept fumbling the keypad. Maria took the phone from him, entered his details and paid via PayPal.

'Come on, come on,' Tadhg said as they waited for the payment to be processed, their eyes glued to the screen.

It finally went through and they both sat on the bed in shocked disbelief as they read the interview with a man called Matthew Bolger about how Dani De Marco had destroyed his life nearly two decades ago. How the twenty-three-year-old single mother from Dorchester who had babysat for him and his wife since she was a teenager became infatuated with him after her own marriage broke down. And how, to his eternal shame, he'd had drunken sex with her one night when his wife was away.

Maria's breath caught as she read how, as a result of that night, of 'the worst mistake of my life', this man had lost his marriage and his career. He spoke of how Dani had made his and his wife's lives hell, calling his cell-phone and their home line constantly, and hanging around outside the clinic where he worked as a speech and language therapist until he threatened to take out a restraining order against her. The harassment had stopped for two weeks, and he'd hoped it was over and he could focus on trying to salvage what was left of his marriage. The next he heard of Dani De Marco was when two Boston PD cops showed up at the clinic one day. They informed him he had been accused of grooming her and having sex with her when she was under the age of sixteen and told him that he needed to come down to the precinct with them.

Bolger was quoted as saying he contacted the *Boston Globe* after his sister read about the accusations Dani had made against an Irish teacher on IrelandCentral. He wanted to try and prevent her from ruining anybody else's life. Alongside the article, the *Globe* ran a photo of a much younger Dani and another more current one taken from the Justice for Jessie Facebook page.

'It's hard to describe how much of a total nightmare that woman made our lives. She turned into a psycho almost overnight after we slept together. She became completely obsessed. She stole one of my sweatshirts off our clothes line and sent my wife a photo of her wearing it with nothing else on, saying I had given it to her. And the scariest part of it all for us was that we'd had this lady minding our kids.

'I ended up being charged with statutory rape for sexual activity with a girl under the age of sixteen – it was my word against hers. It was in all the local papers; she seemed to get off on the media attention. My marriage broke down, my wife kicked me out of the house and I lost my job, because most of my clients were children. There were days when I seriously contemplated driving off a bridge, but I knew if I did, everybody would think I did it 'cos I was guilty. And I couldn't leave my kids with that legacy.'

Bolger said Dani eventually dropped her allegations when the cops challenged her on certain inconsistencies in her story, but she was never charged with any crime.

'She got away scot-free with completely destroying my life while I lost my marriage, my home and my relationship with my kids, because I had to move away from Boston to get work. Just 'cos the cops drop the case doesn't mean those kinds of accusations go away. That kind of stink lingers and let me tell you, you find out real fast who your friends are.'

It was all over the Irish papers this morning, tabloid and broadsheet. There was a big discussion about it on one of the national radio morning shows. People texting in, saying it was far too easy to destroy a man's reputation with one false allegation and that Dani De Marco should face charges now. Mary from Ballinteer rang in to say that Mr Bolger and the unnamed north Cork teacher had both done wrong in sleeping with the girl in the first place, when they were in a position of authority over her. They may have held their hands up, but being drunk was no excuse and they still had a lot to answer for, she asserted.

A rape crisis worker came on, pointing out that false sexual-assault accusations were very rare and that in reality, rape was hugely underreported. When false allegations did occur for sexual crimes, the motivations behind them might include fear or a need for assistance rather than malice, she said. This led to a discussion about the barriers victims faced in reporting to the gardaí, the rape crisis woman saying that fewer than one in two people who experienced sexual violence in Ireland would ever tell anyone and fewer still would report it to the guards. It made what Dani had done to that poor man in Boston even worse, Maria thought, when so many people who really had been sexually assaulted, usually by a person known to them, were afraid to tell anyone about it.

Just as the radio discussion finished, Justine called to the house to update them on the situation. She told them that she had been in contact with the chief super's office in Anglesea Street earlier and that the gardaí were planning to speak to Ms De Marco on this matter today. She wasn't answering her phone, apparently, so he was sending someone to the B&B to try and locate her.

The solicitor said she had left the senior garda in no doubt about the devastation Ms De Marco's allegations had wrought on the life of her client and his family. She explained to Tadhg and Maria that falsely accusing somebody of a crime 'with the intent of causing the person to be investigated, prosecuted or punished' was a serious offence, carrying a maximum penalty of five years in prison. A civil action could also be taken against the complainant for defamation of character and Tadhg could seek damages for any harm suffered to his reputation.

It made Maria wonder what the hell had happened to Dani to make her do what she had done. The tide of vitriol had turned swiftly and the American woman was now the one being vilified in the media and online. It gave neither Maria nor Tadhg any pleasure to hear this, despite all the anguish the woman had caused them. Having been on the other side of it up until this morning, it was still far too raw. As far as they were concerned, they just wanted that woman to disappear from their lives and for things to start to get back to normal. As normal as it ever could be after this, at least.

CHAPTER 48

Six Months Later
Irish Examiner

Thursday, 18 July
A twenty-two-year-old American woman suffered a fatal brain injury after falling down a flight of steps in the grounds of Blarney Castle, Cork in January of this year, an inquest has heard.

Jessie De Marco, from Dorchester, Boston, was found dead at the base of the stone steps on the morning of January 12th, by one of the estate staff members.

The inquest at Cork Coroner's Court heard that Ms De Marco, who had come to Blarney in search of her birth father, had made the trip to the top of the castle to kiss the iconic Blarney Stone.

Consultant pathologist Dr Colm Powell said the post-mortem showed massive intracranial haemorrhage as a result of a skull fracture sustained in the fall. A toxicology report showed a moderate level of alcohol in the system of the deceased woman.

Inspector Frank Conneely told the inquest that the deceased had been wearing a pair of Converse All Star High Top trainers with worn soles which could potentially have been a slip hazard.

Cork coroner Ronan McNamara said it was a very tragic case. He assured Ms De Marco's family and loved ones that death would have been instantaneous and she would not have suffered. The jury recorded a verdict of accidental death.

The coroner expressed his condolences to Ms De Marco's mother, Dani, and her family, who were not present at the inquest.

Jessie De Marco's death hit the national and international headlines earlier this year when her mother Dani launched a public campaign seeking justice for her daughter Jessie. She alleged that Dani had been groomed by Jessie's father when he was her teacher in a Boston school in 2001, and she accused the man, now living and working in Cork, of involvement in her daughter's death. She also hit out at the gardaí for being too quick to dismiss her daughter's fall as an accident.

However, Ms De Marco went to ground when it was revealed that she had a history of stalking and had previously made a false allegation of grooming and sexual abuse in the US.

The Garda Press Office released a statement in the wake of this revelation which confirmed that they were satisfied that Jessie De Marco's death had been a tragic accident and that no foul play was suspected.

To date, no charges have been preferred against Ms De Marco for making a false statement to gardaí or for wasting garda time, and a source has told the *Irish Examiner* that it is unlikely she will ever face prosecution in the matter. The man who was the subject of the accusation and who had admitted sleeping with Ms De Marco, his former student, after she had graduated, has no wish to pursue the matter, according to the source, as he and his family want to put the incident behind them.

Maria

The inquest drew a line under the circumstances of the American girl's death, but it also brought it all up again, reminding everybody of the indelible blot on her husband's copybook.

Everything had happened so quickly after the *Boston Globe* article. Dani had fled the B&B the day the article appeared without even letting Noelle know, escaping the media, who were now stalking *her*. Her brother Joe had come over from Boston and taken control of things, arranging for his niece to be cremated and for her ashes to be flown home. He had sent an apology to Tadhg and the family through the gardaí on behalf of the De Marco family, saying his sister had been troubled even before the sudden and tragic loss of her child and he would ensure she got the help she so desperately needed back home.

The Justice for Jessie Facebook page had disappeared, all the abuse and hatred fading into the ether with it. The parody site had been taken down too; they never found out who had set it up, but whoever it was had likely been running scared of a major defamation case.

It wasn't over yet, though. When Maria went up to Ben's room the night after Dani left the village to say she wanted to talk to him, he told her he needed to talk to her too.

She had decided not to tell Tadhg about their son's brush with arson as she felt he'd learnt his lesson, but she'd wanted to let Ben know that *she* knew. He'd broken down in tears as he told her how sorry he was, and that he never wanted anything to do with those boys again; nor did he ever want to go back to that school. She'd held him in her arms and rocked him, her big soft teenager, while the tears flowed down his cheeks. And she waited for him to tell her.

She'd known there was something going on with him. Ever since that day after mass when he'd come flying down the stairs. Roaring at Tadhg that he hated him, that he'd ruined all their lives. *But they're not lies. Are they?* Dad? *Go on, tell them. Why don't you? ... Get a paternity test so and we'll see who's lying and who's telling the truth.* She had been so afraid that Ben had somehow found out something about Tadhg and Dani, something bad enough to make him turn against his father. Bad enough to try to get rid of Jessie. Which was why she'd been so relieved to find out that he was nowhere near the castle that night.

Ben had wanted her to know the truth about his father, but he hadn't wanted to be the one to break her heart by telling her. Her poor boy, living with the weight of that awful secret, with everything else that was going on around them.

What had shocked Maria most wasn't that her husband knew Dani had been pregnant with a baby she claimed was his, or that he had dropped a seventeen-year-old to an abortion clinic and left her there alone; it was that her husband had known who Dani was from that first moment in Casey's and had lied barefacedly to them all ever since. Whether or not he had groomed the girl, she didn't know. He continued to swear black and blue he hadn't, but how could she believe a word out of his mouth now? Especially when the results of the paternity test had shown that he *was* in fact Jessie's father.

Nobody had been more stunned than Tadhg when they found out. He had been so shocked that Maria had gone behind his back and done the test in the first place, forging his signature and painstakingly combing through the hairs on his hairbrush to try to find ones with a root, then doing the same with the round wire brush that Jessie had left behind in the B&B. The website of the company who did the 'peace of mind' testing had informed her that extracting DNA from hair follicles was a much more expensive and complicated process than from a buccal cheek swab, as there would be much less DNA available. The results, which had come back within three days, couldn't have been more conclusive, though. The report left little doubt. There was a 99.9999% probability that Tadhg was Jessie De Marco's biological father.

Turned out she'd been right in her reservations about him taking that test. While the results from a home test would be inadmissible in court, Maria knew beyond a shadow of doubt that if a proper chain of custody cheek swab test had been carried out, the results would have been the same. Her husband had been completely deluded to believe there was no way he could be the father, that it couldn't happen to him. The stupid, arrogant man.

It was desperately sad to think her husband had had a daughter, her children a half sibling and Essie a granddaughter out there all those years who they knew nothing about. It was even more painful to know that she had been so close to them and that they'd never get the chance to meet her now.

There had been talk of a file going to the Director of Public Prosecutions in relation to having Dani charged with making a false accusation, wasting garda time and conspiring to pervert the course of justice. It was decided not to proceed, since the matter had not progressed to a full investigation against Tadhg and since Dani had returned to the US. Tadhg and Maria had made it clear to the guards that they didn't want her charged, even after they heard about the hoax call from a woman purporting to be a former student of Tadhg's, claiming that he had groomed and sexually assaulted her and that she wasn't the only one. That call had been made from a burner phone and the guards had never traced it, although they had a good idea who had made it, given the company Dani had been keeping in the Gab.

Tadhg and Maria just wanted it all to go away. A court case would have involved raking through Tadhg's sexual relationship with his former student and it would have put their family back in the media spotlight. That was the last thing any of them needed, especially Eva, who was back on track with her studying and facing into the most important exams of her life – hopefully all set to go off to university that autumn. And Ben, who was the only other person apart from Maria and Tadhg who knew the full truth.

She still woke in the middle of the night gasping for breath, heart hammering, a couple of times a week. Some nights she was woken by Tadhg kicking and hitting out in his sleep, fighting the invisible monsters that still plagued his subconscious. One night, he had punched her hard in the back of the head, waking them both and bringing tears to her eyes. He had held her gently in his arms, saying sorry over and over, and she knew he didn't just mean for the bang on the head.

It would get easier, as Essie constantly reminded them both. The memory of that awful time in their lives would never go away, but it would hopefully begin to fade eventually, like grief after the death of a loved one. She didn't know the full story either, though; she was better off that way.

When it had come to the crunch, they had been surrounded by a tight knot of friends and family, who had wrapped their love around them. Maria felt a deep sense of love and appreciation for all those who had stood by them during that crisis in their lives, and she had been pleasantly surprised to find that those who hadn't were no loss to them at all.

Tadhg would be going back to St Vincent's at the start of the new term in September, but Ben wouldn't be going with him. He had admitted to his parents that he'd been deeply unhappy there for some time, largely due to the relentless and nasty slagging he endured on a daily basis for being the principal's son – which had started long before any of his tormentors had ever heard of Dani De Marco. He was a far more sensitive and less confident child than his sister. The opposite to her in so many ways. When Tadhg had started to argue against Ben moving school, his usual 'he's too soft, he needs to toughen up if he's going to get on in life' argument, Maria had warned him not to go there. If Tadhg couldn't understand that Ben was never going to be tough, that their boy's softness wasn't a weakness but part of what made him Ben, then that was his problem. She'd been surprised how quickly he'd backed down.

She had got a place for Ben in Leeside College, a fee-paying school in town, where she hoped he might settle better. He seemed to be really looking forward to the new beginning.

When Maria had first gone back to work, the week after Dani left, she had been warmly welcomed by Dylan O'Leary. 'We missed you, Mrs Murphy,' he'd announced. 'Me mam was tellin' me about your husband and that and I says to her I bet that wan is oney makin' up lies, Mam, 'cos Mrs Murphy is really nice and there's no way her husband would go off making a baby with—'

'That's enough now, Dylan, thank you,' she had said briskly, smiling inwardly. 'Although I appreciate the welcome. Now, can you open *Mental Maths* on whatever page you got to while I was gone?'

As the months went by, Maria had found herself thinking about Dani De Marco more and more. About the vulnerable seventeen-year-old version of her that her husband had slept with – he'd admitted she may not have been quite eighteen when they had sex – impregnated and abandoned alone at an abortion clinic. Imagining Eva in that scenario. Although her husband seemed only too happy to put the whole nasty business behind him and move on with his life, it ate away at Maria. That woman had been the mother of her children's half sibling, but as far as everybody else was concerned she had been lying about that too. And if Dani had been telling the truth about the father of her baby, what else might have been true?

The solid keel that had always kept their marriage right-side up had been knocked sideways. Her husband was doing his best to try and right it again, but she sometimes found herself looking at him over dinner at the table or at night while he was watching TV and wondering who the hell he was. This man she thought she had known so well wasn't that man at all, and no amount of apologising and trying to justify his lies by saying 'I did it to protect our family' was ever going to change that. Ben seemed far more willing to accept his father's apologies and excuses than she was; he had been keen to put it all behind him and pretend that phone call he'd overheard had never happened. Maria would need to keep a close eye on him – these things had a habit of festering in the dark, were best taken out into the light and dealt with – but for now, she had to respect her son's wishes and leave it alone.

Maybe some day she too would be able to forgive Tadhg; it was far too soon to tell. She'd never forget, though, and she'd find it very hard ever to be able to trust him again. Not after all the lies. He had made her question whether she'd ever really known the man she slept beside every night.

The most important thing in her mind right now was that their children were okay. What the future held for her marriage, she couldn't say.

CHAPTER 49

Noelle

She had lied for her son when the guards came to the door that day, still no wiser as to what he had been doing the night of the American girl's death. Whether he had been telling the truth when he swore he had no hand to play in it. Or for that matter, in his own father's death. Once doubt got into the mind at all, it tended to spawn – and suddenly, you found yourself questioning everything.

It had all come out in the wash anyway, as dirty laundry inevitably did. One night, about a month after Dani De Marco had checked out of the B&B and out of their lives, taking her madness and mayhem with her, Noelle had heard banging on the door and rushed out, wondering who it could be.

She had been stunned to find Molly there, her hair plastered to the sides of her head, mascara sweeping down her cheeks in a stream of rain and tears. The girl had been hysterical, pushing in past Noelle.

'Where is he?' Molly had cried.

Noelle had felt a cold fist grip her gut.

Please, no, not the baby.

'What's wrong, Molly? Where's Leon?'

'It's not Leon.'

Thank you, God. Thank you, thank you.

'Do you want to take your coat off, Molly, love? You're drowned.' Her cream teddy bear coat was no match for the heavy rain. 'Liam's in the shower, I think.'

Ignoring her question, Molly took off up the stairs, dripping and sobbing as she went.

Noelle stood at the bottom, wondering what the hell was going on and hoping that whatever it was, Liam wasn't to blame.

'Is it true?' she heard Molly roar above the sound of the electric shower. The shower went off and her son made some reply, but she couldn't hear what he said.

'IS IT TRUE? Answer me, Liam.' Noelle had never once heard Molly raise her voice, never mind at Liam.

She took a few steps up the stairs; she had to know what was going on.

'I'm sorry, Molly. It didn't mean anything. Honestly. It was a huge mistake ...'

Ah, no. No, no!

There was silence for a few moments, apart from the sound of Molly sniffling.

'How could you, Liam? How could you do this to me? To Leon?' The girl's voice was filled with pain and Noelle's own heart broke for her, because she knew this pain well. 'And with my fucking aunt?'

'Please, Molly, I was off my head. Amanda's been comin' on to me for ages. It only happened the once, I swear ...'

Noelle sank onto the stairs.

Her aunt? Amanda? Oh God.

She understood then where her son had been the night of Jessie's death. And why he couldn't tell her. He knew how repelled she would be. How ashamed of him. Everything she was feeling now.

What the hell was wrong with these men? Was there something in their genes? How could he have done this to Molly? That beautiful girl, the mother of his child.

How could he have risked what he had for Amanda McMahon with her blown-up lips and fake lashes that were so heavy the girl could barely open her eyes? Amanda was one of Molly's mother's younger sisters, only a couple of years older than Molly. The two of them were close, friends as well as aunt and niece. A double betrayal. The poor girl would never get over this. She would never forgive Liam for it. And neither would Noelle.

The stupid bloody man.

She heard Molly coming out of the room, Liam in close pursuit.

'Stay away from me,' Molly cried. 'And don't ever come anywhere near me again.'

Noelle stood up, waiting on the stairs.

'Please, Molly.' Liam started to follow the girl down.

'Leave her, Liam. She doesn't want to talk to you.' Her son opened his mouth to protest, but then he took in the look on his mother's face and stopped in his tracks, tears pouring down his face now as well.

Noelle put her arm around the young woman she had grown to love and led her into the warmth of the sitting room, where Molly wailed in her arms.

When she was calm enough to speak, she looked at Noelle from eyes dull with pain and fatigue. 'I knew he was cheatin' on me, I just had this feelin' in my gut. I thought it was that Jessie girl. My friend told me he'd been with her in the Gab the night before she died, that he left the pub with her, and when I asked Liam about it, he went all odd with me. Said I was only being jealous and paranoid, and I started to think maybe I was, but then he lied about where he was the next night. He told me he'd been at a party in Deano's, but I got another friend to check with her boyfriend who was at that party and he said Liam never turned up. I knew there was somethin' goin' on, but he swore blind to me that he'd never cheat on me, he'd never be like his father. The lyin' ... He said you'd never forgive him if he did. And I knew that and I really wanted to believe him, but I just knew in my gut ...'

'I don't know what to say to you, Molly love. I'm so sorry and I'm so ashamed of my son. He should have been thanking his lucky stars for bringing you into his life and that precious baby. I'll murder him.'

It was as Molly was getting out of the car when Noelle dropped her home, her shoulders heaving the whole way, that she asked, 'How did you find out it was Amanda?'

'She's pregnant and she's sayin' Liam is the father.'

CHAPTER 50

Dani

She had been at a really low point when she got the first letter. About two months ago now. Nobody would believe her when she tried to tell them that she'd been telling the truth. Whether Tadhg was Jessie's father or not, as Joe and her shrink pointed out, didn't really matter. He wasn't suspected of having anything to do with Jessie's death, and Dani was going to have to accept it was an accident if she was going to be able to move on from this.

Everything had happened so quickly back in Blarney. She had been sitting in her room at the B&B, trying to gear herself up to call Joe and tell him about the message she'd just got from the *Globe*, when *he* rang her. The reporter had been on to him too, looking for a comment for an article that they were planning to print that day, and everything had gone to shit again.

She may not have been able to remember much about her journey from Shannon to Cork, but she didn't think she'd ever forget one excruciating moment of the cab journey back. Or of being holed up in a hotel near the airport like some kind of fugitive, waiting for her flight back to Boston the following morning, while her brother flew over to sort out the cremation, pay all the bills she'd accumulated and bring Jessie home. She had tried arguing with him, to explain that this wasn't like Matt Bolger, but he didn't want to hear it. This wasn't the Joe she knew and loved; this Joe was hard and cold, and very, very angry. If she didn't get into the cab he had ordered for her and onto the flight he had booked, she was on her own, he'd told her. And she had known he meant it.

Her fragile flicker of a dream of starting a new life for herself in Ireland had been snuffed out.

She knew now that her brother had been stressed out of his mind about her, on top of being exhausted from worrying about his own newborn and Mamma, who had been calling him incessantly, ranting hysterically. He'd had so much on his plate, and he was grieving the death of his niece too – they'd always been close. No wonder he had been so angry with Dani. The last thing he or the business needed was all that stuff with Matt Bolger being brought up again – more negative publicity generated by his younger sister.

After Jessie's funeral, he had told her he wanted to sit down and talk to her. She had known it was probably about her plans to return to work: she hadn't been back since the day before the cops had called to her door to break the bad news, didn't know how she was going to face going back. The weight of her grief was crippling at that point; she could barely even stand upright. It *had* been work he'd wanted to talk to her about, but not her old job.

When he told her he didn't think it was a good idea for her to come back to the restaurant, she had just nodded dully, not caring about anything at that point. She hadn't even been able to imagine trying to make conversation with customers, to smile and laugh and act normal when just getting out of bed took so much energy. She was back living with Mamma, who blamed her for Jessie's death, and rightly so, she'd believed at the time. She hadn't one friend in the world to turn to. With Joe turning against her as well, she was finding it very hard to see any point in going on.

When her brother told her he didn't think it was a good idea for her to stay living with their mother either, she had looked at him in horror.

'I'll stay in my room, Joe. I won't be any trouble, I swear. Please, don't make me move out, not now.' She spent most of her time in her room anyway.

The thought of having to find some place new to live, to share with strangers again, was even worse than the scenario of living with a mother who didn't even attempt to hide her loathing anymore.

Her brother had moved closer to her then, put his arms around her and for a moment, when she closed her eyes, she'd imagined he was Pops, comforting her the way he always had when she was upset.

'I'm not goin' to make you do anything, honey. I just don't think it's good for you livin' here. Myself and Laurie have been talkin' and well ... I don't know what's wrong with Mamma, why she treats you the way she does, but it's not right, Dani. I'm going to get you the help you need. I know the drinkin', the bad relationships, all of it ... well ... Mamma has an awful lot to answer for, but she never will. I've tried talkin' to her in the past about it, but she just can't see that she's the problem, not you. That she's always been the problem.'

Dani had broken down completely then, sobbing for the child who had been rebuffed so many times when all she'd wanted was that basic human necessity, the love of her mother. Unconditional.

'We want you to move in with us.'

She had shaken her head; she couldn't intrude on her brother. He had his own family now, the last thing he needed was his fucked-up black sheep sister living with him. And it wouldn't be fair on Laurie either.

'Just hear me out, okay? You know the way we renovated the summer house? Well, we were going to rent it, but we don't really want strangers trampin' through our yard and it was Laurie's idea ... We thought it could be the perfect little home for you, just until you get back on your feet, you know? Or for as long as you like if you're happy there. It's really cosy. Here, look ... I took photos for you.'

The tears had started again as her brother scrolled through pictures of the cute little white clapboard house with its compact kitchen/diner, its neat ensuite bedroom decorated in lemon and white and its bright lounge with the wood-burning stove. The lounge looked out onto the yard, with its stunning red maple tree, and the garden her green-fingered sister-in-law tended to lovingly.

'You could add your own touches. Paint the walls a different colour, maybe. I could help you. I know it's all very white and plain, but you could make it your own. It would be your home.'

She had shaken her head, too choked up to get the words out. To say it was perfect and she wouldn't change a thing. It couldn't be more different from the gloomy, cluttered rooms of her mother's apartment, a place that had never really felt like home to her, and not at all since Pops was gone.

Since then, things had been very up and down. She had struggled to cope with the deluge of grief that had hit her before she even left Ireland, on top of the shame and humiliation she felt over all the Matt Bolger stuff coming up again. Dr Leibowitz, in her gentle, compassionate way, suggested she might need to give herself a break, that she was far too hard on herself and that this wasn't surprising, given how her needs hadn't been met as a child. That for whatever reason, her mother hadn't been able to give her the love she needed and deserved. That before she could even begin to deal with the grief over Jessie's death, she had to try to unpack the complexity of her relationship with her daughter while she was alive, and with her own mother.

At eighteen and totally out of her depth, Dani had been so relieved when Mamma had stepped in to look after Jessie; it had taken the therapist to point out that instead of teaching Dani how to mother her baby, she had stolen that role away from her too, cruelly poisoning her daughter against her. That she had lost out both on being mothered and on being a mother.

She had known Mamma was trash-talking her to Jessie behind her back, just like she had done to Pops. Belittling her, making her out to be a fool, a *grassa, stupido scemo*. The day when Jessie was about ten and Dani had turned up at the apartment, a hungover mess with a fat lip and a fractured cheekbone, dragging all of her belongings behind her in two trash bags, and her daughter had protested against having to share her bedroom with *la donnaccia*, she knew. A child that age wouldn't have had that kind of language in her vocabulary, wouldn't know what a slut, a *jezebel*, was. Her nonna did though, and so did her two grandaunts, who still visited daily with their boastful tales of *their* kids being made partners in their law firms or being named best orthopaedic surgeon in *Boston Magazine* or making gazillions in Silicon Valley.

When Dani had been caught at the age of fifteen sucking the cock of an older guy under the bleachers in the gym at her high school while his buddy waited for his turn, her mother's solution – rather than get her the help she was so clearly crying out for after the sudden death of her beloved Pops – was to tell her she was ashamed to have given birth to such a *piccola sporco puttana* and to move her to an all-girls' school – and directly into the sights of Michael Murphy. Dani had so many goddamn issues by then she might as well have had prey stamped onto her forehead.

There were days when she could see that the psychiatrist was right. That her bad behaviour had been a cry for the love she hadn't got as a child. That old chestnut. What she had felt for Michael and for Ricky and all the other men she thought she had loved hadn't really been love at all, but her way of trying to fill the yawning hole inside.

Matt Bolger had been different, though. He was the one man she had really loved and she'd been so sure he felt the same way about her too. He had shattered her heart into pieces and on the back of so many other rejections in her life, she had cracked, unable to cope with such immense pain. What she had done to that man was horrifying and shameful and she would never stop regretting it, although Dr Leibowitz was hopeful of bringing her to a point of not just understanding why she did it but of forgiving her damaged twenty-three-year-old self. And of seeing that all of the men she'd been involved with had taken advantage of her vulnerability, her willingness to try and twist herself into a shape worthy of their love when, in fact, she had been more than worthy all along, and probably too good for most of them. Those were the days when she felt hope.

There were other days, though, when she thought the shrink was deluded, that she was utterly worthless, a drain on her brother and his wife, and that it was all hopeless.

It had been on one of the bad days that the first letter arrived. She'd just got off the phone from Mamma, who had called to ask when she was going to visit next. Ironically, her mother hadn't been at all happy when she'd heard about Dani's plan to move into Joe's garden house, saying she didn't want to be left in the apartment on her own and suggesting that she should move in with her son and his wife too, given her advancing years. Joe and Laurie had swiftly vetoed that suggestion. Her mother's sisters were still going strong, albeit feebler and wrinklier now, their daily meeting of the coven still taking place, and her complaints about being lonely in the evenings weren't met with much sympathy. Dani called to her once a week, bringing groceries and staying less than an hour each time, before returning to her own place, her first real home. That was as much as she owed her mother, as far as she was concerned.

She had been sitting on a wooden Adirondack chair on her tiny porch with a glass of iced tea when Laurie had come down the garden, the baby in her arms and a couple of pieces of post for Dani in her hand. Her sister-in-law had handed her adorable niece over to her and gone inside to help herself to some tea. The baby gurgled up at her and Dani felt her heart melting as it always did when she set eyes on this child. So like Jessie at this age with her huge brown eyes, that spiky shock of dark hair; the cousin she would never get to see. The early months and years with her own baby were a blur for Dani, pushed aside by Mamma, further into the embrace of booze and men who didn't treat her right, and she would never get them back now. Sometimes the pain of that threatened to break her, the sadness too heavy to bear, but other times, like now, as Maya squeezed her finger surprisingly tight in her velvety little hand, the love she felt for this little person overwhelmed all of the negative emotions. Sometimes she thought this bond with her niece was a gift that Jessie had sent her: Jessie and Pops, both in cahoots up there somewhere, watching out for her.

Another unexpected gift had been the friendship that had developed between herself and Laurie, who was a regular visitor to her little cabin, sometimes with Maya, sometimes alone when she wanted a break from the baby and her own house. They came to realise that they had a lot more in common than they could have imagined: Laurie had come too from a dysfunctional home background, although it was her father who had been the problem. Dani understood now what her brother saw in this special woman who had shown her more kindness in the past few months than any other woman in her life. She had helped Dani to draw up some goals to aim towards, although she didn't feel strong enough yet to start all of them: kick the booze (not ready), start looking after herself better by eating healthier (a work in progress) and introduce some exercise to her daily routine (she had started taking the baby for a walk in her pram every day, baby steps as Laurie said). She had also marched her into the salon where she got her hair done, insisting on paying for her hair to be brought back to the natural shiny colour that 'a lot of women would kill for' and making Dani promise to stop ruining it with box dyes.

Her sister-in-law sat on the other deck chair across from her, sipping her iced drink and smiling at the baby, who now had a tiny fist clamped around a clump of Dani's hair.

'Be careful. She pulled a pile of hair out of my head yesterday – I think I got a bald patch now.'

'That's okay. I got plenty to spare – don't I, my little angel face?' Dani had realised she was using the kind of cutesy baby voice with Maya that she had found so annoying when Noelle did it back in Blarney.

'So myself and Joe have been talking ...'

'Should I be worried?' she said, smiling. She wasn't really worried: she trusted her brother and his wife, and they had assured her that this was her home now for as long as she wanted, even if that was for ever. Their stunning, triple-decker brownstone was in the beach-meets-city area of Savin Hill, one of the most covetable sections of Dorchester, and they had lovingly renovated it; they weren't planning on moving. In the few months since Dani had lived here, she had grown to love the area, with its beaches and the series of parks known as the Emerald Necklace that made her think of Ireland. She had a number of favourite places: Codman Square for Jamaican food, McKenna's Cafe for breakfast, Phillips Candy House for a chocolate turtle, and Greenhills Bakery. The staff at Greenhills knew her by name now and she liked to go there for coffee, often picking up a loaf of Irish brown bread to take away to remind her of Cork.

'We just want you to think about it, okay, but you know how I'm planning to go back to work next month?'

'Yeah.'

'And we have Maya's name down in that daycare place on the corner?'

'Yeah. Do you want me to drop her and collect her? That's no problem.' She was going to have to think about getting back to work herself soon so she could start paying Joe and Laurie some rent. She was enjoying the slower pace of life and early nights, often sitting for her niece – no more bar-hopping or waking in strange beds – but this situation couldn't continue indefinitely.

'No, well that would be great too, but how would you feel about looking after Maya for us? At home.'

'Me?'

'Yeah. My mom used to look after kids when we were young – some of them were like part of our family – and me and Joe were thinking we'd like that for Maya, you know? Instead of being in a busy daycare with staff changing all the time, we'd love if she could be cared for in her own home. And, well, we think you'd be the ideal person to do that, if it was something you were interested in. She adores you and you adore her, so we wouldn't need to worry about her getting used to a new person, and we'd pay you well. If it's not for you or you don't feel up to it right now we'll understand, but please just think about it.'

Dani looked down at the baby in her arms, who gazed back at her expectantly, as if awaiting her answer. 'I don't need to think about it, Laurie. It would be a privilege to look after this precious angel. Thank you,' she said, her voice breaking, 'for trusting me to ... after all the trouble I've caused ...'

Laurie stood up and wrapped her arms around her. 'Thank *you*, Dani, this means the world to us. Of course we trust you. You're so much more amazing than you know, you know.'

It wasn't until later after Laurie had taken Maya home for her nap that she had seen the post on the counter inside. The large envelope on top with her name and address in unfamiliar handwriting on the front. The Irish stamps.

CHAPTER 51

Dani

When she had opened the envelope, she'd found two smaller ones inside, both with her name on the front, one in the same writing as the big envelope. She'd opened that one first.

Dear Dani,

I hope you are doing okay, or as well as can be expected under the circumstances. You may have read my husband's letter by now, but if not, the other letter is from Tadhg and it speaks for itself.

I hope you don't mind me writing to you as well. I spent a lot of time wondering whether I should, but I just haven't been able to get you – and what happened to you and my husband's part in that – out of my mind. I contacted your brother Joe through your solicitor to ask if it would be okay and he said he thought it would, but feel free to rip this up and throw it in the bin if you want to. I would, however, urge you to read Tadhg's letter, because it's the very least he owes you.

I am writing to say I'm sorry for what you have gone through because of my husband's shameful and regrettable actions, some of which I only became privy to after you left the village. I am saddened by and ashamed of what he has done, the full extent of which he has outlined in his own enclosed letter.

Some of This Is True

My children and I were shocked to find out the results of the paternity test, which I did behind his back, and to realise that, as you had been trying to get everybody to believe, Tadhg was the man Jessie had come to Blarney in search of. I am sorry we didn't believe you, although I hope you can understand why: we were lied to very convincingly by a husband and father we thought we could trust. A man who has always been good to us but sadly turned out not to be the person we thought he was.

Tadhg's shock at discovering that he was the father of your child does appear to be genuine, and while I certainly don't expect you to feel any sympathy for him, he must now live with the loss of a beautiful daughter he never got to know, as a result of his own cruel, selfish actions when you told him you were pregnant.

My daughter Eva and my son Ben talk about Jessie all the time. Not a day goes by when they don't wonder about her, or say they wish they could have got to know her, especially Eva, who always wanted an older sister. She cut Jessie's photo out of one of the newspapers and framed it. She keeps it in her room and has convinced herself they're a bit alike around the eyes, although the rest of us can't see it. I don't have any answers to give them, sadly, but I just wanted you to know that Jessie is in all of our thoughts and we all wish we could have got to know her. She seemed like a real character – a strong, determined young woman, just like her mother. I like to think that in your situation, I'd have fought just as hard as you did, for my daughter.

I hope you have some of that strength and determination left over for yourself now and that you can somehow learn to live with the unimaginable loss you have endured.

Yours sincerely,
Maria Murphy

Dani had read and reread both letters so many times since that day, especially Maria's. Tadhg's apology was bittersweet. She was glad he had written, although she suspected his wife had, if not forced him, at least strongly encouraged him to do so. But it was too little, too late. If he had supported her all those years ago when she had told him she was pregnant, who knew what kind of a life she and her daughter might have had? It was unlikely she and Tadhg would have stayed together, but she might have been able to offer her child a more stable environment, to be a better mother, if he hadn't just seen her as a problem to get rid of. If he hadn't been so arrogant as to think it couldn't have been his child, as if trouble couldn't touch him. *The mighty Tadhg Murphy.*

The old Dani would have taken this letter straight to that reporter in the *Globe* and asked him to print the proof that she had been telling the truth. Tadhg hadn't admitted he had groomed her, but he had said he was very sorry that he'd sent her the wrong signals, which he 'hadn't meant to do but clearly must have', and that he really had seen potential in her writing. He had groomed her. There was no doubt in her mind about that now; she may have exaggerated slightly about the age it started, seventeen, not sixteen, but either way she was still a child. Her self-esteem eggshell thin. The new Dani had no interest in stirring everything up again, though.

She checked the clock on the electric oven in Laurie and Joe's kitchen. Maya was contentedly kicking on her play mat and they had about an hour before they needed to leave for mom and baby group. Dani had been surprised at how much she looked forward to the group, the last place she'd ever have expected to make new friends. Melissa, who was older than most of the others and grandma to an adorable toddler called

Zane, had come over to welcome her on the first day, when Dani had been hovering in the doorway of the church hall, deliberating whether to turn on her heels and make a run for it. She had only missed one day since then, when Maya had the sniffles. She had grown close to Melissa, who had no time for the milestone competition of some of the moms in the group, as well as Latonya, an older first-time mom to a beautiful little girl called Dream, who Melissa had taken under her wing when she was struggling with post-partum depression – she was one of the funniest people Dani had ever met. The three of them had met a few times now for coffee and lunch outside the group, and they were planning a trip to the cinema this weekend without any babies, which Dani was looking forward to. She was babysitting tonight for Dream while Latonya went out on a date. Dani had no interest in men these days, and even if one came along, she wouldn't have time, she was so busy.

If Jessie could see her now, she'd never believe it. Changing diapers and washing bottles, swapping late bars and chasing men for early nights and the cinema with her new friends, exchanging letters with her birth father's wife. She leafed through the photos she had picked out and chose her favourite three: one of Jessie as a baby on a swing beaming madly into the camera, another of her on her communion day with chocolate smeared all over her face and a ten-dollar bill clutched in her fist, and one of her at her twenty-first, smiling as always, happy and beautiful in her short red dress, her thick curls tumbling down her back. Yes, they were perfect. She put them into the envelope and picked up her pen.

Dear Maria ...

EPILOGUE

Night after night, I lie awake, tormented by the image of her lying at the bottom of those steps.

By the what ifs.

Would she have survived if I'd called an ambulance?

Had she lain there terrified and in pain, dying slowly, crying for her mother?

When I eventually found out that nothing had been going on between her and Liam, that my gut had been right but that it had been far worse than I had ever suspected, I had seriously considered ending it all. If it hadn't been for Leon, I probably would have.

I'd worked so hard to try to break free from the stigma of being one of the McMahons from Millview, to make a better life for myself and my child. With Liam, the man I adored. So there was no way me and Leon were going to be abandoned like Mam and me and my brothers.

I called her name, beckoning her up the hill at the side of the church that day. So perfect with her Kardashian curves, her shiny black hair and glowy skin, a takeaway Centra coffee in her hand.

'Hi, Molly. This is very cloak and dagger, isn't it?' she said.

The smile wasn't long freezing on her lips when I told her I knew who her dad was. Instructed her to meet me at the castle at three, at the Wishing Steps in the Rock Close. And to keep it to herself. That I'd have to leave Blarney if it came out that I was the one who told her.

I entered the castle grounds about ten minutes early, squeezing through a gap in the fence used by local kids for gatting in the woods. Leon was strapped to my chest, sound asleep.

It was already dusky beneath the cover of the trees, it was unlikely our privacy would be disturbed. She was waiting at the top of the steps when I arrived. And then I let her have it. Nothing to do with knowing who her father was. But she'd better pull her manicured claws out of my fella.

I'd expected her to be a bit pissed off that I'd lured her there under false pretences, but I hadn't expected her to totally freak out.

'What the hell is wrong with you?' she had yelled, fury in her eyes. 'I came here to find my father. That's all I care about. Not gettin' it on with some fuckin' guy. I was totally bombed last night! We'd been doing shots and I could barely stand. Liam just helped me home. To his mother's guesthouse, where I'm staying, you crazy bitch.'

Could she be telling the truth? Suddenly I felt stupid. Why hadn't I just confronted Liam in the first place when I heard he'd been seen cosied up to the American girl in the Gab, and leaving with her? The girl was sneering at me now, her lips curled in disgust, as if I was some kind of psycho. And that's what got my temper going.

'*I'm* a crazy bitch? You're the nutter comin' over posting your private business all over the place.'

'Ha!' The girl laughed. 'We'll see who the nutter is when I tell Liam and Noelle about this. Luring me to the middle of the deep, dark woods to accuse me of trying to steal your boyfriend.' She laughed again, mockingly. As if I was someone to be jeered at and pitied.

Like being back in school all over again.

How's Mad Molly Mac?

Would you ask your Uncle Ger if he could sort me out with a bag of horse, Moll?

Who's your Aunty Mandy's jockey this week?

It was the laugh that did it.

I shoved her hard in the chest.

I'd only meant to shut her up, to take that smirk off her perfect face. I instinctively reached out a hand when she lost her footing.

It all happened so fast then, her legs pedalling frantically in the air, that inhuman shriek of terror as she fell backwards into the narrow concrete stairwell, the heavy thump of soft-tissue-wrapped bone smacking into solid stone, the sickening crack as she hit the ground at the bottom, and then nothing.

I stood in the ringing silence, both hands clamped over my mouth, howling inside.

Then I took a couple of steps, leaned forward slightly and I could see her. She wasn't moving.

I looked around in panic, no-one around. Shaking so hard, I peered back down. No movement, no sound.

Oh Jesus!

Is she dead?

Should I call for help?

What the hell do I do?

As my mind stuttered, my legs took over and started running.

I'd never set out to harm that girl; I'd never harm anybody. I'd just wanted to stop the teasing, the words coming at me like blades, cutting deep into my softest parts.

Was I tempted to confess? Of course I was, especially when I saw the hell the Murphys were going through. And a couple of times, I came very close. But then I thought of my baby having to grow up with the stigma of having a killer for a mother, even if it hadn't been deliberate. A mother who was in prison. The mocking would be so much worse for my gorgeous innocent boy, his life ruined just for being my son.

Isn't your mam Mad Molly, the maddest of the Mad Macks?

Be careful on the stairs, lads, Leon Mac is behind ye.

I wouldn't tackle him too hard if I was you, boy, he'll set his mam on ya.

So I kept my mouth shut and was glad I did when it all came out about Dani De Marco and she was all but hunted out of the village.

I wish it had been the American girl Liam had cheated with. We could have got over that. And she could still be alive, gone her way with just a warning to keep her hands off my man. Not only have I lost him, but Amanda too, who was like a sister to me.

What's done can't be undone, though. And if being a Mac has taught me one thing, it's that we're survivors. I'll get through this one day at a time, maybe even come out stronger for it.

As for Liam and Amanda … As my mother always said, revenge is a dish best served cold.

ACKNOWLEDGEMENTS

The publication of every book is a collaboration, but none more so than this, my third book, for a variety of reasons, including a delightful cocktail of chronic pain and low mood, with a generous dash of perimenopausal brain fog (at least, I hope that's what it is) thrown in for good measure.

If this book had a difficult conception, labour and delivery, then I was fortunate to have the best obstetrician and midwife combined in my incredibly talented and endlessly patient publisher/editor Ciara Considine at Hachette Ireland to hold my hand, mop my brow and coax the baby out. Thank you, Ciara.

It's such a pleasure to work with the Hachette Ireland team who are always so encouraging, supportive and good at what you do. Heartfelt thanks to Jim Binchy, Ciara Doorley, Elaine Egan, Joanna Smyth, Ruth Shern, Siobhan Tierney, Stephen Riordan and Shauna O'Regan. To Clare Stacey of Head Design, for your fabulous cover design. To my agent Faith O'Grady, thanks for always being at the end of the phone or email, and for believing in my writing. To copy-editor Katie Green, I'm in awe of the job you do, nipping and tucking at a manuscript until it's as tight as it can possibly be. To Assistant State Pathologist

Margot Bolster as always for the benefit of her invaluable expertise, and to Alan Crowley, Crime Scene Examiner, for advice on my fictional crime scene, thanks so much for sharing your time and knowledge. As always, any errors are my own and generally for dramatic effect.

To Philip Comyn, Cork City Coroner, thanks for your help with my research into what happens when a young person dies abroad and a parent has concerns about their cause of death.

To Marie O'Halloran, AKA Casey King, author and crime fiction advisor for her invaluable advice on the garda investigative side of my research.

To Ciara O'Callaghan, Deputy Principal of Scoil Chroí Íosa, Blarney for so generously helping me with my research into the typical daily schedule of a primary school teacher.

To Audrey O'Sullivan, Operations Director of Ormond Quay Paternity Services, thanks for your advice on paternity testing. Any deviation from the norm is mine and made in the interest of fiction.

To my lovely friend Marian McCarthy for allowing me to borrow her late mother's name for Essie, and to my other lovely friend and multi-talented author Kitty Murphy's adorable dog Rupert (the pavement-eater) for inspiring the name of the dog (albeit deceased) in my book.

To my fellow Irish murderesses, I'm honoured and thrilled to have been so warmly welcomed into a gang of such lovely, talented and fun women.

To all of the fabulous book bloggers out there: you have no idea how much a positive post or comment can revive a struggling writer's spirits. Thank you for the time and the effort you put into what you do, all for the love of books. To the bookshops, booksellers and librarians around the country who work so hard and are so passionate about books, thank you so very much.

To my podcast co-host on *Natter with Kate and Michelle*, the wonderful Kate Durrant, thanks for joining me on this nerve-wracking, yet exciting and fun journey way outside both of our comfort zones. To the lovely Alan Johnston, Marketing Director of Bookstation Ireland, our *Natter* partner, and to our enviably coolheaded and talented producer Jack Regan of Trend 7 Media – it's been a pleasure working with you both over the past year. And to all the lovely authors who have come on to the podcast to natter with us, and everyone who has listened, thank you so very much for all your support.

To my family and friends, I feel incredibly privileged and grateful to have you all in my life. To Greg, and our beautiful children, Lucy, Jake and Kiana, I love you all so much. And to my little buddy Brody, who sits under my desk every day as I work, I love you more than everybody else in the world combined. Only joking! (Sort of.)

And most of all, to you the reader. Thank you as always from the bottom of my heart.